Damon Stepped Closer
and Temple Trembled
at His Nearness.
"You Are Cold," He Said Softly.

The warmth of his touch spread through her like warm honey. Damon ran his hands along her arms, and again she shivered though not from the chill of the night.

"Temple, Temple," came Damon's husky whisper. His lips came down on hers with an urgency which shocked them both. Temple felt a wave of desire unleash deep within her.

Damon raised his dark head, his ebony gaze intent upon her face. He reached out an unsteady hand to stroke the soft curve of her cheek, and she swayed against him, causing him to draw in his breath sharply.

He knew there would be no turning back—he had to make her his own.

Dear Reader,

We, the editors of Tapestry Romances, are committed to bringing you two outstanding original romantic historical novels each and every month.

From Kentucky in the 1850s to the court of Louis XIII, from the deck of a pirate ship within sight of Gibraltar to a mining camp high in the Sierra Nevadas, our heroines experience life and love, romance and adventure.

Our aim is to give you the kind of historical romances that you want to read. We would enjoy hearing your thoughts about this book and all future Tapestry Romances. Please write to us at the address below.

The Editors
Tapestry Romances
POCKET BOOKS
1230 Avenue of the Americas
Box TAP
New York, N.Y. 10020

Destiny's Embrace

Sheryl Flournoy

A TAPESTRY BOOK
PUBLISHED BY POCKET BOOKS NEW YORK

Books by Sheryl Flournoy

Flames of Passion
Destiny's Embrace

Published by TAPESTRY BOOKS

An *Original* publication of TAPESTRY BOOKS

A Tapestry Book published by
POCKET BOOKS, a division of Simon & Schuster, Inc.
1230 Avenue of the Americas, New York, N.Y. 10020

ISBN: 0-671-49665-4

First Tapestry Books printing February, 1984

10 9 8 7 6 5 4 3 2 1

POCKET and colophon are registered trademarks of Simon & Schuster, Inc.

TAPESTRY is a trademark of Simon & Schuster, Inc.

Printed in the U.S.A.

Acknowledgments

My beautiful daughter *Sharlette*, who is truly a gift from
God. She has opened a new and wonderful world to
me. She is far wiser than her tender years. Her love and
unique understanding mean so very much.

Marcia Caltabiano, whose friendship I greatly value.
We share a tie that is binding, that is infinite and
immortal. Her friendship is as an anchor, giving stabili-
ty and assurance.

Kay Garteiser, for all the love she has given, for her
friendship that is precious and complete. She is someone I can count on without question—she understands,
cares and really listens. With love and thanks for being
such a very special lady.

Barbara Keenan, whose friendship means much. She
inspires and encourages. The lady holds the corner on
enthusiasm.

Author's Note

In this novel I have used a subject matter that is part historical fact and part fiction. The historical events described herein are as accurate in their occurence as I was able to make them.

I wish to thank the following authors whose books provided the information that made this book possible. The actual historical events, including characters, dates and locations, were obtained from the following:

Carlton J. H. Hayes, *Modern Europe to 1870*
Christopher Hibbert, *Garibaldi and His Enemies*
Cambridge University Press Library Editions, *The Cambridge Modern History*, Volume XI

The author also wishes to thank the following libraries and librarians for their assistance in securing the needed reference books to help make this book possible:

Harris County Library, Fairbanks Branch; librarian Ann McCarthy
Houston Public Library, Hillendahl Branch; librarian Peggy Bailey

And a special thanks to Ann Baker (Ann's Books, Etc., Houston, Texas) for her invaluable assistance as well as her friendship.

The reader must bear in mind throughout this book that the names "Sardinia" and "Piedmont" are both used to designate the state in northwestern Italy. This area was ruled by the royal family of Savoy, whose head had since 1720 been officially entitled "King of Sardinia."

Technically, Sardinia and Piedmont were different areas of one state known as the "Kingdom of Sardinia," Sardinia being an island and Piedmont being the mainland about Turin.

Destiny's Embrace

Prologue

France, June 9, 1851

THE YOUNG MAN STOOD MOTIONLESS, HIS DARK EYES intent upon the lovely creature before him, a smile touching his lips as the gentle sound of laughter met his ears. Damon's black-violet gaze followed each movement of the young girl as she ran barefoot across the clover-blanketed field in pursuit of a fluttering butterfly. Her arms were lifted in abandonment and her lovely face was raised to the sun, whose golden rays played about her fine features.

Her glossy, honey-brown hair shone with a rich glow, the long, silken mane streaming behind her as a gentle breeze danced about the sun-kissed curls. She was a beautiful child—a child soon to become a woman—and Damon, at age twenty and two, found his heart held captive by this striking young beauty.

1

Once again laughter spilled from the girl's full lips; then, suddenly, she stopped her merriment. Placing a hand above her eyes to shade them from the sun, she stared upward at the furry creature perched on a low-hanging limb of a tree. Cocking her head to one side, she placed one hand on her hip and addressed the subject crouched there.

"Sebastian, what are you doing up there?" she demanded pertly. "Come to me." The tiny ball of fur made no move, its only reply a timid cry. "Here, kitty," she coaxed, taking a step closer. "Come, Sebastian." The cat meowed louder, its claws digging into the bark of the tree.

"Oh, you silly cat!" she sighed. Reaching down, she pulled the rear hem of her long skirt forward and between her legs, tucking it into her waistband. "You should not climb trees if you cannot get back down," she admonished the animal.

As she spoke she began to climb the tree, and when she reached the branch from which the frightened creature watched her warily, she stretched her small frame along the limb, slowly reaching out for the kitten. He was a bit too far away and she edged closer.

"Come, kitty, come to Temple," she cooed gently, stretching one hand toward Sebastian. Without warning the little fur-ball hissed at the hand attempting to grasp it and retreated even farther. Temple inched closer, her soft voice coaxing, reassuring. Her knees gripped the rough limb, securing her hold as she concentrated on her task.

Once more she reached for Sebastian and her sudden movement caused the cat to start and spring forward. A tiny claw flashed out, finding its target in the soft flesh of the outstretched hand.

The girl cried out, lost her grip and plunged downward, groping at the air. But the dreaded hard thud of meeting the ground never came. Strong arms broke her fall and held her with assured strength, a warm safety.

Temple opened her eyes to stare into the depths of eyes as soft as velvet, as dark as midnight. The young man made no move to release her, nor did he speak. She was held spellbound as she studied the handsome face so close to her own. His raven-black hair was windblown and he had a proud, straight nose, a strong jaw and a crooked, disarming smile.

Even at the tender age of thirteen Temple felt for the first time the stirrings of a woman's attraction to a man. Never had she seen a man so handsome and, as their eyes met, she was innocently bewildered by the warm, unfamiliar feeling she experienced.

Slowly the young man set her on her feet, steadying her as she stumbled slightly. Only when he swept one bronzed hand across his brow and a crimson trickle spread through his fingers and

3

trailed down his cheek did Temple recover from the spell.

"You are hurt!" she exclaimed, raising her small hand to the wound. Her fingers gently touched the open cut, her touch tender.

"Naught but a scratch, little one," came his low, velvety voice. The sound tugged at Temple's young heart. She detected an accent but could not place its origin.

"But it should be seen to. There is much blood and the cut may be deep," she responded with concern.

He leaned over from his towering height and placed a finger upon the gold, pearl-studded brooch pinned to the shoulder of her dress. Temple glanced down to see droplets of blood staining the oval brooch that had obviously caused his injury.

Quickly she bent down and tore a length of cloth from her petticoat. This she folded and carefully pressed to his bleeding brow. Her hands trembled and she bit at her lower lip as the stranger winced at the pressure. Again their eyes met, gazes mingling, and time stood still.

"Temple!" The magic moment was broken as Erin, her governess, came rushing toward them. The older woman noted the man's injury and took control, instructing the girl to summon help.

As Temple turned to do as she was bid, she heard the stranger assure Erin that there was no necessity, that he was quite all right and would be on his way. Bowing in a gentlemanly manner to the woman, he turned and, with a backward glance at Temple, smiled brilliantly and departed.

The young girl stood watching as the handsome stranger walked briskly across the field and disappeared from sight. She was unaware that she held her breath, confused by an ache in her heart that she had never known before. She knew that she would never forget him, that she would dream of him in the passing years. In her heart was a silent cry, "Will I ever see him again?"

This stranger had stepped into her life, touching her in a way she was still too young to understand. He had touched her heart, a heart most susceptible to warm impressions that were alien to her tender years.

Temple was still a child, pure and innocent, but one waiting upon a shore. She was on the verge of embarking upon a new and wonderful journey, a new awakening. She could see his eyes, still feel his touch upon her flesh, hear his voice, inhale his scent—he would be with her always, even though she knew not from whence he came. She had never even learned his name.

Sardinia, June 9, 1851

A man knelt before the freshly turned earth, his head bent in silent grief as tears rained down his cheeks. His hands were spread flat upon the moist, flower-covered grave and his whispered words could not be heard above the sigh of the wind.

"LaDonna, my love. LaDonna, I am sorry." He turned his face heavenward, his lips trembling, his eyes dark with despair. "Dear God in Heaven! *Why?*" he cried brokenly. Again he bowed his head and wept, his shoulders slumped and shaking, and did not hear the approaching footsteps.

For a moment the newcomer stood watching with hatred in his narrowed eyes. Then he spoke.

"You do not belong here, Harris!" he lashed out with deadly venom.

The grieving man looked up at the speaker standing over him, dressed in black from the wide-brimmed hat on his dark head to his black boots and holding a riding crop in his black-gloved hand. There was an eerie silence for a moment before the black-clad man took a step closer.

"You!" he hissed. His fingers tightly gripped the crop as he pointed to the new grave. "She is there because of *you*. I curse the day she met you! Damn you for her love of you. You killed her and you shall pay for doing so!"

"I loved her, Rosco," answered the mourner. "She—"

His words were cut off as Rosco raised his hand and brought the crop down upon Harris's head

6

with a vicious blow. Again and again the younger man felt the sting of the crop.

"Speak not of love!" Rosco shouted. "Damn you, Nathan Harris! Damn your soul to hell!" With each blow the distraught man cursed, venting his own grief. "My beautiful LaDonna is no more. She lies there beneath the cold ground, never to smile again, never to breathe again. *You* should be there! *You!*"

Nathan slumped forward onto the grave, his face and shoulders bleeding from the cruel attack. Whether due to respect for the older man or love for LaDonna or both, Harris did not know, but he had not warded off the painful lashes.

"You have a daughter, as had I," Rosco Silone bit out, holding the crop in midair, his dark eyes burning into Nathan. "I swear vengeance; you shall pay for my daughter's death! I will have payment for your wrongdoing, for the pain you have caused. I demand your only daughter in exchange for the life of mine."

Harris remained silent, the pain in his heart far greater than the physical pain Silone had inflicted. The avenger lowered his crop and, with a long, ragged breath, continued his tirade.

"My daughter was just twenty and one when you took her from me, Harris. When *your* daughter reaches that same age, you will hand her over to me, thereby making restitution for my loss. Your daughter will become a Silone! She will wed Damon, my only son, my sole heir!"

7

Nathan rose to his feet, his troubled gaze meeting the black eyes so full of fury, but before he could speak, Silone rasped out his final words.

"If your love is as true as you vowed to her in life as well as in death and, now, to me, the life of your flesh and blood is not too much to ask. Look there, Harris." Silone inclined his head toward the grave. "Your blood, drawn by my hand, spilled upon my daughter's grave. Shall yet another body be given to the earth? Your life now, or that of your child eight years hence? Payment in death or in life? Which shall it be?"

Gazing with tear-filled eyes upon the earthen mound, the suffering Nathan made his peace with LaDonna, asked God for understanding, strength and forgiveness, then turned to face Rosco.

"You shall have that which you ask, Silone. God forgive me! Temple will be yours at age twenty and one."

Chapter One

AN URGENT POUNDING ON THE DOOR BROKE THE repose of the wee hours, piercing the stillness of the night.

Temple leaped from her bed, threw on a silk wrap and, stumbling through the darkness, somehow made her way down the stairs to the front door. Breathlessly she pulled open the heavy door and stared questioningly at the man who stood on the threshold, illumined by the street lamp.

"I am John Thomas," the stranger informed her as he removed his hat respectfully. "I am a very close friend of Nathaniel Harris. Are you his daughter?"

"I am," replied Temple, wondering why the man would be calling at such an odd hour.

"Nathan has fallen ill and is at my house. A doctor is with him and I felt that I should come for you. Could you come right away?" His tone was grave and his kindly face colorless. A worried frown creased his broad brow.

Temple's face paled and her knees weakened at the thought of her dear father being ill, yet she hesitated. She did not know this man, nor did she know if there was truth in his words.

Suddenly Erin was at her side, her arm reassuring about Temple's slender waist. "Mr. Thomas," Erin acknowledged the stranger. "Will you please come in? It will take but a moment and Temple and I will be ready to accompany you to her father."

Temple noted the man's quiet "Thank you, Erin," which proved that Thomas was not a stranger to the household. Having only recently returned home from her finishing school, Temple did not know all of her father's friends.

The two women hurried up the stairway and dressed in haste, returning minutes later to join John Thomas for the carriage ride to his home some miles distant.

En route, Temple learned that her father had suddenly become ill while he and his friend were visiting in the latter's study. Without warning, Thomas told them, Nathan's breathing had become shallow, then labored, and an acute pain had gripped his chest. He had then slumped forward in his chair and Thomas, with the help of a servant, had got Nathan upstairs and into bed. A doctor who lived in the area had been summoned and was with him.

Upon arriving at Thomas Hall, Temple followed her father's friend up the wide stairway and to the room where Nathan lay gravely ill. She knelt by his bedside and clasped his cold hand.

"Father," she whispered brokenly, "it is I, Temple. You are going to be all right." She spoke fervently, willing it to be so.

Nathan opened his eyes and smiled weakly, applying the slightest pressure to the small hands that gripped his own. "Temple," he managed, but he was much too weak to talk. "I must—"

"Shush, Father dear," Temple broke in. "You must rest now. Do not attempt to talk."

"My . . . lovely . . . daughter . . ." The words came just above a whisper and Nathan seemed to be in a state of agitation. It was evident that he felt a compelling need to communicate with her. "I must . . . tell . . . most important . . ."

At a loss as to what was bothering him, Temple assured him that she would be close by and that they could talk later. Her father smiled weakly, closed his eyes and drifted off to sleep.

Doctor Tiber followed Temple from the room and closed the bedroom door behind him. "My dear," he began, "your father has suffered a serious heart attack and is very near death. You must be prepared for this eventuality; you must be very strong. Above all, he must be allowed to remain where he is as it would be most unwise to attempt to move him."

"How long—"

"There is no way of knowing for certain, but I fear it could be soon."

11

Temple bowed her lovely head in sorrow and thought of the time she had spent in school, away from her beloved father, the many months they had been apart when they could have been together. He was all she had, almost all she could remember having, as her mother had died when Temple was only seven years old. Now she was losing the only person in the whole world who belonged to her.

She loved Erin, but Erin was not family. The governess had come to live with them about a year after Temple's mother had died. Nathan had realized his child's need of female companionship and had advertised for a governess. He had engaged the eighteen-year-old Erin because he felt that Temple needed youth and gaiety rather than a sour old battle-axe tutor. In fact, one of the latter sort had applied for the position the day before Erin had appeared and Nathan could not fail to note that Temple had withdrawn from the older woman but had responded to Erin with warmth and eagerness.

Now Erin quietly appeared and wrapped her arms around Temple to lend her the comfort she knew was needed. She well knew that the younger woman was a very strong individual—in every respect except where her beloved father was concerned.

John Thomas stepped from a door opposite Nathan's room and spoke to them. "Temple, I have made arrangements for you and Erin to

12

remain here as long as is necessary. The doctor has informed me that Nathan must not be moved, and as my dear friend, he is most welcome in my home until such time as he might be allowed to return to his own home. This room," he indicated the door he had just come through, "will be yours. Please make yourselves comfortable. You also are my guests."

"Thank you, Mr. Thomas, thank you very much," Temple answered warmly. "Now, I would like to return to my father."

It was dawn when Temple left her father's side, wearily making her way across the hall to her own bed. She kicked off her slippers and dropped, exhausted, upon the bed, still fully clothed. Minutes later she had fallen into a deep sleep.

Temple awoke in the strange room in the late afternoon and after a moment of confusion remembered with a start where she was and why. When she learned that Doctor Tiber was with her father, she let Erin persuade her to walk in the garden. Exacting a promise from her friend that she would be called as soon as she was allowed to sit with Nathan, Temple found her way to the beautiful rose garden.

The sinking sun tinted the sky with long fingers of rainbow colors as Temple strolled among the roses toward the rear of the garden. It was there that John Thomas found her a few minutes later, seated on a stone bench beneath a large tree.

"Temple," John said in a hushed tone, seating himself beside her. "It is most urgent that I speak with you." Warm tears welled in the girl's large brown eyes. She felt a tightening around her heart and wondered fearfully if her father had passed away.

"My dear, your father has not long," Thomas began. "Doctor Tiber has said that he only has a few more hours. Shortly after you left him this morning, Nathan suffered another attack."

Temple sprang to her feet with the intention of racing to her father but John stopped her with a hand on her arm. "The doctor is with him, child, and you cannot see him. As soon as you are allowed to, Erin will come for you." He patted her hand sympathetically, then pulled her gently back to sit on the bench.

Sensing an undefined apprehension about Thomas, Temple stared into his kind but troubled eyes.

"Mr. Thomas, you seem to be trying to find a way to tell me something unpleasant. I assure you that I can bear anything. Nothing can be worse than losing my father."

"I am not at all sure of that, Temple," Thomas said and sighed deeply. Then, with a tremendous effort, he went on. "Before you go to Nathan, there is something you must know. He tried to tell you last night, but he was much too weak to explain what it is that he must ask of you."

He rose to his feet and paced slowly back and

14

forth in silence for a few moments before he resumed. "I have known Nathan Harris for many years. He is a good man and he óbviously has done a commendable job of raising you. After your mother died it was necessary for him to put you in boarding schools since he had to be gone for months at a time. Believe me," he looked at Temple earnestly, imploring her to understand, "he never liked leaving you but you are old enough now to understand that it was his job that kept him away from you. He had to go where he was needed, although you needed him, too. It tore him apart!"

Temple listened in silence to this man whom she knew to be her father's friend. What he said was true, she knew it in her heart. Nathan Harris had been both father and mother to her and she knew beyond the shadow of a doubt that he loved her dearly.

"Some years ago," Thomas was saying, "Nathan was on a job in Italy where he met a young woman and fell deeply in love with her, his first love since your mother. Her name was LaDonna and she rekindled the fires of love that Nathan had thought never to experience again. After they had been seeing each other for a few months, LaDonna had to return to her home in Sardinia. Unwilling to lose her, Nathan, at LaDonna's insistence, followed her there and they remained lovers. A few brief months of happiness was all that they had.

15

"LaDonna learned that she was carrying Nathan's child and when she told him, he pleaded with her to marry him. He had asked her several times before to be his wife but she had repeatedly told him that she could not marry him. Your father truly loved this girl and wanted both her and his child. He pleaded for weeks that they be married and finally she told him that she was wed to another. Nathan was deeply hurt; he was like a man possessed. He vowed to find a way for them to be together, but before he could manage that, LaDonna died."

Temple sat in stunned silence. She had never dreamed that her father had been romantically involved since her mother's death. But, of course, those many years ago she had been only a child and Nathan would have thought she would not understand. Suddenly realizing that Thomas had not mentioned whether or not her father's love had been reciprocated by the unknown LaDonna, Temple felt that she must know.

"Did this woman love my father, Mr. Thomas?"

"Oh, yes, my dear! Theirs was a mutual love and a profound one! However, Nathan did question her love for him later when he learned that LaDonna was *not* married to another man. Nor had she ever been."

"But, if she loved my father, why did she lie to him?" The words were wrung from Temple. She seemed to feel the pain her father must have felt.

16

"Fear," Thomas stated flatly, "out-and-out fear!"

"Fear of my father? But why?"

"No, my child. It was fear of *her* father! It was not until the day of her funeral that Nathan learned all the facts." Thomas dropped heavily onto the bench beside Temple. "LaDonna had told Nathan that her name was LaDonna Callas and that she had no family. They always met in secluded places or at Nathan's rooms. But in truth, she was LaDonna Silone, only daughter of Rosco Silone. She had lied out of fear for Nathan, should her father learn the identity of her lover."

"Oh, how awful for them! For my father," she whispered feelingly.

"Yes. LaDonna knew that Rosco was a hard man and very strict, and she feared him as much as she loved him. She also knew that Nathan was an American, a man from a supposedly wild, half-tamed country, and that Rosco would never permit his only daughter to marry out of her class.

"Silone is a proud aristocrat from the old country, bound by heritage and tradition. And in his eyes, Nathan Harris was definitely not in their class!" Thomas paused and Temple, remembering that he had said that her father had "learned all the facts," questioned him further.

"What were the other facts that my father learned, Mr. Thomas?"

"Besides learning who LaDonna really was, Nathan learned that she had died as the result of a miscarriage. It had been his love, his seed, that had caused her death. Or so your father believed. The only other fact, and one that gave Nathan little comfort, was that she called for him with her last breath. That was how Rosco learned the identity of her lover."

"Oh, Mr. Thomas!" Temple cried painfully. "My father has suffered alone all these years! Had I only known, if he had told me, perhaps I could have been some comfort to him. He should have known that I would understand!"

"You were not old enough at the time, my dear, or I feel that he would have confided in you." Thomas shook his head wearily. "I have never seen a man so distraught. And old Silone— he was like a man demented! He damned near killed Nathan when he showed up at the cemetery, beating him with a riding crop as Nathan knelt, grieving, at LaDonna's grave. He cursed your father and swore vengeance, swore that Nathan would pay for causing LaDonna's death!"

After a few moments, Thomas continued in a quiet voice. "You see, Temple, Silone is a Sard. He comes from Sardinia, an island in the Mediterranean, an autonomous region of Italy. And the Sards are among the most dour people on earth! They are marked by intractable sternness, they are proud and hard and unforgiving—at least, Silone is. The Sards believe, literally, in the 'an eye for an eye, a tooth for a tooth' philosophy."

Thomas sat quietly for a moment, running a

hand through his graying hair. "Temple, do you understand what I am getting at?"

The girl shook her head, wondering why Thomas was telling her all these things at such a late date. She did not understand what Rosco Silone could have to do with the present situation. All she wanted was to go to her father, and she thought John Thomas's story could very well wait until another time. With barely concealed impatience, Temple started to rise but Thomas stopped her and resumed his narrative.

"The years have been hard on Nathan, he has been through so much. And he has mourned for LaDonna all these years. So it is time for him to rest, Temple, time for him to make his peace! He can only have that peace, child, with your help. And, please believe me, your cooperation is absolutely necessary!" He looked at her beseechingly.

"I do not understand, Mr. Thomas, why you are telling me this story now. It all happened a long time ago. May I go to him now? He needs me—"

"Yes, Temple," Thomas broke in, "Nathan needs you now more than ever. It is because of this need and because of what is about to happen that you had to know the whole story." As the girl opened her mouth to speak, John held up his hand to silence her. "Listen to me, child, please! Nathan made a promise to Silone all those years ago, a promise that Silone will see that he keeps."

"What kind of promise?" Temple asked uneasily.

"As Nathan knelt at LaDonna's grave, Silone brought down his wrath upon your father. Silone vowed his revenge and demanded the life of Nathan's only daughter for the life of LaDonna, Rosco's only daughter.

"Rosco's words were, 'My daughter was just twenty and one when you took her from me, Harris. And when *your* daughter reaches that same age, you will hand her over to me, thereby making restitution for my loss. Your daughter will become a Silone! She will marry Damon, my only son, my sole heir!' "

With a deep, troubled sigh, Thomas concluded, "It was *that* promise, *that* payment, to which your father agreed."

"No! No! He would not! My father would *never* agree to such an absurd thing!" Temple was in a state of mild shock, unable to believe what she had heard. She twisted her hands in distraction. "Please—please tell me it is not true!"

As the full impact of John's words penetrated her confused mind, Temple told herself that what he had told her was untrue, that her father would never commit himself and *her* to such a ridiculous agreement! They were Americans, from the land of freedom, and her father had instilled in her from a very early age a strong belief in freedom of speech, freedom of choice—in freedom!

Realizing that John Thomas was holding her

hands, she pulled free of his hold. "You are lying, sir," she accused, tears spilling over her flushed cheeks. "Please, you must tell me this is not true!"

But Thomas remained silent and Temple could see stark truth in his eyes. There was a strained silence for a few moments before John shook his head sadly.

"My dear child! I only wish that I could!" he began slowly, his kind eyes pleading for her understanding. "But by some cruel quirk of fate, Rosco Silone has appeared to claim that which he considers payment for the debt he believes Nathan owes him, the payment that your father agreed to."

Temple shook her head, her chin trembling, and her mouth formed the word "no" but no sound came forth. Then she turned and ran blindly from the garden to her father's room, hoping desperately that Nathan would refute John's story.

Pausing outside, Temple drew a long, deep breath and tried to regain her composure before presenting herself to her ailing father. As she entered the dimly lit room, a vaguely familiar man stepped from the shadows, his tall, willowy form seeming to dominate the place. Temple's breath caught in her throat. She was faced with the truth—Rosco Silone!

To her frenzied imagination, Silone was Satan, the avenging dark angel, waiting at the gates of hell to reach out his avaricious hand to plunge her into the licking flames!

"Temple?" Nathan Harris's faint call startled her, bringing her back to the present, and she quickly crossed to her father's bedside.

"Yes, Father, I am here," she crooned softly, taking Nathan's outstretched hand. "You must rest now. I will be right here as long as you need me."

"John? Where is John?" Nathan questioned weakly.

"Mr. Thomas is right outside, Father. He will be in shortly, but now you need to rest."

"No, honey, John must witness—" Nathan's dull blue eyes met Temple's. "Please do not hate me, my darling. Please try to understand what I must ask of you." He halted; the effort to talk seemed to drain his strength. He tried again. "Try to understand . . ." The words trailed off as Silone stepped forward.

Temple felt her knees begin to give way and her sharp intake of breath caused her father to tighten his hold on her hand as if to give her inner strength.

"Temple," Silone addressed her in a low, masterful voice, nodding his gray head. "It is good to see you again after all these years. I am most sorry that it must be under adverse circumstances."

"Mr. Silone," she acknowledged his presence in a choked whisper.

Nathan tugged at his daughter's hand, bringing her full attention back to him. "Temple, there is a long-standing debt that I owe to Rosco. I—I must . . . you must . . ." He clutched his chest and coughed in a painful spasm.

"Shhh," Temple soothed gently. "You must not try to say any more, Father, you are too tired. You must try to sleep and we will talk later."

"No, Temple . . . baby . . . you have to listen to me . . . now! It is very important that you know . . . and fully understand what I am asking—" Again the alarming cough racked Nathan's weak body.

"I know, Father, dear." Temple was amazed at her outward calm when she was quaking inside. Her tear-bright eyes lifted and searched Rosco Silone's face before she leaned forward to place a tender kiss on her father's ashen face. "I have heard the story from Mr. Thomas and know what I must do."

"Then you consent to fulfill this damnable agreement? You will not . . . not hate me for what I so foolishly allowed myself to be coerced into?" Nathan's eyes pleaded for Temple's understanding and reassurance.

"I love you, Father! I have always loved you and always shall! You may rest assured that I will pay your debt and will harbor no resentment toward you. And *never* could I hate you! With God as my witness, I make these promises to you!"

Although Temple's words were hushed, they rang with sincerity in the still room. Those tender promises caused a sudden mist to cloud the vision of the cold, hard Silone.

Nathan smiled in relief at his only child, then raised his eyes to the waiting man. Rosco read unmistakable truth in the dying man's eyes as well as in his words, which vibrated with honesty.

"I loved your daughter, Rosco, loved her more than *you* are capable of understanding. And LaDonna loved me! I felt your pain, your loss— oh, not as a father, but as a man who truly loves a woman. For that I grieved, for that I stopped living a little less each day!"

Nathan paused and the room held an eerie silence. The dying man knew that his time was short and there were things he must express while he still could. His weakened voice had grown strong.

"Now I give you my flesh and blood, my heart, my life," Nathan continued, "and as God above is *my* witness, I have kept my promise. Now do what has to be done." And now the words came dangerously low but clearly heard by all. "Damn you, Rosco Silone, damn you! See that Temple never suffers, see that she is happy! The child does not deserve anything less!"

Silone stepped to Temple's side, taking her cold hand in his own. She bravely raised her brown eyes to the dark, haughty black ones that held hers.

"She will be a Silone, Nathan, and she will have a good life. Of that, I can assure you." Even Rosco Silone could not guarantee more, Temple thought, not once allowing her intent gaze to waver from his.

At that moment John Thomas entered, followed by a priest who held a paper in his hand. The paper was extended to Silone and, upon reading the document, Rosco nodded his head in approval.

Thomas set a quill and an inkhorn on the table nearby as Rosco handed the paper to Temple. She accepted it with trembling hands, her brown eyes wide and questioning on his face.

"This is the marriage certificate, Temple. My son's signature is already affixed," Silone informed her. "You must make your mark—"

Temple stiffened with pride and resentment as she coldly stated, "I am well educated, sir. I can both read and write, among other accomplishments. My father saw to that!"

There was a flicker of admiration deep in the black eyes for the young woman's spirit as well as for her cool composure in an uncomfortable situation. He smiled inwardly at the thought of arrogant, volatile Damon and this proud young beauty who showed such a high opinion of her own dignity. Silone wondered fleetingly at the wisdom of this union he had demanded. For the son was as forceful as the father. There would definitely be a clash of wills.

Turning to Thomas, Silone spoke. "John, you and I will be the witnesses, and *you*," he spoke into the shadows of the room where he himself had been standing when Temple had first entered, "you will stand for the groom."

As the unseen stranger stepped nearer, Temple felt her senses reel. Dear God, she thought in panic, was it to happen just like this? Right now? She had never seen Damon Silone and here she was being married to him—and by proxy, at that! She kept her eyes averted from the man who now stood beside her in the duskiness of the room. How could they do this to her!

The unknown Damon Silone was not even going to be at his own wedding, Temple thought angrily. Was he not even interested enough about the woman he was to marry to be present? Of course not, she told herself sensibly. If he were any kind of a *man* he would be as strongly opposed to this kind of arrangement as she was!

So she was to stand next to a man she did not know and repeat sacred vows that would bind her to another for the rest of her life. It was cold and inhuman, her heart cried, calculated and unfair!

At Rosco's murmured instruction, Temple reluctantly leaned forward and placed the marriage certificate on the low table. As she reached for the quill she met the watchful eyes of her father. His face was pale and drawn and there were tears on his cheeks. She knew that she must do this for

Nathan; she must repay his debt and release him from his torment.

Her heart pounded heavily in her breast. She swallowed the hot tears that choked her throat, dipped the quill into the inkhorn, scrawled her name upon the damnable paper with a shaking hand and thrust it toward Silone with asperity.

Temple reached for her father's hand, needing the physical contact, the assurance of his love for her. She glanced toward the tall stranger but could only see a shadowy form outside the faint circle of the dim lamplight.

"Who giveth this woman in wedlock?" The low words of the priest began the ceremony.

"I, Nathan Harris, the girl's father." With those words Nathan handed his daughter's cold, limp hand to the man who stood in the near darkness. Did she imagine it or did she actually see a glimmer of a smile in Nathan's dull eyes? And was there not a sudden softening of her father's drawn lips as he breathed "thank you"? Were the words of gratitude meant for her? No, she realized in confusion; her father's eyes were riveted on the stranger.

Her hand was clasped in a firm hold and the warmth that emanated from that unknown hand was strangely reassuring. She felt as if she were adrift on a vast, dark sea and the grip on her hand was her only lifeline. Again Temple glanced upward at the man who now held her hand. For some odd reason it seemed important that she see his face but, again, she could not make out his features.

"Do you, Temple Maurine Harris, take Damon Ross Silone . . ." The words flowed on and when they ceased, Temple answered unwillingly and in a choked whisper, "I—I will."

As she spoke, the stranger's hand squeezed hers gently and he ran his thumb over her numb fingers. She found the gesture oddly reassuring.

"And does Damon Ross Silone take this woman . . ." When the pause came, a deep rumbling voice that held no uncertainty stated, "He does!"

Temple felt that if it were the man who stood beside her, this stranger who held her hand so securely within the warmth of his own, this man whose face she could not see—if it were *this* man to whom she was being wed, she would not mind so much. There was a gentleness and understanding that seemed to flow from him to Temple through their clasped hands. And something more, something indefinable.

Then she heard the final words of the ceremony. "I pronounce you man and wife. You may seal the pledge."

Temple obediently turned to the stranger and offered her cheek for his kiss but found herself being pulled against the hard length of the man's body as his lips came down on hers with such pure tenderness that her heart tripped in its beat. The warm, gentle mouth moved over hers with a slow and tranquil deliberation and Temple found her body molding itself to his embrace, her lips returning the kiss with an equally fervent response. She heard a low moan deep within his throat and her soft moan answered his.

Suddenly the kiss was broken and the stranger set Temple gently but firmly away. For a fleeting moment the strong hands held her upper arms and then released their hold, the man's fingers trailing slowly down the length of her arms. She felt drawn to him as if an unknown force were pulling her back, some power urging her toward his embrace.

Frightened, Temple turned abruptly away from the stranger, still feeling the pressure of his lips upon hers. The blood coursed hotly through her veins and her heart was beating like a wild thing in her breast. She felt shaken and utterly confused.

"Forgive me, my darling daughter." Nathan's weak plea broke through the chaos of Temple's emotions and she tried to concentrate on his words. "Be happy, Temple," he whispered as she knelt at his side. "I know Damon Silone . . . he is a man like none you have ever known. Give yourself time . . . and you will love him . . . you see, honey . . . Damon has . . . always . . ."

Nathan's words had grown more faint as he spoke and now they died away as he drew his final breath. Those were Nathan Harris's last words to the daughter he loved so dearly. Temple slumped, grief-stricken, over her father's body and cried out in her sorrow. Looking back, she would always remember the comfort of those strong arms, the arms of a stranger, as he reached out, held her and soothed the raw, cutting pain in her aching heart.

Chapter Two

TEMPLE TWISTED THE WIDE GOLD WEDDING BAND that encircled her slender finger. The band was uncomfortable; it seemed to weigh her hand down. A noose around her neck would have been preferable to the gleaming circlet of gold that bound her to a stranger! A man she did not know, had never seen.

A marriage by proxy! Leaning her weary head back against the plush upholstery, Temple moaned beneath her breath, "Something like this just does not happen to someone like me!" The moan and choked whisper caused a look of deep concern to cross Erin's face.

Yet Temple could bear witness that things "like this" *could* happen to her. It *had* happened and the fact that she was finding it hard to believe, not wanting to believe it, made no difference, none at all!

"Temple," Erin spoke softly, reaching out a compassionate hand to grasp the hand of her friend. "This is something that cannot be

31

changed, therefore it is something that you must accept."

"But I cannot, Erin. This marriage goes against all that I believe in. Marriage should take place between two people who love, not be forced upon those who do *not* love! No! I shall *never* accept it!"

Realizing the futility of further admonition, Erin lapsed into silence and focused her attention on the loading of their trunks, watching with admiration the rippling muscles of the dockhands as they hoisted their heavy burdens. Only ten years Temple's senior, Erin was far from immune to being attracted to a rugged, virile man. In fact, she had enjoyed a mild flirtation with one of the seamen on the voyage from France to Sardinia.

Staring unseeingly out the small window of the carriage lost in thought, Temple did not see the pretty, dark-haired girl approach, nor did she hear at first when the girl spoke to her.

"*Signora* Silone? *Signora* Silone!"

Slowly the voice floated into Temple's consciousness and she turned to the speaker who stood just outside the carriage. "*Signora* Silone," the young woman began, "I am Sophia, from the Villa Silone. *Signore* Damon, he asked that I meet you, as he himself could not come." Sophia took a deep breath before continuing, "The *Signore*, he had to go to Nuoro for business and the *Signora* will be met by his father at the villa. I am to accompany you there."

Temple smiled vaguely at the young woman. "Thank you, Sophia. If that is my husband's wish—"

My husband! Dear God, she thought, will I ever get accustomed to that? She must remember that her name was no longer Temple *Harris.* She must learn to respond when addressed as *"Signora* Silone." She was now the wife of Damon Ross Silone—*the* Damon Silone, as her friend, Carla, had so excitedly shrieked when told that Temple had been married, and to whom.

"Damon Silone of the shipping industry?" Carla had asked, her enormous blue eyes wide with excitement. *"The* Silones from Sardinia? Oh, Temple, how fortunate for you! And how happy you must be!"

Happy? Suddenly Temple had felt that never again would she know happiness. She wondered if she would ever again laugh, even smile, with genuine pleasure. No, not when her whole world had been turned upside down, her entire life planned for her without a thought for her wishes. Happy! No, there would be no happiness in her future, but she had not told Carla this.

Both girls had heard of the Silones all their lives; the name was known internationally. Temple had, at a young age, met Rosco Silone, who had founded the family's shipping business many years before and gone on to make it one of the largest in the world. She had not been favorably impressed by the man. There had been something about him that she had disliked, an undercurrent of ominousness she could not quite identify.

Temple recalled now that Rosco never laughed and she remembered his eyes, eyes that were of the deepest black-violet. She felt a distinct uneasiness about Rosco Silone. Something about him made her tense and nervous.

A sudden lurch of the carriage brought Temple's thoughts back to the present as the steady rhythm of the horses' hooves and the turning wheels carried her ever closer to the Villa Silone and the life that had been forced upon her. She noted that Erin was studying her closely, deep concern shadowing her soft gray eyes. Temple gave a strained smile, nervously tucking a stray curl behind her ear.

"Do not worry so, dear Erin," she managed to say, her voice strained. "Everything will be all right. And if you find that you are not happy here, you can return."

"But I would *never* do that!" Erin informed her in a choked voice. "I would never leave you."

"But Erin, you need not concern yourself with me any longer. I am not the child who was placed in your charge many years ago; I am of age and—and now I am a married woman. You have your own life and, though I asked you to come here with me, you are in no way obligated to remain if you are unhappy."

There was a brief silence as the two women

regarded each other thoughtfully. Then, in a soft voice, her words measured, Erin spoke.

"I have watched you grow into a beautiful young woman, Temple. I have cared for you, understood you, taught you. Yes, that was my duty, you were my responsibility, but . . ." The older woman's voice shook slightly as she went on. "But I have laughed with you, cried with you, shared your secrets and your dreams. I never thought of you as merely my charge as I—I learned to love you."

Erin's gray eyes clouded and her lips trembled. "You have always been more like a younger sister to me. You see, I had no family when your father engaged my services. I was always happy with you. Nathan gave me a home, a family, without knowing that he did so. You are all I have left!"

"Oh, Erin," Temple cried, hugging the other woman. She had never known the depth of Erin's feelings, never realized that she felt so strongly about her and Nathan. And what Erin had said, "you are all I have left," was exactly what Temple felt about her and was one reason she had asked Erin to come with her to her new home.

With tears shining in her brown eyes and her small chin quivering, Temple whispered brokenly, "I am very glad that you are here, Erin. *You* are all that *I* have left, as well! And your being by my side has made this whole outrageous nightmare bearable. Having you near will make it easier. I know that I will always have your love and understanding. I did not ask you to come with me as my governess; I wanted you with me, Erin, I need you."

Tears came to the dove-gray eyes and a gentle smile curved Erin's lips as she took Temple's hand in hers. "Everything will be all right, my dear. We do have each other and together we will ride out any storms we may encounter."

"Yes," Temple replied uncertainly, then, her voice stronger, "Yes, we will!"

Temple knew that her first glimpse of the Villa Silone would remain forever in her memory. It was breathtaking. The stately manor house rose before them surrounded by the lush greenery of the hillside. The whitewashed, two-storied stone house stood proud and beautiful. To the reluctant young bride peering apprehensively from the approaching carriage, the Villa Silone seemed to beckon to her in warm welcome.

The carriage drew to a halt before the wide steps leading up to the large double doors and the driver handed Temple out, steadying her as she stepped to the cobblestone drive. Breathing in the sweet odor of the olive groves mixed with a tangy citrus scent and another unfamiliar fragrance, Temple believed for just a moment that she could be content in this lovely, quiet countryside, living in the gracious old manor. Maybe, just *maybe*, life here would not be so awful.

As those thoughts passed through Temple's mind, the villa's wide door swung open and Rosco Silone stepped out, his dark eyes cold and his mouth a grim, thin line in his hard face. At the sight of him, Temple's pleasant thoughts came to an abrupt halt.

How she disliked this man who had come unexpectedly and uninvited into her life, bringing her world crashing down about her. A man who had hurt her dear father, had destroyed his life and now hers; a vain, arrogant man who had seemingly appointed himself to play God, bringing more pain, more unhappiness, into the life of another Harris!

No! Temple thought vehemently, this could never be home! There would never be any love or happiness here. Always she would remain a stranger, forever on the outside looking in.

Sudden tears choked her and she bit back the helpless cry that threatened to break from her lips. In utter dejection Temple mounted the steps toward the hated man and the open door of the Villa Silone.

Temple crossed the wide portico, her slippered feet moving silently down the wide steps and over the soft green grass and along the narrow path leading from the villa. The sun blazed overhead, its warmth touching the lush hillside. Her face was flushed and her heart beat with excitement at the new and unknown land. A faint breeze stirred and the fragrance of the countryside filled her nostrils.

She moved about the courtyard, lightly touching the silvery-green leaves of the hedge, then bent to smell a fragile yellow blossom. Plucking the delicate bloom, she raised her gaze, taking in the flowering trees that seemed to spread out forever. The sweet, heady fragrance of the blossoms filled the warm afternoon air.

Temple had to admit that the Villa Silone was truly a beautiful place. At present she was alone with her thoughts, her emotions. Erin had begun the task of unpacking and settling them in but Temple felt the need to walk, to be alone, away from the damnable Rosco if only for a brief time before she had to face her new life.

She walked on, enjoying the cool breeze as it wafted through the trees and across the rolling land. Temple was not aware that the beautiful trees that covered the landscape with their silvery-green foliage and gnarled trunks were fruit-bearing olive trees, one source of the Silone empire, that the small, greening fruit constituted a crop of fundamental importance in the daily life and fortune of the Villa Silone.

The low hum of voices reached Temple's ears and she moved on through the trees and stepped from the shadows of the branches into a small clearing. Shading her eyes from the sudden glare of the sunlight, she squinted to adjust her vision to the brightness. A low wooden fence separated her from another cluster of trees and she moved forward to rest her arms along the top rail as she stood watching several men and women working. They were plucking the small, oval-shaped fruit that nestled among the green leaves and placing it in large baskets.

Scanning the rows of trees, Temple saw more people, some on ladders among the branches, each going contentedly about his task. She smiled as she saw small children with long sticks beating at the lower branches, then scampering to gather the green fruit as it rained to the earth. Their happy laughter mingled with the huskiness of an old woman's singing as she slowly helped them to gather the filled baskets. The old woman signaled to some young men near the end of the row and they came racing to lift the baskets into a nearby wagon.

Then Temple saw him. He sat assured and proud astride a great black stallion. The gentle afternoon breeze lifted his dark sable hair, leaving it in unruly, yet attractive disarray. Temple's keen gaze drank in the rock-hard muscles of his broad shoulders beneath the sweat-drenched white shirt. His shirt-sleeves were rolled up and his strong, tanned arms, although relaxed, displayed a steely strength. The lean, muscular legs were clad in tight, fawn-colored breeches and black, knee-high riding boots.

He sat motionless and Temple realized that he was watching her as intently as she was studying him. He made no attempt to move from his place in the clearing, nor did he acknowledge her presence in any way other than his steady, piercing gaze.

Temple felt a strange tingling claim her body. She knew that from this distance he could not possibly know that her very body was trembling from the sudden sensual tension that his presence caused. But when a slow, disarming smile touched his lips and he nodded his dark head slightly, she knew that he was acknowledging her existence and her open staring. Her heart suddenly raced out of control and her breath became ragged as she blushed hotly. God, what was she doing? Never before had she been so brazen; never before had a man affected her in this manner.

What would she do if he should come toward her . . .

As if the thought were a wish granted, the man nudged his horse forward and approached Temple as if in slow motion. She watched wide-eyed as the handsome man astride the impressive stallion moved gracefully and purposefully toward her. Reining in his mount before the speechless young woman, he slipped one long leg across the animal's broad back to rest easily on the saddle horn and leaned forward as if to get a closer look at Temple's lovely face.

He smiled lazily, the beautiful, curved mouth revealing even, white teeth and the hint of a dimple in his left cheek. He spoke not a word, merely let his dark, midnight eyes roam leisurely over her small frame with open male approval.

In turn, Temple studied the handsome stranger before her, noting the haughty, angular face with its deeply etched features, strong jaw, proud straight nose and full, sensuous mouth. Once more a tremor ran through her body as their eyes met and held.

The wind stirred once again, lifting the thick black hair from the man's brow to reveal a small scar above his right eye, the thin line disappearing into his dark eyebrow. There was such power in the man, such magnetism emanating from him that it almost frightened Temple, yet she found it breathtakingly exciting.

Temple ran her tongue along her lower lip in a nervous gesture and his gaze focused on the slightly parted lips. He leaned down and drew the yellow flower from her trembling fingers, raised it to inhale deeply of its fragrance, then brushed the delicate petals across his lips. With a fluid movement he then leaned down once more and tenderly brushed the blossom across Temple's own lips and tucked the lovely flower into the silkiness of her honey-colored hair just above her ear. As the petals brushed over her lips it was as if his lips had brushed hers, and the intimate gesture stirred her senses, stilled her breath and brought a low moan from within her to escape her parted lips.

Raising his scarred eyebrow in a questioning

arch, the man traced his forefinger along the gold band that encircled Temple's finger. His warm breath fanned her face as he spoke.

"Buon giorno, Signora." His voice was a deep, velvety sound that seemed to caress her senses, causing Temple's heart to lurch. She stared speechlessly at the intriguing stranger. His smile widened as he ventured, *"Avete capito?"* When she remained silent, he asked in English, "Do you understand?"

"N-no," Temple stuttered, then remembered that when the maid had spoken to her in the native tongue, Rosco had replied in their language that the *Signora* did not understand. Drawing from memory, Temple added uncertainly, *"Non capisco."*

The dark eyes never left hers as he studied her lovely, puzzled face. Then a low, husky chuckle rattled deep in his throat and the midnight eyes twinkled as he sought to enlighten her.

"I said, 'Good day, Madam.'" He spoke in beautifully smooth English with just the hint of an accent. But it was his eyes, not his voice, that held her; they were piercing and alive with challenge. She seemed to be drawn into the black-violet depths of his eyes and felt that she was drowning in their liquid darkness.

"You are a Silone?" Temple's words were more a statement than a question. She felt that only a Silone would have such fathomless, such *black* eyes.

"Yes, I am a Silone," he admitted, running a hand through his raven hair. "But tell me, my little beauty, how did you know?"

"Your eyes," Temple answered a bit breathlessly but without hesitation. "They—their color—it is most unusual."

This seemed to amuse him for he threw back his head and laughed heartily. The vibrant sound set the blood racing in Temple's veins. Still smiling, he said, "Ah, yes. The damnable Silone eyes. They are a hereditary trait that comes down to us from Rinaldo Silone, fifth or sixth generation back, I think it is. They say that not one male Silone since old Rinaldo has been born without the uncanny black-violet eyes."

He sighed heavily, his hand tapping the hilt of the riding crop that he had tucked into his boot. His gaze lifted and swept the countryside as if he were deep in thought, then swung back to Temple.

"And you, Madam? Who might *you* be?" he asked quietly, his tone hushed.

"Temple," she answered simply. "Temple . . . Silone," she added, nearly choking on the words, her eyes downcast.

"Silone? You, with your warm brown eyes and honey-colored hair?" the man countered, his smile bringing his dimple into play. Shaking his dark head, he went on, "No, this I cannot believe."

"Believe me, sir. Although I, myself, am still

43

finding it difficult to believe. I keep wishing to awaken and . . . and . . ." There was a brief pause during which the man remained silent and watchful, and then she whispered, ". . . and find that it has all been a bad dream."

Still the man waited silently. Moments later Temple raised her head and said vehemently, "Only that will not be. I *am* a Silone! Rosco Silone saw to that! And he cared not whom he hurt in doing so. He was interested only in accomplishing that which he had decreed should be!" Then she added quietly, "The marriage —it was arranged . . . it was a marriage by proxy. . . ."

Her tear-bright eyes met the dark ones of her attentive listener as if pleading for understanding. Why she had told him all this she did not know, but to her surprise Temple saw a flash of genuine concern in the depths of his dark, watchful eyes.

"Surely you are not telling me that you are married to Rosco Silone!"

"No, I am wed to his son," Temple explained quickly. "But I have not yet met him—"

"Ah! Damon!" he broke in.

"Y-yes, *Damon*," she stammered, her hand wiping at the tears that were now swimming in her eyes. Suddenly realizing that before her was a Silone, a relative of her husband, she thought that perhaps he could tell her something, *anything*, about the stranger she had married.

44

"You know Damon?" Her gaze was both questioning and hopeful.

"But of course!" he chuckled, watching her closely.

"You know him well?" Temple asked.

"*Very* well," he assured her, then added, "I would say that I know Damon Silone better than *anyone*, even his father."

Then please, *please* tell me about him, Temple pleaded silently. Tell me that he is a kind man and not hard and unfeeling, like his father. Oh, please tell me that my life here with him will not be completely miserable!

"Is Damon . . . is he a kind man?" she ventured.

There was a brief silence before he answered and Temple realized that she was holding her breath.

"A kind man? I believe so," finally came the quiet reply. His head was bent and he absently toyed with the riding crop, then pulled it from his boot.

"Is he cruel? Is he a hard man, like his father?" Temple persisted.

"At times . . . he can be." It was spoken with studied quietness, as if the man were weighing his words, thinking about his reply.

Temple wondered if he might at some time have borne the brunt of Damon's displeasure, if he had perhaps witnessed some cruelty of the man she had married. Yet he had said he thought Damon was kind.

"Please, can you tell me—" she began again.

"Anything more, little one," he broke in softly, but his voice trailed away and stilled. Piercing her with his eyes, he gently traced an imaginary path along her cheek with the handle of his riding crop, another intimate gesture that caused Temple to suck in her breath sharply.

"Anything more about your husband, *Signora Silone*, you shall learn in good time. I am quite certain that you will be enlightened, Madam, about the things you wish to know about him."

And with that, he swung his leg back across the horse and, settling himself in the saddle, touched his crop to his brow in salute and cantered away. He did not look back at the open-mouthed Temple he left staring after him.

Chapter Three

"Oh, Temple, you are back!" Erin's concerned voice met her as she entered the house and Temple turned to see her friend descending the stairway.

"Yes," she replied as she slowly began to mount the stairs. "I felt the need to be alone, to sort out my emotions." Temple's thoughts were still very much on the dark stranger.

"And did you?" Erin questioned, noting the faraway look in the younger woman's eyes.

"Did I what?"

"Sort out your feelings?"

"Uh—no. No, I merely managed to confuse myself even more," Temple answered honestly, with a bewildered shake of her head. "I do not understand, Erin . . . there was a time when I knew my own mind, a time when I could *control* my feelings!" As the two women spoke, they made their way along the wide upper corridor.

"I am married against my will to a man whom I do not know and *certainly* do not love. I have

47

been brought to an unknown country to begin a new life with that man." Temple paused, then with a deep sigh, she murmured, "Tied to one stranger and attracted to another!"

"What?" Erin came to an abrupt halt, her eyes wide with shock and disbelief, her hand clutching at Temple uncertainly.

"Oh, Erin! I met a man!" Temple turned to her breathlessly, her face flushed and stars in her large brown eyes.

"When? Where?"

"Never have I seen a man so handsome," Temple went on as if Erin had not spoken. "His eyes are the color of midnight . . . his smile—oh, Erin, his smile . . . it takes my breath away!"

"Oh, Temple!" Erin groaned in despair. This would not do! Not at all!

". . . and he rode a beautiful black horse . . ."

Even though Temple's words tumbled on, Erin was not listening. What was the girl thinking of? As if the whole damnable situation was not bad enough already! Lord, but the child did not need any more of Rosco Silone's wrath brought down on her! Before they had sailed there had been many harsh words between Temple and Rosco, even scenes during which they had confronted each other with raised, angry voices and clenched fists.

Temple had snapped that she wanted no part of Rosco *or* his hideous son, no part of his damned villa *or* his country! And Rosco's words had been delivered coldly and deliberately: he cared little for her desires and less about her emotions; she was married to a Silone and there was no changing that fact, no going back. He had threatened to put her bodily aboard the ship to Sardinia, and if necessary, to lock her in her cabin and place a guard at her door.

The verbal duel had gone on for days until Erin had stepped in, calming Temple and gradually convincing her that what was done was done. As unbearable as the situation was, Erin had had to admit there was nothing Temple could do save accept her fate. Not that Rosco had won and Temple had lost, but it was a battle that had ended before there ever was a war plan.

Temple was married, and that was that! She would go to Sardinia to her husband and make the best of her life, she had decided. She knew the truth of Erin's words and although Temple's spirit still rebelled, she had faced the inevitable.

"I shall go, Rosco Silone!" she had spat as if to rid her mouth of a bad taste. "I will go only because I have no other choice. But, damn you, I shall make you wish you had never forced this marriage on me!"

Erin had seen the fury in Temple's brown eyes, the shaking of her small body, the clenching of her fist, and had smiled inwardly at her spirit. And she had also seen the hard set of Rosco's mouth and the fire in his dark eyes as he, too, witnessed the fury of his new daughter-in-law.

They would always be on opposite sides, Temple and Rosco, always be on a collision course. A battle royal would forever wage between those two and Erin would not have wagered on the outcome. The son of one and the husband of the other, how would Damon Silone mesh into the lives and temperaments of these two bitter enemies?

Erin's thoughts returned to the present. On her first day at the villa, just hours after her arrival, Temple had met a man whom she apparently was enamored of. Sweet Christ! What was to happen now?

". . . would that not truly infuriate Rosco Silone?" Temple was asking triumphantly and with her hands on her hips she gave a pure, clear burst of laughter.

"What was that?" Erin questioned, having heard only the latter part of Temple's ravings about the handsome stranger.

"Him being a Silone, do you not see?" Temple supplied with a grin.

"A Silone? *Who* being a Silone?"

"The man!" Temple fairly shouted. "The man I just met. He is also a Silone."

"How—how do you know this?"

"He told me, Erin. Or rather *I* told *him.*" Temple's voice was filled with excitement and her words confused Erin, who was finding this whole drama most difficult to follow.

"*You* told him?" she ventured. "And how—"

"His eyes, of course! Although I have only seen Rosco's eyes, the stranger's eyes were the same uncanny black-violet. Only *his* eyes were not cold, not hard with that unfeeling darkness. They —they were bright with an alertness, a knowing. They had the power to pull you right into them." Temple's brown eyes sparkled with golden tints, then deepened with anticipation as she silently vowed to see the stranger again, somehow.

"Oh, Erin," she continued, "it was such a warm feeling, one I have never before felt, only dreamed of." She hugged herself, allowing the welcoming warmth to once again flow through her.

"This can only mean trouble," Erin murmured to herself distractedly.

Temple walked about the huge bedchamber, her eyes resting upon each feature. The walls were ice-blue in color, the floor was covered with a darker blue rug and the curtains were the same dark blue. She noted the arched marble fireplace and ran her fingertips across its cool surface.

The room was quite beautiful as well as comfortable. There was a large, four-poster bed with light blue tester and spread, two upholstered side chairs and a washstand, dressing table and bureau all richly polished to enrich the warm tones of the mahogany.

Temple stepped from her slippers and she wriggled her toes, burying them deep within the welcome softness. She padded across the floor and stood before the dressing table, studying her image in the mirror.

The girl staring back at her looked tired and so very unhappy. The shadows of unwelcome circles showed beneath her eyes. Her cheeks even looked somewhat sunken. The journey from France had been trying and the food barely edible. Running her fingers through her tousled hair, Temple sighed and moved to the bureau. She would change into a fresh gown before going down for dinner.

She pulled open the bureau drawer and her eyes widened in disbelief; she stood staring down, her fingers hovering just above the open drawer. Temple blinked her disbelieving eyes as if to clear her vision and with trembling fingers she touched the smooth fabric, then withdrew first one, then another garment from its resting place.

"No!" she whispered. "Oh, no!" The objects of her discovery were men's shirts. Quickly she opened another drawer and found men's undergarments. The next drawer held her own undergarments and the last, her blouses.

She raced to the dressing closet and stood frozen as her eyes beheld her own garments hanging on one side and men's clothing on the other. Lined up on the floor were her slippers and two pairs of men's riding boots.

Slowly Temple backed away from the closet and sat heavily upon the bed. There was no doubt that the articles belonged to Damon—her husband! "Oh, dear God!" she groaned aloud. This was *his* room! Erin had put away Temple's belongings in *his* room, had arranged everything neatly alongside his things. Husband and wife! She was to share this room—this bed!

Suddenly she sprang from the bed as if it had moved beneath her and clamped a hand over her mouth to silence the cry that rose in her throat. Her heart was beating wildly and she could hardly breathe.

"Erin!" Temple screamed in a panic-filled voice. "Erin-n-n-n!"

Only a short way down the hall, Erin started at the urgent cry and dropped the china music box she was unpacking. Temple! It was Temple's voice, that ear-piercing cry.

Erin raced down the hall and flung open the door to see the younger woman standing in the middle of the room, her eyes wide and unnaturally bright, her body trembling.

"Temple!" she gasped, hurrying to her side. "What is it, dear? What—what has happened?" Erin grasped the girl's shoulders in alarm, giving her a slight shake. But Temple only stood silent and trembling. "Temple! Tell me what is wrong!" she demanded, her own voice fearful.

"This is Damon Silone's room!" Temple choked out, pulling away from Erin's hold. She pulled a shirt from the drawer and waved it in the air. *"His* clothes! *His* things!" Temple threw it to the floor as she crossed to the dressing closet and jerked a cutaway coat of dark blue velvet from its hanging place. *"Damon's* room, Erin!"

Erin had wondered about Temple's reaction upon learning that she shared her husband's bedchamber. She knew that the girl was not ready for this and would declare such an arrangement totally unacceptable. But all Erin's pleas, all her arguments to Rosco had fallen upon deaf ears.

"She is Damon's wife!" he had told Erin firmly. "His wife in *every* way!"

So Erin had unpacked Temple's clothes and placed them alongside those of her husband as Rosco demanded.

Now, gently pulling Temple toward the bed, Erin sat upon it, tugging the reluctant girl down to sit beside her. "Temple, my dear, please listen to me," she began in a calm voice. "You are married to Damon—"

"I will *not* share this room with him!" Temple gritted and leaped up. "I will *not* share that bed!" she fairly screamed, pointing at the object of her disapproval.

"But you *must,* Temple!" Erin tried to reason with her. "A man and wife *should* share a room—a bed—it is only natural."

"Natural?" Temple countered hotly. " 'Natural,' yes, when they love each other and when— when they *wish* to be together—to be man and wife!" She brushed the tears of anger from

54

her eyes. "*This* is not such a marriage! And I *will not*—"

"Rosco has decreed it," Erin cut in quietly. "I tried to reason with him, Temple, but he would have none of it, he would not listen."

"Rosco Silone can go straight to hell!" Temple raged, heading for the door that Erin had left standing open. She raced out into the hall and was halfway down the stairs before Erin reached the upper landing.

"Temple! Wait!" she called urgently, but Temple was beyond listening, beyond caring. Erin closed her eyes and breathed a silent prayer. There was no stopping Temple when she was in such a state and Erin envisioned the two adversaries hurling angry words, maybe even coming to blows, even drawing blood! At that thought, she hurried down the stairway.

"Rosco Silone!" Temple hissed as she flew into the study, ready to do battle. But the room was empty. She wheeled about and charged down the short hallway. "Rosco Silone!" she bellowed, her fury rising by degrees. She met a startled young housemaid who looked at her as if Temple were daft. The little maid flattened herself against the wall and made the sign of the cross. Surely the new *Signora* would be murdered by the older *Signore* Silone, she thought. *No* one had ever shouted at him so.

Temple rushed past the maid and threw open

the double doors to the library. Rosco stood haughtily before her, a brandy snifter in his hand, his heavy eyebrows raised questioningly.

"Damn you, Rosco Silone! *Damn* you!" she gritted, her clenched fists beating the air, her eyes shooting golden fire. "You go too far! I was ordered to wed your son—a man who cared so little that he was not even at his own marriage ceremony! I stood by and watched my father die as he pleaded that I fulfill his damned, stupid 'promise' to you. A promise that should never have been demanded, a promise that *certainly* should never have been honored!" she spat in blazing fury. She glared unafraid, unflinchingly, into the amused black eyes of the man who towered above her.

Rosco had already admitted to himself that he liked the spirit his son's wife displayed. Not only that, he actually respected her fiery temper and the fact that she was not afraid of him, not one whit! There were very few people who had ever dared to stand up to Rosco Silone. This chit of a girl did not give an inch in their personal warfare. Yes, he thought, he had made a very wise choice for his son. Already she had the characteristics of a true Silone!

"You took my life, my freedom, and gave it to your son whom I seriously doubt is a *real* man if he allows his father to rule his life!" Temple raged. "You took me from my home to bring me to this—this damnable country—to this house, knowing full well that I never wanted to come here. You have played God with me, Rosco Silone, for the last time! I *will not* live in Damon's room and share his bed! *I will not*—"

"You will do as Damon wishes!" Rosco spoke for the first time, his eyes cold, black chips now, his voice icy. "You are his wife—"

"The hell I am!" Temple shouted. "In name only, and that it shall remain!"

"We shall see, Temple," he told her, placing his empty snifter on the table.

"I hate you! I hate your son!" she stormed, stamping her bare foot in her anger. "I will *never* let him touch me, I will *never* truly be his wife!"

In her rage Temple had not heard the front door open, nor had she heard the sound of the steps on the marble floor of the entry hall. Only Erin had heard and she turned to see a young man enter the library. He slowly removed his gloves and tossed them on a nearby table, casting his riding crop after them. He unbuttoned his shirt and began to pull the shirttail from his breeches, exposing a broad, deeply tanned chest covered by a mat of dark hair. There was a slight smile on his lips as he observed the scene before him, hearing every word, every vow that Temple uttered.

Erin was taken aback by the sheer handsomeness of this man who stood there, feet braced wide apart, hands on his narrow hips, dark eyes twinkling with a mysterious gleam. Surely this was not Damon Silone, Erin mused. But if not

Damon, who? Rosco's gaze suddenly lifted from the irate Temple to stare over her shoulder.

"Damon!" Rosco greeted his son with a broad smile. "Your wife, I fear, is quite a hellion!"

Erin groaned to herself and Temple whirled to stare straight into the midnight eyes of Damon Silone. The knowing eyes stared back, the smile on his full lips widened.

"Hello again, little one." Damon's tone was low and husky, the sound causing Temple to tremble and her heart to pound hard against her breast. Her knees threatened to buckle beneath her.

"Oh, my God!" was all she could say and even that came out as a choked whisper.

Damon stepped nearer, his gaze taking in every detail of Temple's appearance from the wild disarray of her honey-colored hair to her bare feet. She did not move as he stopped only inches away from her. God, he thought, but she was beautiful. Even more beautiful in her anger than she had been this afternoon in the groves.

And she had been standing there venting her anger, unleashing her hatred for Rosco's son, vowing never to love him, never to be his wife! Damon chuckled, for he had seen the hunger in those brown eyes, had read the longing there. He had felt the heat from her body and knew, without a doubt, that her vows would be most difficult to uphold.

Temple was thinking the same thing. Her attraction to this man was overpowering; one look into the depths of his dark eyes and she was aflame with desire for him. He was so handsome, so virile. All he would have to do was touch her and she would be lost. She had known that this afternoon when she had first seen him—this afternoon! The mysterious stranger was her husband! She had asked this man questions about Damon Silone when *he* was Damon Silone! She had made a complete fool of herself—*he* had made a fool of her! Oh, how he must have enjoyed the encounter, how he must have laughed at her.

Anger swept over Temple like a raging tide. He had known who she was and—

"You!" she hissed and before Damon could move, Temple lashed out, her hand meeting his cheek with a fiery, resounding slap that rang out across the room. Erin watched in wide-eyed horror and Rosco's mouth dropped open in pure astonishment. And before anyone had time to react, Temple fled the room. The slam of the front door echoed along the hallway moments later.

Erin made no move to follow. She stood rooted to the floor in stunned surprise, as did Rosco, both staring at Damon. He raised his hand to his reddening cheek. His fingertips touched the corner of his mouth and came away moist with blood. He ran his tongue over his smarting lip and gazed down at the crimson stains on his fingers.

Then, to the surprise of both Rosco and Erin, Damon threw back his handsome head and laughed. It was a deep, throaty sound and his body shook with his laughter. Blood *had* been drawn, Erin thought, but Lord, not in the manner in which she had imagined! And Damon had borne the brunt of Temple's fury, had suffered a blow from her hands, yet he stood there laughing! Erin shook her head. It did not make sense to her at all.

Damon's twinkling eyes met the shocked ones of his father and as he spoke there was still laughter in his velvety voice.

"You are right, Rosco, she *is* a hellion!" Damon agreed. "But, God! Is she not beautiful? She has a fiery passion that I shall enjoy to the utmost, a spirit worth taming, but not breaking." Again he chuckled and added, "The war is on, Rosco, and she is damned well worth the fight!"

Damon Silone walked to the liquor cabinet, poured himself a brandy and stood studying the swirling amber liquid that reminded him of Temple's sparkling eyes. A tender smile touched his sensuous lips and he walked to the open door and lifted his brandy snifter in salute to the young beauty who had lashed out at him in such passionate anger.

Again the throaty chuckle sounded as Damon turned back to his still silent audience, raised his snifter once more in a silent toast to the pair, then tossed down the golden liquid in one gulp.

Chapter Four

ERIN PAUSED JUST OUTSIDE THE LIBRARY. THE DOOR was ajar and she could easily hear the voices that were raised in anger.

"Business be damned!" Rosco's voice boomed. "You have business here at the villa."

"Nothing that I cannot attend to when I return," Damon replied, his voice gritty. "I shall be gone seven days, maybe longer."

"You have a wife—" his father began.

"I have no wife, Rosco," Damon countered, his tone steel-edged. "I have merely given my name to the woman—and at your insistence, I might add. Because of heritage, out of obligation, as you have so often reminded me."

"Temple is to be your wife, Damon, in every way," Rosco stated firmly. "It will *not* be a marriage 'in name only'!"

"You will have no more, Rosco, so do not demand more. I have given you what you wanted —given you your revenge. Nathan Harris's daughter is married to your son, she now bears the Silone name."

Damon slammed his glass down on the table. There was a long minute of silence before he continued speaking.

"'Vengeance is mine,' saith Rosco Silone! 'An eye for an eye!' You have waited eight long years for the sweet taste of revenge and have now obtained it by ruining a girl's life, binding her to a marriage of which she wants no part and—God in Heaven!—I have played a part in bringing it about. The whole thing sickens me! I want no more to do with your plans!"

"Come now, Damon. I have seen the way you look at Temple. You are attracted to the woman you married—you desire her."

"She wants no part of me!"

"You can have whatever you want from her, Damon, she is your wife," Rosco persisted.

"I will not force myself upon her. Not now— not *ever!*"

"I want grandchildren from this union, Damon." Rosco's voice was low, almost weary.

Silence hung in the room. Neither spoke, neither moved. The atmosphere was charged with emotion.

Finally Rosco broke the silence, his voice a near plea. "Grandchildren."

"Only if she comes to me, Rosco, only if Temple comes to me—wants to be my wife."

"But, Damon—" Rosco attempted, only to be cut short by his son.

"I have pressing business, Rosco," he barked and strode toward the door.

Erin slipped quietly down the hall, hoping that Damon had not seen her, had not realized she had been eavesdropping. Opening the front door, she stepped outside and went in search of Temple.

Temple stood motionless, her gaze fixed upon the beautiful woman in the painting. There was a sadness about the beauty that tugged at Temple's heart. Dark, blue-black eyes stared back at her, a wistful half-smile touched the full lips and long, black hair cascaded over the bare shoulders. The warm, tanned skin looked as smooth and rich as the wine-colored crushed-velvet gown. Temple studied the small gold locket suspended on a narrow black ribbon that graced the young woman's slender neck. The delicate hand of the girl in the portrait lightly touched the gold locket in a loving, almost reverent manner.

"So this was LaDonna," Temple whispered in a strained voice, her own hand reaching out to touch the locket in the painting. "You are the woman my father loved, the woman he lost and grieved for during the last years of his life."

Tears stung Temple's eyes and spilled over to trickle slowly down her cheeks. Her heart ached for LaDonna, for her dear father, for herself. She felt so alone.

She had wandered along the wide upper corridor in the early hours of the morning, coming upon LaDonna's room by chance. Entering the room, Temple had felt as if she were trespassing—the room had apparently been kept just as the beautiful LaDonna had left it. The large bed was draped with a pale pink spread, laden with satin pillows of soft white and pink on which rested a porcelain doll with finely painted features and dressed in a blue silk gown. There was also a dog-eared, leather-bound diary and an ivory lace kerchief that still held the faint scent of rose petals.

Temple had scanned the room with keen interest, not daring to disturb any of the articles from their resting places. Then she had peered into the adjoining sitting room and had immediately sighted the painting on the wall. LaDonna Silone gazed back at her, and it seemed to Temple as if her eyes held understanding of Temple's dilemma and even sympathy about her ordeal.

LaDonna was gone from this room, from this house, from her loved ones. The thought saddened Temple unbearably.

"I am here," she began in a choked voice, "here in your house, married to your brother at the demand of your father! And I am here, LaDonna, because of you." Temple brushed the tears from her cheeks with the back of her hand, shook her head wearily and looked into the dark eyes of the portrait. "Yet I cannot hate you. I—I cannot even hate Damon as I swore I would. If I *could,* it would be so much easier," she admitted honestly.

She stared down at her clenched fists in despair and a sob wracked her body. Again she turned to the beautiful image. "Do you not see?" she pleaded, as if the girl could hear her, would answer. "I *want* to hate Damon, I do not wish to be attracted to him and yet—yet—I am! He had touched my heart before I knew who he was! It is not *fair.*" Temple wailed and the voice did not seem to be her own.

"Not fair!" Temple repeated wearily. "I cannot fight when every emotion, everything within me reacts to him with such overpowering responsiveness. The attraction is so strong that it—it threatens to possess me."

She turned from the painting and crossed the dimly lit room. As she reached the door and grasped the knob with a shaking hand, she looked over her shoulder.

"Was the love you shared with my father worth all the pain, all the bitterness, that has spanned the years? Was it so precious and fulfilling that it should, after all these years, cause even more pain, more bitterness, for yet another Harris? For the only child of your lover? Why must *I* suffer for the love you and my father had, for which you defied your own father?"

Having completed her one-sided conversation, Temple sighed heavily and left the room, closing the door softly behind her. She made her way back along the darkened hallway in the empty wing of the Villa Silone toward her own room, where she threw herself across the bed, her eyes wide and unseeing.

Five days! It had been five days since her arrival at the villa. Her mind went back to that day, to the first time she had seen Damon, not knowing who he was. And that awful scene in the library, the moment when Rosco had spoken to his son and Temple had turned to meet those black-violet eyes, when the husky voice had said, "Hello again, little one."

How many times in the last five days had she relived that embarrassment! How many times had she recalled Damon's handsome face and lithe frame, how often had his words of greeting echoed in her dreams, as well as her waking hours! Damon's caressing voice—

With a low moan Temple rose and walked to the terrace doors and stood staring out into the night. A night that seemed too still, too quiet. A half-moon drifted in and out of the milkiness of the clouds and only a few stars winked in the dark sky.

She clutched the curtains and closed her eyes tightly as she willed back the remembrance of how she had struck Damon in her embarrassment and anger. Unwillingly she recalled how she had fled the room and, fearing that Damon would follow her, run from the villa into the darkness of the night, seeking refuge in the gardens.

But Damon had not followed nor had he sought her out later. Erin had been the one who found Temple, much later.

"Damon has left," Erin had explained as she took Temple's hands in her own, reassuring her as she led the way back to the big house. "He told his father that he had pressing business."

And when Temple had asked how long Damon would be gone, Erin had looked at her with concern, an unreadable expression in her eyes, and replied, "A week, maybe longer."

Temple's heart had seemed to stop its beat as her thoughts rushed forward. *Would he come back?* And she had felt faint, overcome by panic, at the thought that he might not.

"Are you, Damon?" she whispered now into the darkness, tears burning her throat. "Are you coming back?"

Suddenly Temple felt very lonely and it seemed that she was only half alive. Her overwhelming loneliness drove her out of the room and, opening the double doors, she stepped out into the night. Her bare feet were soundless as she made her way over the cool stone terrace and down the steps leading to the gardens.

The moist grass dampened her bare feet as she walked. The moon slipped from behind a bank of feathery clouds and washed the earth with its silvery glow. A gentle breeze stroked cool fingers over Temple's body through the ankle-length, white satin nightgown she wore.

She listened to the whisperings of the night and watched the shadows dance about the garden and over the groves. Her emotions were confused, her thoughts on Damon. Temple had vehemently sworn to hate the man she had been forced to marry, had vowed never to be a *real* wife.

Then she had turned to meet his eyes—those dark, piercing eyes that belonged to the handsome stranger she'd met in the groves—and that unfamiliar current of excitement had flowed between them. The very presence of the man had stirred her, his hard, lean body and his windblown hair—how she had longed to run her fingers through that thick, midnight hair. Her heart had beat in wild wonder and she had yearned to lose herself in his embrace.

Now, as she walked alone in the beautiful, moonlit garden, she could think of nothing but the man who was her husband. How could she keep her vow to hate this man to whom she was so strongly drawn? How was she to combat her longing, when all she wanted to do was to reach out to him, to touch him? She frankly admitted to herself that she could not hold out long against him, against herself!

Even now Temple longed to be held close by Damon, embraced by the warmth of his arms. What would her life be like with this new awareness? Did she truly want to be Damon's wife, after all? Would he want her? He had been forced into this marriage as she had been. Did he resent her as she had resented him? There were so many questions and it was all so terribly confusing!

Damon had left the villa only hours after meeting his new bride. Had it been because he hated her for being the cause of his entrapment in marriage? Or could it have been because of her abominable temper, her outrageous behavior?

Sighing, Temple reached down and touched the fragile petals of a rose bud, her fingers tracing the flower gently as she recalled how Damon had taken the blossom from her fingers that first day. Remembering the intimacy of the gesture, Temple's heart hammered within her breast and again she felt an unnamed sensation in the pit of her stomach.

There was a gentleness in Damon, as well as a passion that could be furious whether awakened by anger or by desire, by hate or by love. Temple lifted her gaze to the changing sky. Damon had known anger, even hate, she felt certain. And, being the virile man that he was, he had also known desire. But love? What about *love?*

And she had to ask herself why it would matter to her if Damon had known love. She honestly did not know why it mattered, but it did.

Temple shivered and crossed her arms about her. Suddenly, without turning, without being told, she sensed Damon's presence. As the breeze fanned her, Temple's nostrils were filled with the heady, male scent of him—an odor of tobacco, scented soap, the out-of-doors.

She neither moved nor spoke. Damon had made no sound, no attempt to let her know that he was there, yet Temple knew that he was there somewhere in the shadows.

Damon stood watching. Temple had not heard his approach, for surely she would have retreated hastily, thereby acknowledging his presence.

This beauty is my wife, he was thinking, and I want her. I have wanted her for more years than I like to remember. God, how he had tried to get her out of his mind, out of his heart. He had fought his need for her, had turned to other women in an attempt to expel his passionate yearning for her.

But neither the passing of years nor other women had lessened his desire. Temple had only been a child of thirteen when she had first captured his heart, and the memory of that lovely creature, the gentle sound of her laughter as she ran barefoot across a clover-blanketed meadow, had remained with him through the years. Damon smiled tenderly at the remembrance, noting that even now Temple was barefoot. He recalled the striking young girl with her face lifted to the sun. Now standing before him was that same beauty grown to womanhood and it was the soft moonlight that bathed her delicate features in its silvery glow.

Damon ached with a burning need for Temple, a longing that stemmed from his long-ago enchantment and had grown into an all-consuming desire.

But Temple hated him, hated who he was. She had been forced into an unwanted union and he had heard her vow that she would never love him. Dear God, how would he be able to fight his constant desire to reach for her, to take her to his bed, to make her his own?

Damon was a strong man and a hard one, but Temple—his desire for her could break his defenses. He had said that he would not force her, that she must come to him. Yet all the while his resolve battled against that part of him that impelled him to go to her, to make love to her. But his better judgment urged him to bide his time, for this was something worthy and, though at the moment beyond his reach, something that might be attained at some future time.

Therefore he had gone away, seeking refuge from Temple's nearness and his temptation. Lying with another woman only hours after he had left the villa, he had realized that he could not take that woman, that he had no desire for any woman save Temple.

Now, as he stood watching her in the garden, the moonlight danced over her skin and set her hair aglow and the smooth satin of her gown caressed her supple curves. His own flesh flushed with the heat of desire, his body was taut and his heart beat wildly against his rib cage.

His need was too acute. He would have to leave again, get far away from her lest he break his own resolve. He drank in her beauty for a long moment and turned to leave.

"You came back."

Temple's low voice floated upon the night breeze and Damon stopped short, then turned slowly to meet her gaze. He stared deep into her soft, velvety brown eyes and his heart lurched. What an overpowering impact this woman had on him! She had known that he was there—how long had she known?

Damon made no reply. After a brief silence, Temple spoke again.

"I—I was afraid you would not come back." The simple statement puzzled Damon, in view of her previous behavior.

Drawing a deep, ragged breath, Temple tightened her arms about herself and Damon saw that she was trembling. A single tear glistened in the moonlight as it coursed down her cheek and Damon had to restrain himself from reaching out to her. Sweet Christ! She was tearing him apart, wreaking havoc with his emotions.

For a long minute the two stood as if in a trance, gazes locked, each waiting for the other to make a move. Then Damon broke the silence, his voice low.

"I left word that I would be back. Were you not told?"

"Yes—yes, I was so informed, but . . . after

my behavior . . . I wondered if you would—"
Her voice suddenly stilled as a sob threatened to
escape her. "But this *is* your home and my
presence has no . . ."

Damon watched her closely, his lips curving in
a slight smile. Christ, but she is magnificent, he
thought, sensing her inner battle between pride
and vulnerability. He studied Temple's striking
beauty. Her hair fell in a thick, silken mass about
her shoulders and her warm brown eyes were
openly yet warily watching him. His attention was
drawn to her soft, full lips. He longed to taste
them, to press their softness to his own.

Damon slowly lifted his gaze from her lips to
meet her questioning eyes. "And would you have
cared, Temple? Would it have mattered to you,
had I not returned?" he asked softly, observing
her quick intake of breath.

Temple shifted her weight from one foot to the
other, nervously catching her lower lip between
her small, pearly teeth. She did not reply, for how
could she tell him that it *did* matter to her? How
could she possibly admit to him that she had
thought of little else but him during these past
empty days?

Yes, it mattered to her! Could he not see? Did
he not know that she was drawn to him like a
moth to a dancing flame? Dear God! Could he
not feel that current that flowed from him into her
very soul?

Once more their eyes met. Damon had never

imagined that he would be content with one woman for the rest of his life, that he would find one who would stir his passions to a feverish pitch and for whom he would experience such a raging desire. Eight years ago when he had rescued a child beauty from a fall, had looked down into brown velvet eyes that seemed to pull him into their warm liquid depths, never to surface again—he had not known that that lovely child would one day be his wife, the woman he would want for always.

Temple! She was a gleaming memory that the years could not dim. She had unknowingly wrapped a silky cocoon about his heart, sheltering a longing for her that had endured across the years and now had emerged as a deep passion.

Temple's mind reeled with her thoughts. What was Damon thinking, she wondered; was he hating her, assessing her as his adversary? She scanned the clear-cut features of his handsome face, his mouth that was curved in a half smile.

She could love him, she thought in surprise. Again she felt that strange sensation deep within her that was becoming all too familiar. Could it possibly be the beginnings of love? she asked herself. Had Damon any suspicion of her feelings? He had awakened desire within her and now her heart cried, I want you, Damon Silone! I want you to want me!

She wondered what it would be like to have him make love to her. What kind of a lover would he be—a passionate one, she felt sure. Would he be gentle—

"Your eyes are quite amazing," came Damon's husky whisper. "They can be keen and wary at the same time, yet they can turn all soft, wistful and dreamy." He stepped closer and Temple trembled at his nearness. "You are cold," he said softly and reached toward her, his hands clasping her upper arms.

The warmth of his touch spread through her and her knees became weak. Damon ran his hands along her arms, reveling in the feel of her smooth skin. How he wanted her! Could she not know? Did she not feel his body tremble with his need?

"You should return to the house." Damon spoke just above a whisper.

"Yes," Temple answered, but she did not move. She could not tear her gaze from his hypnotic, black-violet stare. Again she shivered, though not from the chill of the night.

Damon removed his coat and placed it about her bare shoulders, lifting her mane of honey-brown hair. Its silkiness flowed through his fingers like finely spun gold as he freed it from the collar of the coat. The touch of her fanned the fires raging within him and, clenching his teeth, he groaned raggedly as he crushed her to him, burying his face in the softness of her scented hair.

"Temple, Temple," he moaned in a strained

voice. *"Mio Dio, io desidero voi!"* His lips came down upon hers with an urgency that shocked them both and Temple felt a wave of desire unleashed deep within her, willing her to respond to Damon's heated touch, his searching kiss as he held her trembling body pressed along the length of his hard frame. Her senses reeled and her heart hammered recklessly within her breast. Never had she known that a kiss could be like this!

Damon raised his dark head slowly, his ebony gaze intent upon Temple's lovely face. There had been raw, unbounded longing in her response, an answering to his hungry, questioning kiss. His heart raced wildly and his own body began to tremble as Temple slowly opened her passion-drugged eyes to meet his frankly stunned gaze. He stroked the soft curve of her cheek with an unsteady hand, sending a shiver cascading down her spine. She swayed against him, causing him to catch his breath sharply.

The emotional current flowing between them was charged with intensity, the force so violent that it staggered Damon. He had not meant to touch Temple, had not meant to kiss her—but once he felt her silken flesh, breathed in the heady scent of her hair, he had lost control. Now, with his mouth moist with the taste of her kiss, he knew there would be no turning back—he had to have her, to make her his own! He would bind her heart to his, her love to him as securely as she had already captured his.

Chapter Five

A SUDDEN, FRANTIC SHOUT SHATTERED THE STILL-
ness.

Caught up in the spell, neither Damon nor
Temple had noticed that the night sky had taken
on an orange-red glow, nor that the night breeze
had become unusually warm.

Damon spun from Temple, his body taut and
alert, his eyes taking in the uncanny glow that lit
the sky.

"My God!" His voice was strained and low.
"My God!"

"Damon! What is it?" Temple cried in alarm.
She grasped his arm, frightened, seeing the anguish in his face.

Again came the frantic call, *"Fuoco! Fuoco!"*

"Stay close to me!" Damon ordered, turning
back to Temple and gripping her arms painfully.
"Stay close, do you understand?" His dark eyes
brooked no argument and she nodded her head
quickly. "There is a fire in the villa! *Fuoco*—fire!"
he explained hastily.

Then, taking her hand in his, Damon ran back along the garden path, Temple trying desperately to match her steps to his long strides.

Not knowing exactly where the fire raged, Temple's immediate thoughts were of Erin and her safety. Then her mind raced on to the beauty of the big house, Damon's home, his birthplace. The house that had seemed to welcome her, to beckon to her to make it her home. She could not bear the thought of the Villa Silone falling victim to such a catastrophe.

As they emerged from the gardens and onto the open grounds, Temple saw that great swirls of smoke had begun to rise and cloud the sky and angry orange flames rose higher and higher, illuminating the darkness. With relief she realized that the fire was not at the big house, but at the stables beyond.

Temple had to fight for every breath she drew, for her lungs seemed to fill with smoke. Everywhere people were fighting the rushing fire, trying to keep it from spreading.

Erin stood beside Temple in the human chain, passing buckets of water, hand over hand, to douse the flames that raged rapidly through the stables. The night was now filled with a threatening, intense heat and the sky was lighted by flying sparks.

Temple's arms felt as if they would surely break and her neck was stiff and ached almost unbearably. She wiped the sweat from her brow and upper lip with the back of her hand, leaving streaks of soot on her drawn features. Just when she thought she could not possibly go on, someone relieved her and she stumbled a few feet away, falling to her knees in sheer exhaustion. Temple glanced down at her ruined gown, her blackened hands and arms, then pulled Damon's coat closer about her.

A small cry escaped her and tears flowed down her ash-stained cheeks as she watched the flames lick at the trees and the rooftop of the secondary stable that housed the breeding stock.

"Please, dear God," she prayed in agony. "Please do not let it spread."

A scream startled her and Temple sprang to her feet, looking in the direction from which the cry had come. She could not understand what the young girl was saying but she saw where she was pointing. A flaming limb from an overhanging tree dangled dangerously above the breeding stables, spitting sparks that danced about the roof. Suddenly the limb came crashing down to rest atop the stable.

Fear gave wings to her tired feet and Temple sped toward the stable with only one thought in mind—to get the horses out. She could hear the frightened cries of the mares, the anxious pounding of hooves as they beat at the stalls, trying to escape.

Only a few of the workers had seen the hungry

flames as they began licking at the stable roof and as Temple burst through the large doors she was followed by a few men from the villa. She ran to the first stall, thrusting back the bolts and opening the gate, then ran on to the next. She worked like a demon as she made her way down the long corridor. Behind her the men coaxed the frightened horses to safety.

Faster and faster the fire spread, catching at the dry hay in the loft. The blaze was burning angrily, out of control, and the girl worked feverishly toward the last stall, the stall that housed Damon's pride mare, Spirit. But when she reached it, the latch was jammed! It would not budge. The mare reared, her nostrils flaring, her eyes wild with fear. Her hooves slammed against the walls of the narrow stall.

"Whoa, girl," Temple spoke to the mare. "You'll be all right, I shall get you out of here safely." Her fingers worked at the stubborn lock in a frenzy.

"Oh, God! Please help me!" Temple cried in despair as she saw the flames creeping closer and closer. Suddenly the lock gave way and the gate swung open, and the frightened girl reached for Spirit. The mare plunged in panic and backed up, and Temple, pressing her small frame between the animal and the side wall, caught hold of Spirit's mane and pulled, urging her from the stall. Her spoken plea to the mare was a strangled cough as smoke singed her throat. Still she tugged at the mare, compelling her to make her way toward the open doorway.

"Just a little farther," Temple coaxed, "just a little farther."

The heat was almost unbearable, the smoke suffocating. She felt dizzy and lightheaded. By now bits of burning hay littered the stable floor and Spirit balked at the sight.

A spark from the floor caught at the hem of Temple's gown and she beat at it with her hands, momentarily releasing her hold on Spirit's mane. The mare reared dangerously, her hoof grazing Temple's brow, then thundered through the remaining space to the open door and out into the night as if pursued by demons.

There was a sudden, cracking sound and Temple's eyes flew to the burning beam overhead. She stood transfixed, her eyes filled with horror as the beam came crashing downward. Her shrill, terrified scream filled the night.

Damon beat at the flames with a water-drenched blanket while Rosco, at his side, threw buckets full of water. He had turned his attention from his chore at one point, his eyes seeking out Temple, and had seen her handing water buckets along the line from the water supply to the burning stables.

She had looked so small, so tired, but at that moment Emil, the butler, had relieved her and Damon had seen her stumble to the ground in exhaustion. His heart went out to her and he mentally applauded her brave spirit.

Damon fought on to suppress the spreading fire, grateful that due to fast work and the early alarm his men had been able to get the stock out and headed to the pastures far away from the inferno. His muscles ached and his eyes burned from the thick smoke.

The air he breathed was hot, filled with ashes and heavy with the blackness of smoke. Once more his gaze sought Temple, but she was gone. He scanned the water line. She was not there. Damon's eyes darted about the grounds and then he saw that the breeding stables were also aflame. He ran toward them, calling to Rosco to carry on.

Darting among the men and the horses they were attempting to lead to safety, Damon entered the burning building and through the dense smoke he saw Temple struggling with Spirit.

A sudden, cracking sound brought Damon's unbelieving gaze to the flaming beam overhead and then back to Temple's face and the terror in her eyes. As the burning timber broke free and came hurtling downward, Damon threw himself forward, diving toward Temple.

Her scream rent the air and the two fell to the floor as the heavy beam crashed, striking Damon's lower body a glancing blow and coming to rest just inches from them. Damon gritted his teeth against the searing pain in his leg and his pain-glazed eyes rested on Temple who lay beneath him, her eyes closed, blood and soot mingling on her brow.

The fire was now sweeping along the stable, the heat unbearable. Damon got unsteadily to his feet, lifting Temple in his arms. The pain in his injured leg was almost intolerable as he put his weight on it, but he clasped his precious burden close against his heart as he staggered through the raging flames to safety.

Emil ran toward his master with Erin at his heels.

"I will carry my wife," Damon told Emil as the faithful servant attempted to lift Temple's inert body. Then he limped and stumbled across the grounds toward the house.

"But, *Signore,* you, too, are injured," Emil exclaimed with concern, keeping step with Damon. "If you would only allow me—"

"*I* will carry her!" Damon reiterated sharply. Realizing that Erin was following them and guessing at her anxiety, he spoke kindly to her, requesting that she run ahead to fetch clean water, cloths and whatever she thought might be needed to minister to the girl.

Entering the house, Damon carried his wife up the stairs and into their bedroom, placing her gently upon the bed. He sat beside her and his long fingers were gentle as he examined her brow to determine the extent of her injury. Impatient for Erin's return, he stripped off his shirt and began to wipe the blood from Temple's forehead and cheek.

Erin hurried in with a basin of warm water and a cloth and would have made use of them but Damon quickly took the cloth from her. Dipping it in the water, he tenderly bathed the wound, his face white and strained.

As he worked he spoke to Temple in a low, soothing voice. Erin could not understand the words he spoke in his native tongue, but she moved closer, her eyes on the girl's pale face stained with blood and soot.

Erin watched as Damon brushed the hair from Temple's brow. How gentle his movements were, what tenderness he showed as he bathed the wound and his dark eyes held such warm emotion that Erin caught her breath.

He really cares for her, she thought, a warm feeling stealing over her. The man that Temple had married *loved* her; Erin smiled serenely at the knowledge.

"Erin," Damon turned to her, "find Emil and have him send for a doctor." Turning his attention back to Temple, he continued, "My wife needs to be seen to at once. Tell Emil to go himself if necessary."

Without a word Erin left the room in search of Emil.

Damon rinsed the cloth and washed Temple's face again, removing more soot and grime. She was so pale, so limp that he was frightened. He rose from the bed and stood looking down at her. She *had* to be all right, she had to be safe!

He had died a thousand deaths when he had entered the burning stables and seen Temple struggling with the terrified mare. He had called to her to leave the animal, to get herself to safety, but she had not heard him above the cries of the frightened animals, the shouts of the men and the roaring of the flames.

Damon walked to the window and, placing his hands on either side of the frame, leaned his brow against the windowpane, his eyes searching the night. The sky still glowed with a reddish light and people raced about, fighting the now dying blaze.

He knew that he should be down there but could not bring himself to leave Temple's side. He rubbed absently at his throbbing leg. He had feared that he would be too late to save her as he saw the burning spar break loose and come hurtling down.

Although he had moved with lightning speed, it had seemed to him that his movements were in slow motion. He remembered Spirit rearing . . . hoof grazing her brow . . . Temple's stricken face . . . the fear . . . her scream . . .

Staring over his shoulder, Damon studied the lovely girl in his bed. His wife! The woman he had always wanted. So quickly she could have been taken from him. The vivid memory of the flames reaching out to engulf her, to take the life from her—he knew that he would not have emerged from that flaming inferno without her.

"You do not know, my darling," he whispered, "how very much you mean to me. My life would have no meaning without you, there would no longer be any reason to live."

Damon moved back to the bed and reached down to stroke Temple's cheek lovingly.

"You are my life, my dearest, and one day I shall be yours," he said softly. Bending over, he brushed his lips against Temple's and, as he did so, breathed, "One day!"

Temple's moan brought Erin hurrying to her side.

"Temple? Temple, it is I, Erin," the woman said in a low whisper. "Can you hear me, dear?"

The girl opened her eyes and smiled weakly, lifting a hand. Erin grasped her outstretched fingers, tears running down her cheeks.

"Oh, Temple," she cried, her voice trembling.

"Dear Erin," Temple whispered. "Why the tears?"

"You have had me so frightened," Erin choked, wiping at the tears. "When you did not regain consciousness . . . you lay there so still, so pale. . . . Oh, Temple, it has been so awful!"

"How—how long?" The girl spoke slowly. Her throat ached and felt raw.

"Three days! Three awful days!" Erin replied. "You have not so much as moved or uttered a sound. The doctor said that it could be some time, but *three days!*" As she spoke, Erin wrung her hands and paced the floor in her agitation.

"Erin, do stop pacing," Temple scolded with a shaky laugh. Then she added, "The fire—was it bad? Was there much loss?"

"The main stable was lost," Erin began, sitting on the edge of the bed. "A few horses were injured, but not badly. The breeding stable can be salvaged, but a portion will have to be rebuilt. Some of the workers were slightly injured, nothing serious. Only you were hurt badly." A brief pause, then she added, "And Damon."

"Damon?" Temple sat bolt upright, her eyes wide and her mouth agape. The sudden movement caused her head to spin and she brought a trembling hand to her brow. "Damon hurt? Oh, Erin! How badly?"

"Do not upset yourself, Temple," Erin advised, pushing the girl back down upon the bed. "You are not—"

"Tell me, Erin!" Temple demanded. "How badly hurt is Damon?"

"A few minor burns on his upper body and hands." Erin spoke quietly and matter-of-factly. "The doctor said they would heal and not leave any scars. It is his leg that is the worst. He has been in a lot of pain from that injury."

"His leg? But what happened? Burns, I can understand, but his *leg?*" Then, as if the thought had only occurred to her, Temple cried out, "Oh,

Erin! Damon's leg is not broken, is it? Or worse? Is—is he crippled? Oh, I could not bear it!" Weakness washed over her at the mental picture of Damon astride Spirit and the thought that perhaps he would never again be able to ride through the groves and look over the beauty of his lands.

Beads of cold sweat broke out on Temple's forehead and her face was deathly pale. Erin quickly sought to reassure her.

"No, no, Temple! It's nothing so terrible. Damon's leg was struck by the falling beam when he threw himself on you in the breeding stable," Erin explained, her eyes intent on Temple. "Your husband saved your life, Temple. If that beam had hit you—" She could not finish the thought.

"So Damon was injured because of me," Temple said thoughtfully after a moment, her tone solemn. "I—I did not know. I did not see him in the stable. I was trying to save Spirit. . . ."

Damon had saved her life, had risked his own for her. He had been badly injured in doing so. Had Erin told her everything? Could it be that Damon was more seriously hurt than she had intimated?

Suddenly Temple knew that she had to see Damon. She had to see for herself.

"Where is Damon?" she asked breathlessly.

"In the room directly across the hall," Erin answered, watching Temple closely.

Erin had known Temple for too long not to see

that she cared for Damon. The man had touched her heart even before Temple knew him to be her husband. There was an attraction between the two that could not be denied. And had Erin not witnessed the injured Damon carrying Temple securely in his arms, close to his heart, from the burning building, even though he was in great pain himself? Had he not refused to be relieved of his burden, and had Erin not seen the tender concern in his dark eyes as he ministered to the girl?

And Damon had remained beside her bed while the doctor attended to his own injuries. He had taken no heed of the kindly doctor's advice that Damon should rest, nor had he taken the medicine for pain. It had not been until the wee hours of the morning that Erin, with Emil's help, had persuaded Damon to take any nourishment other than black coffee. Though all the while in excruciating pain, he had remained at her bedside waiting, watching and sometimes dozing from exhaustion.

As a last resort, Erin had slipped some laudanum into the rich broth that she had coaxed Damon to drink. And when he had become sufficiently drowsy and disinclined to argue, she had summoned Emil and between them they had managed to carry Damon across the hall and put him to bed. He had slept for some twelve hours.

"I must see him, Erin," Temple exclaimed, rising from the bed. "I must go to Damon." She grasped the bedpost to steady herself, but waved Erin away when her friend moved to her side. "No, Erin, please. I am only a bit weak, otherwise I am fine."

"Temple, you should stay in bed awhile longer. You can see Damon later. I promise you that he is in no danger. I have told you—"

"But you don't understand," Temple broke in impatiently. "Do you not see, Erin, that I have to do this?" Wrapping a flowing satin robe about her slim body, she looked at the older woman earnestly and continued, "Damon was injured because of me. I must see him for myself, I must *know* that he is all right. Please understand."

"Yes, dear, I understand." Erin's tone was low.

As she watched Temple move slowly across the room and the hallway, she added, in the same low voice, "I understand far more than even *you!*"

Chapter Six

"CAVOUR IS NOT EASILY DISHEARTENED."

Damon's tone was low and he sighed wearily.

Temple's hand stilled on the doorknob. The door to Damon's room was slightly ajar and she could easily hear what was being said.

"No," Damon continued, "Sardinia, in *his* mind, is but a prelude to a far more ambitious plan. He is determined to achieve political union of the entire Italian Peninsula under Victor Emmanuel II."

"But the obstacles are so great!" replied a masculine voice tinged with a French accent.

"They are indeed," Temple's husband confirmed. "But that will not stop him. He has endless determination, as well as being a powerful man. Cavour will succeed in obtaining that which he seeks."

"I hear he has had some mysterious conversations with our friend Garibaldi," the strange voice stated. Yet to Temple it seemed more a question, as if the man were waiting for Damon to reveal something more.

"Yes," Damon spoke knowingly, "I have been so informed."

"My God! The man patronizes secret societies, meets with Napoleon III and now Garibaldi! He is cooperating with the King in the reorganization of the Sardinian army. Cavour has utilized his diplomatic talents to enlist foreign aid for Sardinia. He uses his power daringly to achieve his ends. What will he do next?"

"Next?" There was a shadow of a smile on Damon's lips and amusement in his eyes. Shifting his weight in the large bed, he replied, "Next he plans to cement the alliance between Sardinia and France. He has made up his mind that France and her assistance will be the most practicable means of expelling the Austrians from Italy."

Temple had positioned herself where she could see Damon lying upon the bed. She noted that he moved constantly as he spoke, as if he were restless and uncomfortable. Only a thin white sheet covered his lower body, leaving his upper body bare.

Temple flushed at the thought of him lying naked beneath the sheet. The thought excited her, causing a slight tremor to course through her. She felt the heat rise within her at the remembrance of his kiss, his embrace and the wild passion that he had roused within her in the moonlit garden on the night of the fire.

Once again Damon's rich voice reached out to her from within his room.

"Cavour has taken great care and skill in cultivating a friendship with Louis Napoleon. He feels that Napoleon will be of assistance when the time comes. And doubt not that he *will* call upon Napoleon and soon, I feel. Very soon."

"So you believe the time is near?" the visitor questioned in concern. He ran a hand nervously across the back of his neck.

"I do," was Damon's terse reply.

"Then you have information that I have not?"

"No, my friend." Damon sighed raggedly and leaned forward to rub his injured leg gingerly. "No information—just a feeling here in my gut." He pointed to his belly. "And as *I* believe, so do others. The fire was a sure sign that someone is becoming nervous."

"The fire was deliberately set," the other man agreed without hesitation. "Rosco told me."

Temple's heart lurched in her breast. The fire had been deliberate! Someone had put a flame to the stables! But why?

"They are attempting to stop us," Damon was saying. "They will do anything and at any cost. It is still a mystery to me where they are obtaining their information. From whom?"

"One of your men, perhaps?" the stranger suggested.

"No!" Damon stated emphatically. "I trust my men, Pierre, and not one would I believe to be a spy, a traitor!"

"Then *who?*" Pierre asked in consternation.

"Would to God that I knew," Damon replied, shaking his dark head wearily. He sank back, resting his head on the snowy pillow. "I have no answers."

Temple started suddenly as a door opened behind her and turned to see Erin stepping into the hallway. Placing her forefinger to her lips to signal caution, Temple motioned Erin back into the room and followed, closing the door behind them.

Temple stood at the window, staring out into the rain, deep in thought. She had returned to her room and paced about restlessly while she repeated to Erin what she had overheard—Damon's conversation with the man Pierre, about the suspicion that the awful fire had been deliberately set and their belief that someone meant to do more harm.

Of course Erin had scolded her for eavesdropping and had said that it was not any of Temple's business.

"You will do well, my dear, to leave this alone," Erin had told her earnestly, shaking a finger at Temple as if she were still a child.

But Temple knew that she would not let it lie. Damon was frustrated about something and definitely concerned about this spy-informer. He trusted his men, he had said. What men? The workers in the groves, the stables? What was he talking about?

She had heard of Louis Napoleon, Garibaldi and Cavour, of course, well-known, powerful men. And the King! Just what was her husband involved in? What were his dealings with these men and who was the Frenchman, Pierre? Could Damon's association with them endanger his life?

She would find out, Temple decided, if there were any way possible. And what if the information is something you do not wish to know about Damon, she asked herself. That was just the chance she would have to take. Yet deep down she hoped fervently that Damon was not in any danger—and that he was not on the wrong side of whatever it was he was involved with.

Thunder crashed loudly and Temple jumped. She watched as the flashes of lightning lit up the dark sky with a silvery glow and briefly illuminating the landscape.

She turned restlessly from the window to pace the large room again. Thoughts of Damon lay heavily on her mind and she stopped before the fireplace, gazing unseeingly into the red glow of the embers. With a deep sigh, she knelt upon the floor and sat back on her heels, staring unblinkingly into the hypnotic flames.

Damon floated through her thoughts. She remembered his dark eyes looking into hers, his deep voice, the gentle touch of his hands, his kiss. How she wished he were here with her, for the night was long and so lonely.

She would find no rest this night. It was not the

storm, for she had always loved the sound of the rain, the wind, the thunder. Yet she could not find peace tonight.

Temple glanced up at the domed clock on the mantel. Its delicate, golden hands indicated that the time was well after two in the morning. Why was she so restless?

If she were with Damon, she thought fleetingly, nestled close to him, held warm and secure within his embrace—Temple shook herself mentally and stood up, surprised and confused at her thoughts. Where was her common sense? Why should such thoughts possess her?

In her disquietude she once again paced the room, feeling like a caged animal. Her gaze sought the clock once more but only five minutes had elapsed. How slowly time moved when one had nothing *but* time, and how quickly it passed when one had but little time.

Damon. The name was a steady drumming in her subconscious and Temple began to speculate about her feelings for him. Her anger had dissipated and she was not sure just when it had happened. She had melted within his embrace, had welcomed his touch, had thrilled at his kiss. She wanted to forget her bitter words and vehement vows, for in that moment in which she had realized that the stranger in the groves and Damon were the same man, she had also realized that her vows to hate him and to never be happy in this marriage would be difficult to uphold. Her

DESTINY'S EMBRACE

attraction to him, then *and* now, was overpowering. One look into his passion-filled eyes, one touch from his skillful hand, one kiss, and her body was aflame with desire for him.

Finally Temple realized that it was the storm of conflicts raging within her that was causing her unusual restlessness, and she faced the fact that these emotions were the first stirrings of love. Her heart suddenly ached unbearably at the knowledge, because she believed that she alone would love. For Damon had been forced into the marriage as well, and there was no reason to believe that he would fall in love with her.

After a long time, Temple moved on silent, bare feet out of her room and across the hall to Damon's room. She entered the room and paused just inside the doorway, her eyes adjusting to the dimness. Then she quietly closed the door behind her, crossed over to the bed and stood looking down at Damon, her husband—yet not her husband.

A lamp burning low on the bedside table shed a soft glow over the sleeping form. He lay on his back, one hand resting at his side, the other flung upward above his dark head to disappear beneath the pillow. Damon's finely etched features were softened in sleep, his black hair an unruly mass of waves. A stray curl lay loosely on his brow.

Temple's heart lurched at the perfection and beauty of this man and she wondered if their son would look like his father. Would he inherit the strong features, Damon's fierce pride? She caught her breath suddenly at the thought.

Dear God! She was wondering about the child they might have together and Damon had not yet taken her to his bed. Not *yet?* Temple had vowed never to be anything more than his wife in name only, and here she was dreaming about their child—a son with Damon!

Temple's heart ached with need for Damon. She leaned closer and could hear his rhythmic breathing and see his broad chest rise and fall. She studied his handsome features, her heart quickening its beat. He was perfect in her eyes, his body sun-bronzed, hard and solid. His tanned skin stretched smoothly over firm muscles. The dark hair on his chest and belly looked soft and she felt the urge to stroke it.

God help me, she groaned inwardly, I want him. Taking a long, ragged breath, she drank in the sight of this virile stranger who was her husband, this man whom she now freely admitted to herself that she wanted.

You rebelled at marrying this man, she reminded herself, had no intention of loving him, swore that you would not do so. Yet in only a few days you have come to want this marriage, to desire Damon, even dream about having his child!

What was it about Damon Silone that awakened within her such a need, such a desire to love and to be loved? He was a mystery, a danger. A man who could have any woman he wanted and take whatever he desired. He was a man worth having, worth loving.

And love him Temple did! The first time she had seen him in the groves he had captured her heart without reason, without question. She had not fought her attraction until she had learned that the man was Damon. As hard as she had tried to hate him after this discovery, she was irresistibly drawn to Damon, helpless to fight her emotions. It was as if there were an uncanny power much stronger than herself that made it impossible for her *not* to love him. As if the two of them were destined for each other, held strong and sure within destiny's embrace.

What would it be like to have this man make love to her, she wondered. Would his love be gentle and warm, or wild and untamed? She felt in her heart that she knew the answer, that making love with Damon would be a sweet, yet savage, experience.

A tightness tugged at her heart. She *would* have Damon, she determined; this dangerous, powerful, handsome and mysterious man for whom she yearned *would* be hers. She would gain the reward of his love and would cherish it always, no matter what she had to do.

She held her breath and reached out a shaking hand toward the sleeping Damon, but her hand paused in midair.

Touch him . . . the words whispered ever so softly within her heart, within her mind. She could reach out, touch him, know the feel of him beneath her fingers and he would never know. It would be something that she could carry to her dreams. Touch him . . . touch him . . . Even the rain beat the tempo of the words against the windowpane.

What would happen if she obeyed the impulse? What possible harm could there be?

The curtains stirred as a sudden breeze rushed in through the window and the gust of wind extinguished the lamp's flame, leaving Temple and Damon in darkness.

Damon lay staring at the ceiling. The rain drummed a tattoo on the window, thunder rumbled in the distance and intermittent flashes of lightning lit the room as the storm decreased.

His leg pained him, the monotonous sound of the rain annoyed him, the bed was uncomfortable and the night threatened to go on forever.

But all these things were not why sleep was eluding him. The reason for his sleeplessness lay mere steps across the hallway.

Temple! The child-woman who had invaded his heart and his thoughts years ago. Temple, now his wife—to finally have her yet *not* have her—and God, how he wanted her. Would he have the patience to wait for her, he wondered.

Damon moved restlessly, trying in vain to find a comfortable position. It had been difficult to keep his mind on his conversation with Pierre, for thoughts of Temple kept drifting along the corridors of his mind. He remembered how very close he had come to losing her in the greedy, hungry flames of the stable fire. Her brave performance during the calamitous ordeal had won his admiration. What a trooper she had been!

The fire! Keats would have learned of the attempt to destroy a good portion of Damon's estate, would know that the livestock had been endangered, which was no doubt what had been intended. But the horses had been saved and would serve their purpose, and the stables could be rebuilt.

Damon and Pierre would simply wait to receive further instructions from Keats. Soon Cavour's plan for war with the Austrians would be launched. After opening Parliament on January 10, Victor Emmanuel II had uttered a fateful phrase: *". . . we are not deaf to the cries of pain that reach our ears from every part of Italy."* His words had spread like wildfire across the peninsula.

Damon had been called on to help recruit volunteers and to teach them to fight. He had readily answered the call and had enlisted the help of his best friend, Pierre Torre.

A few miles away on the grounds of the Villa Silone some fifty men were quartered in a training camp. Each man was eager to learn to fight for the unity of his beloved country. Damon, a master horseman and marksman, spent long, tedious hours training both young and old to be quick and on the mark, to handle a weapon, to ride and sit a steed in battle.

Volunteers had flocked into Piedmont from all over Italy after the King's speech on that day—a speech to which Napoleon had added some touches that aggravated while pretending to moderate its tone.

Damon smiled, thinking of Napoleon's arrogance and aggressiveness. The great Garibaldi had been called upon, for a war in which Garibaldi fought would necessarily be a popular one, far more so than one fought by the regular army supported only by the French.

A clever man was Cavour, Damon thought, invoking Garibaldi's name as a magnet to draw volunteers to Turin. And draw them it did.

On January 24, France and Piedmont had signed a military treaty stating that in the event of an Austrian attack, France would fight on the Piedmont side. Excitement mounted, and the stream of volunteers increased.

So as the men came marching in, rallying to join in an effort to unite Italy, Damon was given the task of training, clothing and arming them and providing each with a sturdy steed before sending them on toward Turin. The Villa Silone was a base both for training volunteers and for breeding and stocking horses for the Sardinian army. The latter was what had been threatened in the fire in an attempt to cripple the army.

February was coming to an end, hundreds of volunteers had passed through and more were coming. The day for war would soon be upon them. Austria was daily becoming more nervous and uncomfortable as her spies relayed news of the movement. The people waited apprehensively to learn that war had been declared.

Damon knew that there would be more trouble, more attempts by the Austrians to destroy strategic locations and facilities. He realized that he and the Villa Silone were main targets because of their alliance with the King. He would have to be doubly careful from now on.

His troubled thoughts scattered as he heard his bedroom door open stealthily, then close just as quietly. His hand crept slowly and imperceptibly beneath his pillow, where his fingers slid easily about the cool handle of his gun, gripping it in readiness with a steady finger resting on the trigger.

Beneath lowered eyelids he watched the shadowy form move toward his bed on silent feet. Just as he was about to draw the pistol from its hiding place the lightning flashed its silvery glow to reveal Temple's shapely figure. Damon relaxed.

The gentle odor of scented soap assailed his nostrils and he breathed in the tranquil aroma as he watched the girl in the dimness through half-closed lids, thoroughly enjoying the sight of her. Why was she here, he wondered. Why, at this late hour, had she come to his room? Had the storm awakened her, frightened her? Or had she merely entered this room by mistake?

Temple came closer, her gown brushing the side of the bed, and stood looking down at him for a long moment without moving. He fought the urge to reach out and touch her, waiting to see what she would do. She reached out toward him, then paused with her hand in midair.

The wind rustled across the room, extinguishing the lamp's flame, and the room was swallowed by darkness. Damon waited, his eyes gradually adjusting to the darkness, his half-lidded gaze intent upon the lovely creature standing beside him.

God, but she was beautiful even in the dimness, a ghostly shadow in satin. The shimmering fabric clung to her supple figure like a second skin and Damon found it difficult to keep his breathing steady and his body still and relaxed. Furthermore, his awakening shaft had begun to rise as heat pulsated in his loins.

Once more Temple's hand moved toward him and his body became alert. Ever so slowly her fingers touched his brow and as lightly as butterflies' wings brushed a lock of hair from his forehead, then shyly traced the contours of his face. The touch was so soft that Damon scarcely felt it, yet it held a molten heat that spread rapidly through his body. Her thumb gently outlined his lower lip and ran on to his jaw and neck.

Damon fought to control the turbulence building in his body. Temple's touch was like fire. He was dreaming, he decided. Temple could not be here, stroking him so tenderly with silken fingers.

He had dreamed of such a moment for so long that now that it was happening, he could not believe it. He could only believe it if he were to touch her, feel her warm skin, feel the beat of her heart against his breast and the length of her beautiful body beside his in the bed.

Temple's hand moved lower as she grew bolder and her palm caressed his wide shoulders and broad chest. She thrilled to the discovery that his body hair was as soft as she had imagined it would be. The feel of Damon beneath her touch as she learned his body made her feel warm and fluttery.

And Damon became consumed with desire as she sensually explored his heated body. Temple was doing wildly delicious things to him, he was completely caught in her bewitching spell.

As her palm flattened against his taut belly and her fingers entwined themselves in the soft mat of hair, Damon caught his breath sharply. Temple started and would have jerked her hand away, but Damon's hand covered hers, pressing it firmly against him as he whispered, "No, do not withdraw."

His eyes were bottomless and dark as they looked deep into hers, and time stood still. Tension stretched between them. Temple's heart beat wildly in her breast, as did Damon's.

"Ah, Temple! Temple!" Damon groaned huskily. "Do not stop your sweet torture." He caught a labored breath, his body shuddering. "That lovely body of yours, your lips, your hands—God, but you set my body aflame! You threaten to consume me with your passionate heat while I am bound by the sweet magic that you weave. I am clay in your hands, helpless with the need of you, the desire for you."

Damon's hand moved hers against him and she felt the muscles of his belly ripple and tighten, heard the rush of breath escape his lips as he closed his eyes tightly. Again Temple attempted to pull her hand away but his grip tightened.

"No," he whispered raggedly, drawing her toward him. At the sudden movement, Temple lost her balance and toppled over to lie across his warm chest. He took her lips with his own, clasping her body urgently to him.

Damon was unable to resist her. His tongue teased her lips, running along them slowly, and as a sigh escaped her his tongue entered her mouth to taste the warm, sweet nectar. Then she was returning his kiss, exploring, responding. She melted against him and shuddered as a white-hot flame licked through her, bringing with it an overpowering desire like warm honey flowing through her veins, intensifying her already aroused emotions.

Damon ran his hands over her shoulders, caressed the nape of her neck and her back, and her smooth, velvety flesh was heated beneath his touch. He rolled to his side, taking Temple with him. And when he would have broken the lengthy kiss she clung to him, her mouth hungry and demanding upon his.

"Temple, I need you," he whispered against her lips, his breath mingling with hers. He caught her lower lip between his teeth, nipping and sucking gently. Stroking her breasts in a slow, soothing motion, Damon brushed a finger softly over the nipples that were now taut and strained against the satin gown.

He caressed her back and hip, his hand never idle upon her body, his touch tender. He reveled in her response as he felt her hips begin to press urgently against him, her body quivering.

His body on fire and his manhood at full hardness as it strained against the sheet, Damon pulled Temple closer to the length of him. With a throaty purr she began moving against him in a sensual, passionate and rhythmic motion, beckoning him to answer her need.

Damon was overwhelmed. He had Temple in his arms, in his bed; Temple, his wife, feeling the same urgent need, the same heated passion as he. An overpowering desire to imbed his ready manhood deep within her womanly softness surged through him. Damon needed to make her his as she should be.

His mouth left hers to trail kisses down her throat and shoulders, and Temple moaned Damon's name, the sound a breathy softness that made him catch his breath and quickened his pulse. He cupped one breast in the palm of his hand, moving his thumb in a slow, circular motion, feeling the nipple hard and erect. He bent his dark head to kiss the swell of her breasts, moving his warm lips over the tender flesh.

Temple's mind was in a turmoil. She had wanted this, had dreamed of this moment, but now that their coming together appeared to be imminent, she was suddenly afraid. Her heart leaped into her throat in sudden terror and her body tensed. She could not go through with this lovemaking!

It was right for her to want Damon, to desire him, she told herself. Yet now as she lay in his arms and felt his passion rising—oh, God! She could not do this, she was not ready! This was the last barrier, the last step toward surrendering to Damon. In her heart she had already broken all her vengeful vows and she knew that she would one day go willingly to his bed. But not yet!

What must Damon think of her coming to his room, coming so easily to his bed? But she was his wife, this was expected, was it not? Oh, it was all so confusing, wanting Damon yet not wanting him. She had only just realized her love for him, admitted to herself that she wanted to be his wife. But things were moving too fast. She knew nothing about bedding a man, pleasing him, nothing about what to say, how to perform. She feared that she would be a disappointment to him and that was something she could never live with. It must be beautiful—for both of them.

"Damon," Temple spoke in a choked whisper as she pushed against his hard chest. "Damon, please! I—I cannot—" Her small hands clenched into fists between their bodies.

Damon stilled, his dark eyes looking deep into her frightened ones. His breath came ragged and hot against her throat, his body rigidly poised above her.

"I—I—" she stammered as a tear coursed down her flushed cheeks and her body trembled beneath him. "It—it was a mistake for me to come to—to your room. Oh, Damon, I am sorry!" she cried desolately, closing her eyes tightly in an attempt to block out his image. "I came—I only came to . . ." The words trailed off into silence.

You only came to *what,* her mind screamed at her. You wanted him; he was in your thoughts, your dreams. *So you came to what?* It was you who took those steps across the hall to Damon's room, you who reached out to touch him. He merely responded to that touch, just as you wished him to! Oh, Temple, admit it—

"You only came here to *what?*" Damon's gentle voice broke into her thoughts.

Temple opened her eyes to see a lazy smile on his lips, his eyes tender and questioning. She blinked, not believing that he was not angry. He was actually smiling!

"To—to check on you," she stammered. Her body gradually relaxed and she unclenched her fists and spread both palms flat against his chest, feeling the steady beat of his heart. She knew with sudden clarity that she had nothing to fear from this man.

"So you only came to check on me, and not to warm my bed."

Temple wondered whether it was a question or a statement; Damon's low, soothing voice seemed to caress her.

"Frightened, little one?" he asked, and she nodded her head. "Temple, my beautiful Temple," Damon breathed as his thumb brushed the tear from her cheek. "You need never fear me, my wife. I am not the monster you imagine me to be—I am only a man."

Temple smiled, her gaze holding his.

"I do not think you to be a monster," she said huskily, the truth of her words shining in her eyes. "And it is not of you that I am frightened, but of myself," she admitted.

"Yourself?" Damon asked incredulously. Then a deep chuckle rattled in his chest as he eased himself onto his side, resting his weight on his elbow as he leaned over her. His black-violet gaze held hers. "And *why*, my wife, would you be frightened of yourself?"

"Because—" Temple broke off, her tongue moistening her lips. The unconscious action drew Damon's eyes to her mouth and his stomach

110

muscles tightened at the remembrance of her kiss. "Because I am confused," she whispered, "frightened of what I was—what I *am* feeling. I—I have never . . . well, I have never behaved like—a wanton."

Damon laughed, the sound pleasant and genuine as it echoed across the room. Temple flushed.

"You responded to me, little one. You have every right to respond to your passion, to be wanton with your husband." His hand slowly trailed over her neck and shoulder and Temple's body reacted with a slight tremor. Damon smiled knowingly. "I want you, Temple. I want to make you my wife in every sense. But I will not force myself upon you. You are a child-woman who longs to be a woman. You have hungers and needs that cry out to be fulfilled, but you are not yet ready for the transition.

"When the time is right, when the woman in you decides that she is ready, I will be here, waiting. Only then will I take from you what is rightfully mine. You have made the first step in that direction, my wife. You came here to this room, to me; you responded to my kisses, my caresses, with equal ardor. I can wait for you, Temple, for my reward shall be the greater. That which comes easily is not near the value of that which is difficult to obtain."

"Damon, I—"

"Shhh, little one," he whispered, placing a finger on her lips. Leaning forward he kissed her tenderly. "Stay with me, Temple," he urged against her mouth. "Lie with me. I ask nothing more than to sleep with you in my arms." His lips moved softly against her cheek and touched the pulse at her throat. "I will not beg, Temple, only ask. Will you stay?" Again his ebony eyes met hers.

Her soft "yes" was a mere whisper as she reached out to run gentle fingers along Damon's parted lips. He kissed her fingertips, catching them within his warm clasp, and drew her to him. Temple's soft form molded itself beautifully against his lean frame and she gave a sigh of contentment, reveling in the feel of his body. She knew that this was where she belonged—here in Damon's arms, nestled close against his heart.

Damon lay relaxed and contented. He closed his eyes in sleep as the gentle fingers of dawn were creeping across the sky, caressing the land with awakening softness, bringing forth a new day.

Chapter Seven

TEMPLE STIRRED AND STRETCHED HER SHAPELY BODY in a feline motion. She buried her face against the softness of her pillow with a muted groan. She did not want to wake up, she wanted to go on floating in this boundless fantasy in which Damon held her in his strong embrace, his lips taking hers tenderly, her body molding to his in their beautiful love-play.

No, she never wanted this dream to end, never wanted to open her eyes to reality. But as Damon whispered love words in her dream, a ringing of harsh voices invaded her consciousness and forced her to abandon her warm cocoon of fantasy.

Again Temple stretched and lay drowsily, listening. Only silence met her ears. A frown knit her brow. What had awakened her?

Reaching out, she ran a hand over the bed. Damon was gone. Had she dreamed their encounter last night? Had she wanted him so badly that her longings had ruled her dreams?

She opened her eyes to the soft glow of morning and sunlight spilling in through the window, dancing about the room. Turning her head, she studied the place where Damon had lain. The pillow still held the imprint of his head.

It had not been a dream, Temple thought. She had come to Damon last night and, though they had not made love, she had stayed with him. She had slept securely and serenely in his arms. She smiled as she remembered his gentleness, his smile.

Temple hugged his pillow to her breast. She breathed deeply, her nostrils filled with the manly scent of Damon. How she loved him—this man of such enigma.

Just as she was about to drift back to sleep, the sound of voices rose and grated upon Temple's ears. That was what had awakened her from her peaceful, dream-filled sleep. She climbed from the bed and crossed to the window. Her gaze rested on Damon's lithe form as he led his black stallion, Rosco following a few steps behind.

The older man's face was angry, his fists clenching and unclenching at his sides. Damon seemed not to notice his father's anger as he checked the saddle and adjusted the stirrups. Temple watched Damon's movements and noted that he was limping.

"Damn you, Damon, listen to me!" Rosco's furious voice reached Temple. "You are injured, you can only cause yourself further harm. Pierre or Jules can see to the training until you are—"

"*I* will see to the training, Rosco. Not only is it

my duty, it is also my wish. My leg gives me little pain. I have suffered much greater injuries. An annoying pain and a bothersome limp will not interfere with what I have to do," Damon asserted.

"Your stupidity is exceeded only by your stubbornness," rasped the elder Silone, "and your arrogance equals both!"

"All hereditary traits, Rosco," Damon said with a grin. "Without them, I might add, I would not be a true Silone."

With those words Damon placed one foot in the stirrup and effortlessly swung his bad leg over the animal's broad back to rest his weight easily in the saddle.

Rosco gripped the reins, arresting his son's movement to urge the horse forward. Damon's dark eyes met the equally dark ones of his father. Neither spoke as a silent battle warred between them. Then Rosco loosed his hold upon the reins and stepped back and Damon nudged his mount with the heel of his boot. The horse took a few dancing steps forward, then broke into an easy lope. Dust swirled in a cloud behind the man and horse.

Temple stood staring at Rosco—the harsh tyrant who had so easily overturned her life, the powerful man whom her father had feared, whom *she* feared. For the first time, Temple felt an emotion akin to pity for Rosco. There he stood, watching his only son ride away in defiance of his wishes. Damon had shown strength, pride and determination of his own.

Suddenly Temple was reminded of the words she had spat at Rosco shortly after her arrival at the Villa Silone. "You took my life, my freedom, and gave it to your son, whom I seriously doubt is a *real* man if he allows his father to rule his life!" But now Temple could plainly see that Rosco did *not* rule Damon. The tyranny he exercised over others was powerless on his son. For Damon Silone was a man who bowed to no one.

Temple was suddenly jolted by a disquieting thought: why had Damon complied with his father's demands regarding their marriage? Why, on *this* instance, had Damon not rebelled? She shook her head in amazement and bewilderment.

At that moment Rosco turned, glancing upward toward the window where Temple stood watching. Their gazes met and held. It was apparent that Rosco realized that she had witnessed his defeat, and his eyes held a mute challenge. Temple's heart tightened in her breast and she felt suddenly cold. She turned from the window, a low cry springing from her lips.

The Master Silone, who manipulated people's lives, who was arrogant and overpowering, was, after all, only a man—yet a man to be reckoned with.

"Damon, you should not have come," Jules Rossini objected as he took the reins from

Damon and tied them about a branch. He watched as his friend alighted from the horse, then placed a large hand on his shoulder in a friendly manner.

"I am pleased that everyone worries so about my health," he remarked, laughter in his voice. "I have been away far too long, Jules. But I am now recovered, save for a slight limp."

"And your bride?" Jules asked in concern. "I hear that she, too, was injured in the fire."

"My wife is well," Damon assured his friend, a faint smile upon his full lips as he walked toward the clearing where his men waited.

Temple was still very much on his mind. He had awakened to find her soft body snuggled against him, her honey-colored hair fanned over the pillow and his shoulder and chest as she rested in his arms.

Damon had lain quietly, his gaze intent upon her lovely face. His heart had quickened its beat and his blood had flowed hotly in his veins, and he had to control his urge to kiss her warm lips, to stroke her satin skin. Instead, he had risen from the bed only to stare down at her sleeping form, a smile touching his lips as Temple stirred in her sleep. A tiny purr had hummed in her throat as she nestled closer to his pillow and reached out for him.

It had taken every ounce of his willpower not to crawl back into the bed and make love to her. He had ridden to the camp with thoughts of his lovely

Temple running rampant through his mind, memories of her hands upon him, her shy touch that had set him afire, the taste of her lips, her silken skin.

And her fright when she realized that she could not go through with their lovemaking! Her gentle brown eyes had been wide and frightened, yet passion-glazed and questioning. They had met his eyes in a silent plea that he understand her fears. He remembered her smile and how her body had molded so easily, so naturally, to his own.

Damon sighed deeply and forced his mind toward the work that awaited him.

Temple watched the activity below the small rise upon which she knelt, concealed by dense bushes. One man was rushing to mount a horse that stood ready, several were engaged in mock hand-to-hand battle and others were practicing sword thrusts. There were shouts of orders, most of them issuing from the tall commander who seemed to be everywhere at once, his bare torso glistening with perspiration in the strong sunlight.

Temple was fascinated by his movements. Damon was obeyed without question and was most assuredly in charge of the situation as he barked orders left and right. The men obviously respected their leader and the watching girl was struck with admiration by this side of her husband.

Damon did not sit astride his horse to oversee the training of these men; he was one of them, a qualified leader who not only showed his men how to tackle their opponents in hand-to-hand combat but allowed them to practice the techniques on himself.

After she had watched Damon ride away that morning, noting the direction he took, Temple had dressed hurriedly and gone in search of Erin. Merely telling her friend that she was going for a ride, she had admonished Erin not to inform Rosco of her whereabouts. Then she had made her way to the temporary stables where a stable hand had saddled a gentle mare for her use.

She had mounted the mare with only one purpose in mind—to follow Damon and learn, if possible, just what he was involved in. Surely she had a right to know. She had felt sure that she would find him and she reasoned that wherever he was it had something to do with his involvement with the King and Cavour, with the talk of war with Austria. She was determined to find out if her husband was in any danger and to protect him, if need be.

Now her eyes rested upon Damon as he wielded a sword in practice combat with another man. The two swords of the men clashed loudly and she gasped involuntarily. Her heart lurched at the thought that Damon might one day be forced to fight for his life against a real enemy.

So enthralled was Temple with the scene before

her, with Damon's grace and skill, that she failed to hear the footsteps behind her.

"Do my eyes deceive me, or have I stumbled upon a wood nymph?" asked an amused voice.

Temple spun about and lifted her eyes to the intruder. Towering above her was a young giant who stood with arms folded across his broad chest. Feeling at a distinct disadvantage, Temple scrambled hastily to her feet and stepped back from the stranger, her brown eyes wide and wary.

Dark blue eyes stared back at her and his well-shaped lips smiled lazily as the man took a step toward Temple. She backed hurriedly away only to be blocked by a huge boulder.

"Do not fear, my lovely, I would do you no harm." The words were gentle, the voice lightly accented. Temple recognized the voice as the one she had heard in conversation with Damon in his room. This must be Pierre, her husband's friend.

She sighed in relief. "You are Pierre," she stated simply.

"And you must be Temple," he replied matter-of-factly.

Temple nodded. For a moment the two stood in silence, appraising each other. Pierre was tall and handsome with light brownish-blond hair that hung loosely about the nape of his neck, eyes that shone with the clarity of polished sapphires, and a strong jaw. His features were striking, his skin warmly tanned, his body trim. Temple thought he looked to be a charmer, a heartbreaker, and wondered how many women had lost their hearts to him.

A slow smile spread across Pierre's handsome face, revealing even, white teeth, and a hint of a dimple played at the corner of his attractive mouth. The smile was so friendly that Temple responded in kind.

Pierre's blue gaze lingered upon Temple. "Until now I had not had the pleasure of meeting the bride of my best friend. But I had learned your name and been told of your beauty—which, I might add, Damon did not in the least exaggerate. So tell me, how did you know who I am?" he asked with keen interest.

"By your accent," she informed him. "I heard you talking with Damon yesterday. He called you 'Pierre,' and I remembered your voice."

"Ah! So it was my accent," he laughed, moving to rest his lean frame upon the boulder. "But many of Damon's friends have accents."

"But *yours* is French—not Italian or Greek," she explained knowingly.

"And you know the difference?"

"Yes. Although I am an American, I was schooled in France."

Temple found it very easy to converse with her husband's friend and began to talk of France.

Pierre heard little as he stared at the woman before him. *Mon Dieu!* but she was a beauty! It

121

was understandable that Damon was so complete-ly taken with her—what man would not be! Such loveliness was not often found.

Pierre had known many women but could not remember one with such an enchanting beauty. Her hair shone like warm honey, her eyes were velvety, soft brown. She had enticing rosebud lips and skin that seemed to have a silken texture. And her body—what a suppleness!

He concluded that Damon was, indeed, a fortu-nate man. And although their friendship more closely resembled the love of brothers, Pierre found that he very much envied Damon his possession of this woman.

Abruptly Pierre turned his gaze from Temple to the sphere of action in the clearing below them. "Are you spying on your husband's activities?" he queried suddenly in a strange voice.

"Spying? Of course not!" Temple flared indig-nantly. She did not like the word "spying" or Pierre's implying that she would do so. *"Observ-ing,* I think, is the correct word! And why I should explain my actions to you, I do not know! It is no one's business save my own!"

"I stand corrected, madam," Pierre apologized in amusement, noting the ring of steel in Temple's tone. How quickly she had reacted to his chal-lenge that she might be spying on Damon! So Damon's wife has spirit as well as beauty, Pierre thought, a combination he definitely liked.

"You have a quick temper, Temple Silone," he

remarked to the indignant girl. "How explosive it must be when your temper clashes with Damon's." He chuckled good-humoredly, shaking his blond head. "You will be good for my friend; he needs a woman such as you. His arrogance sometimes becomes unbearable and his temper uncontrollable."

"Is Damon really so bad? You speak of him as if he is dreadful, as if he possesses a horrid temper—almost as if he were ruthless!"

"He can be ruthless," Pierre stated bluntly.

His words puzzled Temple, for she had seen only gentleness in her husband. She remembered Rosco's words to Damon earlier that morning: "Your stupidity is exceeded only by your stubbornness, and your arrogance equals both!" And there was the heated verbal battle between Damon and the elder Silone Erin had overheard. Of course, Erin had not repeated the conversation, but she *had* told Temple of Damon's fiery burst of temper and had concluded with the fervent hope that she, Erin, would never be the recipient of his anger!

Now Pierre, who readily acknowledged that he was Damon's staunch friend, had referred to her husband's arrogance and temper, admitting that he could also be ruthless.

Temple's troubled thoughts were interrupted when Pierre straightened and stepped away from the boulder. With a sigh, he ran his fingers through his thatch of blond hair.

"It has been a most pleasurable interlude, Temple, but I must go. Otherwise Damon will send a scout or will come himself in search of me. For I was due at camp some time ago." He took her hand and, raising it to his lips, placed a light kiss upon it.

Pierre strode to his tethered horse and swung up into the saddle, but as he turned to ride away, Temple's soft voice stopped him.

"Pierre?"

He looked questioningly at her, and Temple moved toward the horse and rider somewhat uncertainly.

"I—I would prefer that Damon not know—"

His gentle voice broke in as she hesitated. "I understand," he told her softly. "You do not wish Damon to know that you are 'observing' his activities. Am I correct?"

"Yes."

"Then it will be our secret and the first step to *our* friendship. But you must remember that Damon, too, is my friend, and true friendship is based upon trust as well as other virtues."

"That is true," Temple agreed with a vigorous nod of her head. "But I do not yet know my husband well and in this manner I will be able to learn more about him."

"And *have* you learned more?"

"Oh, yes!" she told him eagerly. "I have seen much to admire and respect about him!"

"Damon will eventually learn that you were

here, Temple." Pierre seemed very sure of his words. "However, I am certain that you are more than capable of handling that situation."

Touching his hand to his forehead in a farewell gesture, Pierre urged his mount toward the camp.

And Temple resumed her watch.

Chapter Eight

DAMON RODE AMONG THE GROVES, HIS EYES FEAST-
ing upon the lush trees and the beauty of his land.
He remembered his first glimpse of Temple when
she had first arrived at the villa.

He had watched her walk across the green
earth and stand at the fence to watch the workers,
the warm sunlight dancing on her golden-brown
hair. Her graceful movements had captivated him
and he had studied her intently, waiting for the
moment when she would notice him.

That day would forever be in his heart, in his
memory, as vivid as the day he had first seen her
those many years before. Somehow he had
known, even then, that she was destined to be his,
this child-woman who had captured his heart so
completely.

Pierre rode beside his friend, noting his silence.
Damon had been uncharacteristically quiet this
day.

"Garibaldi was summoned to Turin," Damon
stated bluntly as he pulled his horse to a stop.

"He was called to discuss the formation of the volunteer troops."

"He met with Cavour?"

"Yes."

"Was the meeting profitable?" Pierre questioned, leaning forward to flex his tired muscles.

"Indeed. Furthermore, Cavour took Garibaldi to meet the King. And, as I understand it, Garibaldi liked what he saw of Victor Emmanuel, who was in turn impressed with Garibaldi."

"So all seems to be going well for Garibaldi," Pierre commented.

"Very well," Damon returned. "He was granted a commission as Major-General in the Royal Army of Piedmont and given official command of the volunteers that Bixio and Medici are enlisting. They are to be called the *Cacciatori delle Alpi*."

"Our friend Garibaldi, is he pleased with this outcome?"

"I think so," Damon replied and nudged his mount forward.

"And you, Damon?" Pierre pressed, his gaze intent upon his friend.

"I am pleased for him. Garibaldi is a good man, a loyal friend and a born leader as well as a fierce fighter."

"I was speaking of you, Damon."

"Me? What do you mean?"

"I know that it was your wish to fight with Garibaldi should he receive a command. But those hopes have been dashed by the order that you remain here to continue training the volunteer troops. While your heart was—"

"My heart is here as well, my friend," Damon broke in. "I will do what I have been asked, and I will do it well."

Pierre said nothing more as he rode alongside his friend toward the Villa Silone, speculating about what else was in Damon's thoughts. Pierre had known the man long enough to be aware that something lay heavily on his mind. The pending war with Austria was uppermost in everyone's thoughts, yet Pierre was certain that something else had Damon preoccupied. And after meeting the lovely Temple earlier this morning, Pierre knew where Damon's thoughts dwelt. For his *own* thoughts had hardly left the young beauty.

The sun was low in the sky and Damon was anxious to get home. With all the excitement of a young swain en route to visit his first love, Damon was impatient to see Temple. After their unexpected intimacy last night it had been difficult to leave before she had awakened. But it had been necessary for him to do so in order to arrive at the camp in time to transmit his report to his commander, for the messenger would leave soon after dawn.

Suddenly Damon's attention was caught by an approaching rider on the path ahead. He strained his eyes to make out the figure and his heart lurched as he recognized Temple.

She rode leisurely toward them, her hair flowing in the late afternoon breeze. A bright smile spread upon her rosy lips as she saw Damon. She slowed her pace and Damon hastened his own.

Pierre watched the scene with mixed emotions, then turned his mount toward home, leaving Damon and Temple to meet without an audience. His heart seemed unusually heavy and he realized with alarm that he, Pierre Torre, had been smitten by the beautiful Temple Silone—the wife of his dearest and best friend!

Temple's uncertain gaze met Damon's and her heart soared when she saw the broad smile that lit his face and shone in his eyes. Damon leaned forward and kissed her and, although the kiss was not a long one, it stirred excitement within her.

"I trust you do not object to my riding out to meet you?" She looked at him shyly, her fingers toying absently with the reins.

"How could I object to that which gives me so much pleasure?" Damon replied, his voice husky. He placed his hand over Temple's, stilling her nervous fingers. "Come, ride with me and I will show you the beauty of our villa and tell you the history of this enchanted land."

As Temple listened to his vibrant voice, noting its velvety richness, her heart seemed to expand within her bosom. Each encounter with Damon made her more aware of her love for him.

"Share with me the setting of the sun, little

one. The beauty of sunset and the whispering of the evening breeze will be ours alone."

"Sardinia," Damon concluded, his gaze upon the hillside. "They say that neither Romans nor Arabs, Greeks nor Phoenicians ever subdued her. Such beauty she has! She is proud and strong, alone in the vast blue waters of the Tyrrhenian Sea. She is like nowhere else, lying outside the circuit of civilization."

They stood on a gently sloping knoll on the far side of the groves. The sky was streaked with color as late afternoon hastened toward evening. Broken wisps of clouds scuttled across the heavens, partially obscuring the setting sun. A breeze floated by, carrying the sweet scent of the groves and field flowers.

In the short time she had been here, Temple had already come to love this land. It had welcomed her, embraced her. Her heart ached at the sheer beauty of this land to which she had not chosen to come, the husband who had been forced upon her. And now they were both so much a part of her that losing either would be unbearable.

"It is almost frightening," she whispered, unaware that he had heard her quiet words.

Temple sensed Damon's quick look, his dark eyes watching her. She turned to meet his gaze and her pulse quickened as it always did upon meeting those piercing black eyes. Her throat tightened and her heart raced wildly.

Why did he have such a devastating effect on her, she wondered. Why could she not look at him without flushing and feeling weak, without remembering last night?

Damon moved closer, his arm brushing hers.

"There—there is such magic here," Temple said breathlessly, stepping away. "Something that reaches out, almost beckoning. Do you not feel it?"

"I feel it," he replied, his voice a low, hushed sound. His hands reached out to caress her arms and he turned her to face him. She looked into his magnetic eyes, into those dark, disturbing eyes and found within their depths a silent challenge, a question. A dangerous tension was building between them, a raw alertness.

Temple drank in the handsome face so close to hers. A current seemed to pass between them, a live, hot spark that would ignite at the slightest touch and would burn fast, out of control.

Damon's gaze was drawn to Temple's slightly parted lips. He remembered all too well the melting of her body to his on the night before, the response that had so quickly flared at his kiss, his touch.

God! How he wanted her in his arms again, how he longed to taste her lips. He would have her this time, he was certain. It was there in her eyes, the longing, the yearning. Damon sensed that with only a little encouragement and gentle coaxing, Temple would come willingly into his arms and welcome his lovemaking.

"I want to make love to you, Temple." His voice was a breathless whisper. "I want to make you mine."

Temple felt as if she could not breathe; her body trembled and her knees weakened. She wanted him and he had so easily read her very thoughts!

"Damon—I—" she stammered, her eyes wide and uncertain.

"You want me, Temple, just as I want you."

She slowly shook her head in denial. "N—no," she choked, "I—I—"

"Yes," Damon countered quietly. "It is there in your eyes, in your voice, in the movement of your body." He crushed her to him, burying his face in the scented softness of her hair. "Temple, Temple! Do not deny this!"

He covered her mouth with his own, teasing the soft fullness of her lips until she parted them, allowing his tongue entrance. A low moan sounded within his throat and his arms tightened about her. She lifted her arms and clasped them about his strong neck and molded her body closer to his.

Unnamed emotions flooded Temple's body at the closeness of Damon's hard frame pressed against the softness of her body. She could feel the racing of his heart against her breast. Slowly they sank to the warm grass.

Damon rained kisses along Temple's cheek, ear and neck, setting her on fire. She clung to him, pressing closer, her body coming alive, seeking something more than just his kisses, his touch. His fingers gently stroked her smooth flesh.

Temple lay back as Damon loomed above her, his strong, muscular leg thrown across hers. He leaned closer to gaze into her eyes and she could feel his breath warm against her throat as he murmured in his native tongue. Gently he nestled one firm breast in his hand, its weight pleasant in his palm. He ran his thumb over the erect nipple, bringing a moan from Temple's lips, and he caught his breath at the quickening of his heart's beat and the rising heat in his loins.

"God!" he breathed, the sound a ragged gasp. "You have no idea what you do to me, what pleasurable torture you inflict!"

Again his mouth claimed hers. Temple found herself drowning in sensations as his moist tongue teased the inside of her mouth and her tongue, his fingers eagerly exploring her lush curves through the clinging fabric of her dress. She writhed in response to his probing hands, dimly aware that her skirt had inched up above her knees.

Damon slid his knee upward along the length of her slender legs to her exposed thighs in a slow, maddening rhythm. Sweet Christ! She was driving him insane with her throaty purrs and the abandoned response of her sensuous body. He wanted to feel her heated flesh against his, wanted to taste every inch of her, to drive himself deep into her moist warmth.

He pressed his knee against the throbbing mound between her legs, drawing a husky 'Ohhhh' from Temple's lips as she arched against him in ardent reply.

"Do you feel that, Temple, the bittersweet ache there in the core of you?" Damon whispered fervently.

Temple moaned and bit her lower lip. Again Damon's knee pressed against her.

"There is where I wish to be, joined with you, becoming one with you. Ah, Temple," he groaned. "It will be such a beautiful, savage joining, your passion meeting mine."

His urgent need of her spread through his entire body. He was consumed by a raging passion which was intensified by the answering passion that flowed from Temple, her young body hot and hungry for him.

His eyes holding hers, Damon slowly unfastened the small buttons of her blouse, then slipped it from her shoulders. He cupped the full breasts that strained against her camisole and, leaning over her, placed a kiss upon each rosy crest and ran his warm tongue along the deep valley between them, sending a delicious shudder racing through Temple's trembling body.

She watched his every move, a fierce heat engulfing her. His skillful fingers worked at the fastenings of her skirt and undergarments and then she lay bare before him.

Damon caught his breath sharply at the beauty of her lying naked and willing beneath him. Temple's firm breasts rose and fell with each breath, the nipples dark pink and taut. Her flat belly quivered at his touch. God, but she was beautiful, so damned desirable. And she was his and his alone.

"You are the most enchanting, most desirable woman I have ever known," he breathed, running his fingers over her fevered body. "A fiery passion lurks deep within you and I want to arouse it, to bring it to a roaring flame, an all-consuming need."

Rising to his knees before her, Damon took her hand in his and placed it against his chest.

"Undress me as I have undressed you," he said softly. "It is your right."

"I—I cannot," Temple whispered, a catch in her voice.

"Yes," Damon urged gently as he moved her fingers to the buttons of his shirt. "Yes, you can. You want to see me just as I see you."

"But—"

"There is nothing to fear, little one." He smiled tenderly. "I only want to give you the same pleasure you are giving me." Tracing a forefinger along her parted lips, he went on softly, "Please me, Temple, and your reward shall be richer, I promise."

Shyly her fingers worked the buttons of his shirt. The last button undone, Temple stared at the mat of dark hair that covered Damon's broad chest, the sight sending a rush of excitement through her. It was not as difficult as she had expected and the thrill of his burning eyes upon her, watching her undress him, aroused her even more.

She met his intent gaze openly and he smiled lazily.

"Go on," he urged in a husky voice. "Touch me, explore."

With shaking fingers Temple tugged at the fastening of his breeches and managed to slip them down his narrow hips.

Suddenly her hands stilled and she closed her eyes tightly.

"Damon," she murmured softly, "please . . ."

Damon understood. He rose and removed his boots and breeches and stood before her.

"Temple," he spoke her name and the sound was a caress. "Look at me, do not be ashamed. You want me as I want you. There is beauty in what we are doing."

Slowly Temple lifted her eyes to the man towering above her. She was stunned by his magnificence. As he stood naked and proud before her, she thought him to be beautiful, a living sculpture, that far surpassed anything she'd ever seen in a museum.

His shoulders were broad and muscular. A crisp mat of black hair graced his chest and ran down his hard belly to his manhood, which stood erect and ready. His muscular legs showed strength from long hours of work and riding. His tanned skin glistened with a fine layer of perspiration.

Damon's heart hammered in his chest as he watched Temple's gaze slowly roam over him, her first look at a man stripped of his clothing. She had been shy, uncertain at undressing him, but now as he stood before her, he could see that the sight of his naked body excited her.

Damon joined Temple upon the ground, pulled her to him and kissed her deeply. Their bare, heated flesh seemed to cling. It was time for Temple to become a woman and she would do so willingly, without any regrets. She felt no fear, only heightened excitement. It was as if she had waited her entire life for Damon Silone.

"I have wanted this for so long." Damon breathed her very thoughts. "So very long!"

Temple was aching with the need of him, her body pressing closer and closer to his. The very touch of him, the sight of him, set her aflame. She moaned as Damon covered her body with the rock-hard length of his own, swept away on the tide of passion as her supple body molded to his muscular frame.

Damon looked down at Temple, his black-violet eyes smoldering with passion.

"Oh, Damon . . . Damon . . ." she whispered, her voice a mere thread of sound.

"Ah, Temple, we must go slowly," Damon cautioned gently, trying to control his breathing and the trembling of his body. "But I need you so badly and you are so soft and willing that I am finding it damn hard to maintain my self-control." His words were labored.

Temple's brow knit in confusion and upon seeing this, Damon smiled at her and shook his head slightly.

"A woman's first time . . . it is sometimes painful, little one, and I do not wish to hurt you any more than necessary. But my desire for you is so great, and the sight and feel of you—God, but you feel so good in my arms!"

He took her lips in a long, stimulating kiss. Each drank in the sweetness of the other. Temple began to move against him; a groan erupted from his throat and he tightened his embrace. His fingers trailed along her hip and thigh like a licking flame, each stroke sending shivering sensations through her entire body. She heard a soft, purring sound and realized that the contented sound was emerging from her own throat.

"Yes . . . yes . . ." Damon chanted in a husky voice, urging her on, coaxing her to bathe in the ecstasy of her emotions. Temple writhed beneath him, her body crying out for something she knew only Damon could supply. His fingers stroked and soothed, his tongue teased her parted lips.

"You are ready, little one," Damon whispered, his breath fanning her throat. "Your body is seeking fulfillment of your need, your desire. I can give you so much, Temple." His hands moved over her body as he spoke, his touch like fire.

"All you need do is ask, and I will pleasure you as you never dreamed possible. I will teach you, guide you on an adventure of ecstasy."

Temple moaned and her fingernails dug into his shoulder as she pulled him even closer.

"What is it that you want, Temple? Tell me what you need."

Her body was on fire, her heart beat out of control, her breath came in ragged gasps and tiny, panting whimpers escaped her lips.

"Tell me, little one, tell me," Damon urged, his manhood rigid and throbbing against her.

Temple arched beneath him, her pelvis pressing against his hard member. "Oh, Damon!" she murmured, her hands running over his sweat-dampened skin in a frenzy. "Please love me!" She tried to pull his dark head downward to kiss his lips, yet he held back, a tantalizing smile playing about his sensuous mouth. "I need you. I want you. Oh, Damon, please—"

Her plea was smothered as his lips took hers in answer. He embraced her with a fierce grip and knew that it was time to make her his. His lips traced a path along her cheek and throat.

Damon's knee nudged her legs wider, opening her to him. He positioned himself astride her, bent his head to kiss her deeply, and surged forward with a slow, deliberate thrust to break the maidenhead, the final barrier between them. His mouth upon hers stifled her small cry of pain, then he was moving slowly, gently within her.

Temple had stiffened at the fiery pain that seared her at the moment of Damon's entry. She had involuntarily pushed against his chest but the pain was fleeting and his kiss seemed to drown out the memory of the painful moment. His hands roamed over her flesh and he moved within her, arousing sensations that were bittersweet and consuming.

Glorious tremors vibrated through Temple's body, enveloping her in a lofty exhilaration. Damon led her along the path of fulfillment toward the peak of ecstasy, the most intimate union possible between man and woman, when two hearts beat as one and two bodies become one. With consummate grace and skill he brought to perfection Temple's first act of love, her first surrender.

She became a woman within his arms and knew passion at its utmost, far surpassing her most fanciful dreams.

After some time they had dressed and ridden back to the house. There had been little conversation, each one lost in his own thoughts. It had not been a strained silence that surrounded them, but a satisfying, intimate one.

Upon reaching the house, Damon stopped his horse and leaped lightly to the ground. He lifted Temple from her saddle and slowly lowered her to the ground, allowing her body to glide smoothly along the length of his own. The intimate gesture brought a sharp intake of breath from Temple and caused Damon's body to tremble.

Later, as Temple undressed for bed, her mind was filled with thoughts of her husband and their afternoon of passion. Their coming together had been a beautiful union. They had lain in each other's embrace as the evening duskiness enveloped them.

Damon's lovemaking had been uninhibited and wild, yet tender and passionate, just as Temple had known it would be. He had been unhurried and deliberate in teaching her the art of love. She felt that she could have gone on forever, lost in his caresses, his embrace.

As Temple had descended from the lofty cloud of fulfillment, her passion spent, she had looked about her, comprehending that she and Damon lay naked and uncaring with only the earth beneath them and the sky above. She had been momentarily embarrassed about the brazenness of their action, but Damon had laughed and cradled her closer to his heated body and told her, "The bedroom is only *one* of many places in which to make love, little one."

Temple returned to the present with a start as Damon entered her room to bid her good night. She saw his reflection in the mirror where she sat brushing her long, honey-gold hair and the brush stilled its stroking motions. Their gazes met and held. Neither spoke.

As if in slow motion, Damon approached his wife and, placing his hands on her bare shoulders, turned her to face him. He leaned forward to take her parted lips in a searching kiss and she returned the kiss with abandon.

When his lips would have left hers, Temple clung to Damon and asked him softly, against his mouth, to stay with her.

And as the flame of the lamp burned low, Damon led Temple to the bed and took her in his arms as they sank into its welcoming softness. He made love to her slowly and afterward he tenderly kissed her and whispered her name. They fell asleep in each other's arms.

From that night forward, Temple shared Damon's bed.

Chapter Nine

TEMPLE LAY IN THE SOFT BED FEIGNING SLEEP AS Damon moved soundlessly about the room, dressing quietly in an effort not to awaken her. She smiled inwardly at his thoughtfulness.

Each morning as dawn approached, Damon rose, dressed, dropped a feather-light kiss on her brow and left for the training camp. And, unknown to him, Temple's feet would touch the floor in a run as soon as she heard his departure from the villa.

This morning was no exception. Temple dressed hurriedly and, slipping from her room, made her way on tiptoe down the stairs to the kitchen. Placing meat, bread and cheese in a cloth sack, she hastened to the stables.

Temple drank in the beauty of the new day. The sky held a russet hue and the wind stirred the trees with a gentle rustling, wafting the aroma of the orchards across the land.

Entering the stables, Temple hurried along the stalls, recalling the fire. The scent of freshly cut timber mingled with the faint odor of singed wood. The workers had moved quickly to rebuild the main stables and to repair the breeding stable. In a matter of just a few days, they had removed the blackened rubble of charred timbers, cleared the area of all debris, brought in new timber and spent long hours to return the stables to their original state. Only the memory of that awful night and a lingering scorched scent remained.

Temple saddled her horse, tied her food sack to the saddle horn and prepared to mount. But as she placed a foot in the stirrup, a harsh voice halted her.

"Creeping from the house again, Temple?"

She turned to see Rosco Silone standing in the open doorway.

"No, Rosco," she countered. "I am simply going for an early morning ride."

"As you have *every* morning for the past three days?" he returned smugly. His eyes were dark and unreadable.

"I enjoy riding."

"So it would seem," came Rosco's terse rejoinder.

They stood in silence, their gazes locked, and Rosco was reminded of the day not too long ago when he and Damon had stood at odds in the same manner. And he read the same determination in the depths of Temple's brown eyes that he had in his son's. The realization was disturbing.

"It would be well, I believe, that my son put a

rein on his wife," Rosco stated coldly, walking toward the girl. "You are too spirited for my liking and I have told Damon as much. I have also told him that he must break you, that he must master you before you cause him grief. Yet he goes about his business, leaving you to run rampant, when you should feel the bite of the rein about your neck!"

Temple seethed with anger. Rein, indeed! Master! Break her as if she were a spirited horse and not a human! How she would like to put a rein about this insufferable man and lead *him* about, chastising him with the stinging lash of her riding crop when he balked. She smiled at the thought.

Rosco noted the amused smile and bristled in resentment.

"You shall soon learn your place!"

"And what *is* my place, Rosco?" Temple asked sweetly, her hands on her hips and her chin tilted in defiance. "Am I to play the fragile, devoted, adaptable woman? The subordinate wife!" She laughed now without amusement, her brown eyes hard. "Shall I, as the wife of Damon Silone, be subject to the authority and total control of my husband?"

Mimicking the subservient stance of an underling, Temple begged in a whining voice, " 'May I eat, Damon?' 'May I sleep, Damon?' 'May I breathe, Damon?' *'May I live?'* "

Rosco opened his mouth to speak, but she rushed on.

"Women! You think we are such pathetic little creatures that we must rely on *men* to think for us! What is a wife? You see her as an inferior, docile and weak, pliable to a man's will, yielding to handling or training like an animal. Never someone to be treated as an equal and never to be suspected of having a mind!"

Temple took a step toward Rosco. Her eyes were blazing and her breath came in short, ragged gasps.

"I will not play the role your small, arrogant mind decides that I should! I do *not* rank inferior or second best, Rosco Silone. Neither you *nor* your son will break me! I will not submit to being shaped, formed, or trained, nor will I be intimidated!"

With a sharp intake of breath, Rosco snapped, "You believe yourself to be strong, Temple, but you will soon learn that you are not so strong as you would like to think. Damon is the stronger. He *will* break you—mark my words!"

"When hell freezes over!"

With those words Temple fairly flew into the saddle, turned her horse about and fled the stables. She paid no heed to Rosco's angry voice shouting after her.

Temple rode like the wind, her hair flowing behind her in a golden cloud. She blinked back the tears of anger that sprang to her eyes. Why, oh why, did she allow Rosco Silone to make her so angry! All had been so peaceful in the last few days, she thought, the memory flooding through her of the afternoon when she had met Damon as he returned home from the camp. She recalled his tenderness, his patience and understanding, how they had come together as the sun sank slowly from the sky. It had been beautiful and fulfilling. Later that night they had lain together upon the large bed and again he had made love to her. Afterward they had fallen asleep in each other's arms.

In the past days they had learned much from one another, getting to know each other slowly. She was learning to trust, to love. She could not yet read Damon's innermost thoughts nor could she imagine what the depth of his feeling was for her. That remained a mystery. They were still strangers in so many ways.

Temple skipped lightly down the stairway and walked toward the study. The door was standing open and she saw that Damon sat on the edge of the wide desk, his arms crossed over his broad chest. He glanced up as she paused in the doorway, unsure if she was intruding.

"Ah, Temple," Damon greeted her warmly, crossing to meet her. Bending over, he brushed her lips with his own. "Good evening, little one." Taking her hand in his, he led her into the room.

Then Temple's gaze met that of Pierre Torre.

He was sitting in a wing chair beside the desk. He rose slowly and acknowledged her presence with a slight nod of his blond head.

"Temple, this is my lifelong friend, Pierre Torre. Pierre, my wife, Temple," Damon introduced them, his dark eyes dancing. "But then, there really is no need for introductions when the parties concerned have *already* met."

Both Temple and Pierre started, their eyes meeting. Pierre's eyes held a hint of surprise, while Temple's were full of accusation. Neither asked the question that was uppermost in both their minds.

"A man should be aware that his wife and his best friend are having secret meetings," Damon stated calmly.

"We have not been meeting!" Temple denied hotly, her brown eyes flashing. "Not in secret or in any other manner!" She turned to Pierre. "You told him!" she accused.

Pierre shook his head, his hands spread in a helpless gesture. "No," he told her. "I thought that *you*—"

Damon's laugh filled the room and both Temple and Pierre whirled to stare at him in surprise. Damon reached out and pulled Temple to him, tilting her chin so that she had to look up at him. She stared into his dark eyes.

"Did you believe that I would not find out?" Damon asked in a low voice, and Temple trembled. "Do you think that I do not know what goes on on my own land, in my own house? That I would not know my wife's movements?"

"But Pierre and I—" Temple broke off, her eyes wide and pleading. "We—we have not been meeting, Damon, I swear—"

"Oh, little one," Damon interrupted. He dropped a light kiss upon her nose. "I know that," he said softly. "And I knew that you were there on the hill that day, I know that you have been there every day since. I have had someone not too far from you at all times. Do you believe that I care so little for you that I would not see to your safety?" His arms encircled Temple, tightening about her slender body. "What I do not understand is why you crouch up on that hillside for hours each day."

Pierre had relaxed visibly, noting the lack of anger in his friend's voice.

"I can answer that," he told Damon, his blue eyes bright.

"But you will not!" Temple twisted in Damon's arms to look at Pierre, a warning snapping in her brown eyes.

"Oh? And why not, my little spitfire?" Damon inquired with interest. But Pierre answered for her.

"There is something that, at Temple's choosing, must remain unknown to you and she fears that I might disclose it," Pierre explained, laughing at Temple's discomfiture. "I understand that women are none too keen about letting a man know that they are spying on him."

"I was *not* spying," Temple bristled. "I was watching, Pierre—*watching!*"

"And liking what you saw," the blond man returned in amusement. Then to Damon he said, "She had her eye on a handsome, virile man who walks about half-naked."

Temple caught her breath sharply and shot Pierre a withering look.

"Is this true, Temple?" Damon demanded, his eyes stormy, his jaw tight.

Oh, she could gladly throttle Pierre Torre! How *could* he! Why was he doing this, creating doubts about her in Damon's mind, insinuating that she was desirous of another man? She wanted to slap that silly grin off Pierre's handsome face, but she could not move, for Damon held her too tightly against him.

Pierre watched calmly, amusement glinting in his eyes. It pleased him that his friend had found a woman he adored, one of whom he could show such jealousy. No other woman had ever before affected Damon that way.

Temple remained silent and Damon's anger began to rise.

"Answer me, Temple!" he gritted out. "Is what Pierre says true? Were you there because of a man?"

Temple's chin tilted and she stared into his ebony eyes without flinching.

"Yes!" she admitted.

Damon's breath strangled in his throat and his fingers bit into her soft flesh as he gripped her arms.

"Who?" he hissed, then spat an ear-ringing oath. *"Who is he?* Tell me, for I shall call him out!"

"You cannot," Temple barked, her voice as loud as Damon's.

"No?"

"No!" Pierre and Temple spoke in unison.

Damon looked from his wife to his friend. So Pierre knew the identity of the man who held Temple's attention. He addressed his question to him.

"So you know this man?" Damon's tone was sharp.

"Yes, I know him very well," Pierre answered truthfully, trying hard not to smile.

Temple was shaking with cold fury. Pierre was deliberately baiting Damon! Seeing the undisguised rage in Damon's face, she suddenly became afraid; this was the side of her husband she had not witnessed, the anger that she had been warned of.

"Then *you* will tell me what my wife will not," Damon vowed, "and I shall challenge the cad!"

"That would not be possible," Pierre informed him, amusement now shading his voice.

"Not possible? Why?" Damon released his hold on Temple and, placing his hands on his hips, turned to confront his friend.

"It would be impossible to call *yourself* out."

Damon stared at him agape; then his face paled and his hands fell limply to his sides.

"Myself!" he said in disbelief.

Pierre nodded and began to laugh. Suddenly Temple saw the humor in the situation and a small smile touched her lips.

"Myself! My God!" Damon shook his head in astonishment and looked shamefacedly at Temple. *"I* am the man?" he asked, pointing a finger at his chest. Temple nodded.

Damon unexpectedly burst out laughing, and then she was locked in his steely embrace. She looked up to see his eyes alight and shining as he looked deep into hers.

"Ah, Temple, my beautiful wife," he murmured as his laughter died away. Black-violet melted into brown as their gazes held, their heartbeats mingled and Damon's dark head bent to her.

"Temple, Temple . . ." he groaned as his lips took hers. She molded herself against the length of him, her arms slipped about his neck and she pressed even closer as a tiny whimper sounded within her throat.

Pierre stepped quietly from the room, closing the door noiselessly behind him. His own heart and emotions were confused, a mixture of pleasure and disappointment at witnessing the whispered words, the embrace, the intimacy that Damon and Temple shared.

Chapter Ten

TEMPLE SPRAWLED UPON THE BED, HER BARE FEET dangling over the side, a pillow propped under her head, hands laced together upon a book that rested face down on her stomach. She found it impossible to keep her mind on her reading.

It was raining and Damon had forbidden her to ride out to watch the training. "Find something to keep yourself occupied," he had told her. And all morning she had tried to do just that but had found herself with nothing to do.

Turning over, she rested her chin on the pillow and stared out the window, allowing her thoughts to drift.

She recalled last night's encounter in the study with Damon and Pierre. For the first time she had witnessed her husband's quick temper. Temper? Lord, that was indeed a mild word for his show of anger. It had risen in violence like a raging tempest. All it had taken was a few words fed by an undercurrent of suspicion and Damon's fury had reached full force. Seeing this in him had frightened her. He had been ready to challenge a man for no other reason than that he suspected that Temple was attracted to him. She could still hear the rage in his voice when he had demanded to know the identity of the man—and his stunned expression upon learning that it was himself.

Oh, Damon, she sighed to herself, dare I hope that your display of anger was because you truly care for me, because you are jealous? That your lack of indifference means that a flicker of affection for me exists in your heart? How she prayed that it were so. How she wanted his love!

Temple left the bed to stand before the window. Looking out into the rain, she saw nothing. Her heart and thoughts were some miles away— on Damon.

Had LaDonna's love for Nathan been like this, she wondered. Had it burned as fiercely as Temple's did for Damon? Now she could understand so much more. Her words came back to her, the words she had spoken to a dark-haired beauty captured on canvas—a beauty with a wistful smile and a look of sadness.

"Was the love you shared with my father worth all the pain, all the bitterness, that has spanned the years? Was it so precious and fulfilling that it should, after all these years, cause even more pain, more bitterness, for yet another Harris? Why must *I* suffer for the love you and my father had, for which you defied your own father?"

Yes, Temple now realized, their love *had* been worth everything! It had been precious and fulfilling, worth defying Rosco Silone for. LaDonna had loved Nathan completely, loved him with a passion that had given her the strength, the will to have him, to be with him no matter the cost.

And Temple knew that *she* loved Damon in the same way, with as much passion, if not more. But one thing tore at her heart almost unbearably: Damon did not return her love as Nathan had returned LaDonna's.

The rain had stopped, leaving the grounds shrouded in silvery mist. Raindrops still rolled from the roof and dripped into glistening puddles on the veranda.

Temple heard the sound of approaching horses, then saw Damon and Pierre riding toward the stables. She watched as they dismounted, handed their reins to a stableboy and walked slowly toward the house. Damon's laughter rang out and she saw him throw back his dark head in amusement. He gave Pierre a hearty slap on the back, causing the other man's even tread to falter slightly. Pierre shook his blond head and said something that made Damon's laugh boom out again. The two stopped at the pasture fence and Damon leaned on it, placing his arms on the top railing and one booted foot on the lower.

How handsome he was—how overwhelmingly, physically handsome! Leashed power rippled through his magnificent frame. A savage passion,

a fervent lover lurked behind his facade of civili-
ty. Temple felt warm all over just looking at him.

She smiled happily, pleased that she was the
recipient of that sweet passion, that she knew
both Damons—the proud, courteous aristocrat
and the uninhibited, wildly sensuous man.

As if sensing her scrutiny, Damon turned from
the railing and looked upward to see her standing
at the window. He flashed her a warm smile that
caused her heart to flutter in her breast. She
returned the smile, then on impulse reached up to
touch her fingertips to her lips and blow him a
kiss.

At her action, a look of incredulity came over
his face. Quickly he turned to speak to Pierre.
The two shook hands and Damon headed toward
the house, his steps fluid and graceful.

Temple flushed at her impulsiveness. How
could she have done such a thing? Why had she
made such an intimate gesture? She stood motionless for an endless moment, and then as she
turned from the window, Damon strode into the
room. He walked straight to her and, taking her
in his arms, kissed her tenderly.

"I did not choose that that kiss be lost upon the
breeze," he murmured against her parted lips.
"Such sweetness should be savored and returned." And again he took her lips.

Erin and Rosco sat in silence at the long dinner
table. Only the tinkle of silverware and crystal

accompanied by the monotonous ticking of the oversize wall clock could be heard in the dining hall.

Rosco's gaze went to the clock for the fiftieth time. He was quite irritated; it was a good half-hour past the dinner hour and his son and daughter-in-law had not made their appearance at the table.

Emil entered the room bearing a crystal wine decanter on a silver tray.

"Emil," Rosco growled impatiently. "Do you know what is keeping my son and his wife?"

Erin glimpsed the ghost of a smile on the butler's lips before he gravely informed his master, *"Signore* Silone and his lady will not be joining you and the *Signorina* for dinner, sir." Before Rosco could question him further, Emil hastened to add, "I have been instructed to place a tray outside the *Signore's* room so that they may partake of their dinner in their suite, sir."

Erin thought she saw a twinkle light up Rosco's dark eyes. He placed his linen napkin to his lips to conceal what Erin guessed would be a pleased smile.

Later that evening, as Erin made her way to her room, she passed their room and noted that the laden tray still stood on the low table by the door, its contents untouched.

Chapter Eleven

DAMON SAT BEHIND THE LARGE OAK DESK, HIS DARK head bent over a leather-bound ledger. He wrote his last entry, dated it and pushed himself back from the desk. Lacing his fingers behind his head, he stared unseeingly out the window.

He was bone-weary after a long day of working with the volunteers. The training was strenuous and grueling, but it was all necessary. For when the call for war came, and Damon knew that it was inevitable, his men must be ready.

For the last few weeks he had been returning home late at night and spending long hours in the study preparing his reports for the messengers. He seldom took time to eat properly and had been getting very little sleep.

A light rapping at the door brought Damon's troubled thoughts to a halt and he glanced at the clock. It was an hour past midnight and he smiled knowingly. His visitor would be Temple, bringing him a tray of meats and cheese, for she would have awakened to find that he had not yet come to bed and would guess that he would not have taken the time to appease the gnawing in his belly.

She would be draped in a soft, flowing nightgown, her silken hair falling freely about her shoulders and her feet bare. The woman *never* wore shoes, Damon thought, and chuckled.

The soft knock came, and the door opened quietly. Temple's questioning "Damon?" preceded her as she peeked around the door.

"Hello, little one." He spoke in a gentle voice and smiled lazily.

"I—I thought you might be hungry," Temple explained unnecessarily.

She entered the room, and balancing a tray on one hand, pushed the door closed behind her. As she moved to the center of the room, Damon's ebony eyes took in the lovely sight of his wife. She looked just as he knew she would. Her body was clad in a gown and wrap of pale blue silk, her honey-gold hair shone in the lamplight and, yes, bare feet peeked out from beneath the hem of her nightgown.

Damon laughed aloud, a hearty sound that caused Temple to start and stare wide-eyed at him.

"Oh, Temple, my beauty of a wife." His voice was husky and tinged with amusement. He crossed the room to greet her. "Let me see what surprises you have brought me." Lifting the white cotton cloth, he uncovered the tray to find half a

smoked fowl and slices of sausage accompanied
by fruit and cheese and a loaf of brown bread.

"A feast fit for a king!" Damon exclaimed, and
Temple smiled.

How it pleased her to see him happy, to hear
that lilting, carefree laugh. Damon placed the tray
on his desk, then took a folded coverlet from its
resting place on the settee. He spread the fine
woolen blanket on the floor, placed the laden tray
on the coverlet and settled down beside it. Ex-
tending a hand up to Temple, he asked, "Would
you join me in my repast, little one?"

Temple clasped his outstretched hand and sank
to the floor to sit beside him.

Damon leaned forward and kissed her tenderly. "You, my wife, *should* be in bed, you know,"
he said in mock sternness, then lightly kissed her
nose.

"And *you,* my husband, should be there as
well," Temple retorted saucily.

"I would like nothing better, but I have much
work to do. My days are full as well as some of my
nights," Damon explained with a sigh. "It will
only be for a little while longer, God willing."

Temple's feather-light touch brushed the lines
that furrowed his brow. As her fingers traced his
eyebrow, she once again noted the thread of a
scar above Damon's right eye and wondered what
had caused it.

"You are tired," she whispered. "I worry so
about you. This—this war, Damon, I—"

"Shhh." He placed a finger on her lips, stilling her words. "This war means freedom, Temple, unity for our country. My effort is little compared to what others are doing. I am but one man among many."

"But not *all* men are as important to me as you. I am afraid for you. Someone is trying to harm you, to destroy you and what you are accomplishing."

"Would you like some wine?" Damon tossed the words abruptly at her.

"W-what?" Temple was taken aback by the unexpected question. Had he not been listening to her? She was trying to tell him that she feared for his life and he calmly asked if she wanted some wine!

"I said, would you like some wine," Damon repeated calmly, noting the frustration in Temple's face.

"Damon, how can you sit here so—so unconcernedly and ask if I want wine! Were you not listening? *I am afraid for you—afraid of this war!* Oh, Damon, I—I—" she choked, tears filling her eyes.

Her voice broke, and Damon reached out to take her in his arms, rocking her as if she were a child.

He berated himself under his breath for having added to her distress by his thoughtlessness. "I am sorry, Temple," he soothed her. "Please do not cry. I did not mean to make light of your fears. I know they are very real but, little one, if you allow yourself to dwell upon them your fears will only increase. I have a job to do. This is my country and I will serve her in any way that I can. If I am put in danger, then so be it. I cannot change my convictions or my loyalty."

"But Damon—" she cried.

"I am what I am, Temple," he told her flatly.

She met his gaze, her brown eyes swimming with tears. Yes, she thought, and *that* is why I love you. But that was also why she feared losing him. She could not imagine her life without Damon.

As Temple lifted her arms to encircle his neck, to embrace him, Damon spoke softly, his breath stirring her hair. She did not hear his muffled words and she would not have understood them, for they were spoken in Italian, as he whispered, "Temple, my heart, my life!"

She clung to him, her heart beating rapidly against his chest, and he held her thus for a long time, his touch gentle, his fingers stroking her hair as she cried, wishing that the tears could wash away all her fears.

Finally Damon lifted Temple in his arms to carry her from the study and up the stairs to their room. He tucked her into bed, brushing his lips over hers. Silently she watched him walk to the window to stare out into the darkness. After a while, Damon began to undress and Temple watched the way the moonlight shone through the window to play upon his tanned skin. He turned to Temple and joined her upon the bed.

She went eagerly into his strong arms. Damon kissed her tenderly, running his hand along her cheek, and he whispered, "Go to sleep, little one. Fear nothing, for I am here. We are safe in each other's arms."

Temple closed her eyes and the gentle stroking of Damon's hand soon lulled her into a peaceful sleep.

For some time afterward Damon lay wide awake, his mind filled with questions and the worry of what was to come—the war, his duty and Temple, his lovely Temple whom he loved with an unfathomable passion. Temple, without whom he could not live. For, as he had whispered to her, she was his life!

Later Damon awoke from a fitful sleep for the third or fourth time to stare into the dimness of the room. A warm softness snuggled against him and he tightened his hold about Temple and smiled.

Oh, Temple, my love, he sighed inwardly, what a wonder you are. He brushed his lips along her cheek. Such fire and spirit, such overpowering passion and gentleness. You vowed to hate me, never come to my bed, yet now you come so willingly into my embrace and surrender so completely. Dare I hope that in time you will as willingly and completely surrender your heart to one who loves you with a passion that surpasses life itself?

Damon leaned over to place his lips upon Temple's in a soft kiss.

"I want your love, Temple, I need that love as one needs air to breathe, to survive!" His voice was a mere whisper.

Chapter Twelve

TEMPLE STOOD WITH HER HANDS ON HER SLIM HIPS, a look of frustration on her pretty face. The boy's laughter rang out merrily.

"And just what do you find so humorous, Mario?" Temple asked with mock sternness.

"You, *Signora,*" he answered, pointing at her, and began laughing again. "You look like a boy."

"Why Mario, thank you!" Temple exclaimed, pleased at his words. "That is exactly what I wish to look like."

The youngster's dark eyes studied her closely as she stood before him dressed in his clothing. He had not asked any questions when the pretty *Signora* had asked him for a shirt and a pair of his breeches. He had simply raced away to get them and bring them back to the tack room. The *Signora* had thanked him, set him to stand watch and to warn her if anyone entered the stable, and then stepped into the room and closed the door.

A few minutes later the *Signora* had emerged wearing Mario's clothes, her honey-brown hair tucked beneath an old hat. Mario had never seen such a thing and his momentary shock at the sight of her quickly gave way to laughter at the strangeness of her new appearance.

"But why would a pretty lady like you wish to look like a boy?" he asked now. This Mario could not understand at all. He thought the *Signora* was the most beautiful lady he had ever seen; she even made a pretty boy.

"Can you keep a secret?" Temple whispered conspiratorially, her eyes bright and a mischievous smile on her lips.

Mario nodded eagerly.

"I am going to ride out and join *Signore* Silone's army," Temple told him.

The boy's mouth dropped open and he stared speechlessly at her.

"Do you believe my disguise will work?" she queried. "Do you believe that I can fool the *Signore?*"

"I am not sure, *Signora,*" Mario said nervously, running his fingers through his hair.

"Not sure? But why not?" Temple asked, looking down at her outfit.

"Well . . ." He drew the one word out, then walked slowly around her, eyeing her closely.

"Well what, Mario?" she prodded, turning to look at the boy.

"Your shape," he said bluntly.

"Whatever is wrong with my shape?" she asked worriedly.

"Nothing," Mario replied promptly, his eyes still on Temple's figure.

"But Mario, you just said—"

"You have curves where boys do not, *Signora*, and . . . ah . . ." His face took on a faint red tinge. "Well, other parts, too," he finished lamely. He cleared his throat uncomfortably.

"Oh," Temple said, realizing what he meant. She took one more long look at herself. "I see what you mean," she told him, embarrassment creeping into her voice. She sighed heavily and sank down to sit on a bale of hay, bracing her elbows on her knees and resting her chin in her hands.

Mario did not like seeing the pretty *Signora* look so unhappy. Maybe he should not have mentioned the difference in her shape. He dropped down to sit on the floor near Temple, a straw between his teeth. They sat thus for a few moments.

"What is this? Have you two nothing more to do than to sit about on your lazy bottoms?"

Emil's voice startled them and Temple and Mario jumped guiltily to their feet in unison, bumping into each other in the process. Temple's hat slipped back on her head and the weight of her hair brought the golden-brown mane cascading down over her shoulders.

"*Signora!*" Emil exclaimed, his eyes bulging in surprise. His mouth worked but no words came forth.

Temple smiled shyly and reached down to pick up the fallen hat. Mario looked from his father to the *Signora* uncertainly. Realizing that Temple was not going to explain, he attempted to do so.

"The *Signora* is in disguise," he stated a little too loudly.

"Disguise?" Emil repeated in astonishment.

"Yes. She is—well, she is going to volunteer in *Signore* Silone's army." The boy spoke proudly, his brown eyes shining up at his father.

Emil was aghast and stood staring wordlessly.

"Only she has a problem," Mario went on importantly. "You see, it is her shape. It is all wrong."

Now Emil found his voice. "Mario!" he barked. Temple began to laugh.

"He is quite right, Emil," she agreed, laughter rippling in her tone. "As Mario pointed out, even in boys' clothing I still look very much female. Therefore, my disguise will not work."

Emil knew not exactly what the *Signora* was up to, but he could see how disappointed she was. The woman was different from others, he had realized that shortly after her arrival. But he could see that she was a fine lady and that the younger *Signore* was very fond of her.

Emil often caught the *Signore* watching his lady with a special look in his eyes. She had brought laughter to the villa, which had long been without it. She did not put on airs, the young *Signora,* but

169

worked happily about the house, relieving the housekeeper of her overload. And she stood up to the master, the elder *Signore*, with an undaunted spirit. Emil smiled, remembering the times he had overheard their heated verbal battles. This lady was indeed a welcome addition to the Villa Silone.

Now she was up to something, no doubt something that would shock the younger *Signore* and infuriate the elder. Emil found that he wanted to help her in whatever endeavor she had in mind.

"Perhaps a loose jacket," he suggested, suddenly breaking the silence.

"A jacket?" Temple inquired.

"*Si, Signora,* a loose-fitting jacket. It would hide what the shirt will not."

"Oh, Emil, you are right!" Temple cried excitedly, throwing her arms around his neck. "Thank you, Emil, thank you!"

The man was taken aback by the *Signora's* impulsive show of gratitude and did not know how to react. Mario stood staring agape at the *Signora* hugging his father, his wide brown eyes darting to the stable door to see if anyone else had witnessed this unusual scene.

"Mario, do you have an old jacket that I may borrow as well?" Temple asked him and he answered with a nod. "Then fetch it for me, please." Looking down at her bare feet, she added, "I shall only be a moment. I just have to run upstairs and pull on my boots." She ran from the stables, a trail of laughter floating behind her.

Mario stared at the door as she disappeared, then looked at his father.

"The *Signora*, she hugged you," the boy said in awe, "like you were just like she is."

Emil smiled at his son, a proud look on his face. "I am still trying to comprehend that fact, my son."

"The *Signora*," Mario continued, "she is very special, is she not, father?"

"Very special," Emil agreed, running work-worn fingers through his dark, unruly hair.

Temple rode into the camp. Her disguise must be effective, she thought, for all the attention she drew was a glance here and there. With young men riding in each day to join the cause to unite Italy, one more eager volunteer was not an unusual sight.

She looked about, her eyes searching for Damon, but he was not to be found. Pierre was training some men to fall from their horses and roll quickly to their feet. Others worked with swords and from some distance away echoed the muffled sound of gunfire. Perhaps Damon was at the firing range, she thought. She decided to tether her horse at the main tent where she saw Damon's and Pierre's mounts grazing peacefully.

The flap of the main tent was lifted and a pretty

woman stepped out. Her hair was a fiery russet color and she was dressed in an emerald green riding habit with black boots.

Damon followed her from the tent. Temple's heart turned in her breast and her breath stopped. As she watched, the red-haired woman turned to Damon, placing her hands flat on his chest possessively, and looked up into his face. Damon said something to her and she shook her head.

Then the unknown girl reached up to pull Damon's head downward and kissed him full on the lips. Temple's breath escaped in a rush and her fingers tightened on the reins, causing her horse to dance slightly. She moved closer. Damon reached up to detach the woman's arms from about his neck and moved a step backward. Temple could see that he was displeased, for his face was taut and anger lurked in his dark eyes.

"Do not ever again take the liberty to do that, Della," Damon said, his voice tight and controlled.

"But Damon, darling—" Della cooed and started to step closer, but Damon halted her movement with a steely hand on her shoulder.

"I mean what I say, Della. Do not push me—you will not like the consequences."

Damon suddenly became aware of the horse and rider approaching them and looked up. He stood transfixed, a mixture of emotions chasing over his handsome face. Then he smiled broadly and stepped around Della to walk briskly toward Temple.

Della stamped her booted foot and turned to follow him. "Damon, really!" she said exasperatedly.

Damon stopped before Temple, hands on his hips, and his dark eyes were shining with amusement, his smile bright and welcoming.

Temple stared at him uncertainly.

"What are you about, little one?" he asked softly, the tenderness in those few words causing her heart to quicken its beat.

"You recognized Spirit," she murmured, disappointed that he had known who she was.

Damon shook his head. "It was *you* I recognized."

"But how?"

"Your movements, your gracefulness, your figure. I noticed these even before I saw your face. Such beauty cannot be disguised." He reached up to lift her from the horse and stood her before him, his hands resting at her waist. "Again I ask, what are you about?"

"I wish to volunteer in your army," she told him solemnly, her brown eyes shining.

"Well, little one," he laughed good-naturedly, and took the hat from her head, loosening her silken hair. "I have no doubt that you have the spirit and temperament of a fighter, but," he tilted his head to look at her appraisingly, "I am afraid you are of the wrong gender."

"Oh? Am I hearing you complain that I am a woman?" Temple teased, leaning toward him and batting her long lashes innocently.

Damon smiled lazily and drew her to him, planting a lingering kiss on her full lips, a kiss that sent her senses reeling.

"Is that an indication that I am complaining?" he asked huskily, the light of passion flaming in his black-violet eyes.

Temple's knees went weak and she had to cling to him to steady herself. They were so engrossed in each other that they had completely forgotten Della.

Della had stared narrowly at the boy astride the horse, thinking that Damon was acting most peculiar about him. There was such tenderness in his voice, although she could not hear his words, and the fact that Damon's attention was fully upon this youth irritated Della.

Then he had lifted the rider from the horse and set the creature before him—whatever did he mean by such an action! When Damon removed the dusty hat and a mass of golden-brown waves cascaded down, Della almost choked. Fury surged through her when he pulled the girl into his embrace and kissed her. It was a kiss with meaning, and Della fully recognized that fact.

Her green eyes narrowed maliciously and she immediately decided that this woman would have to be disposed of. In Della's mind, Damon Silone had always belonged to her. She had long planned to be mistress of the Villa Silone and she *would* be, no matter who tried to stand in her way.

She should have remained in Sardinia, Della thought in self-recrimination, and made sure that Damon was under her spell. But so certain was she that Damon would be hers that she had gone to France for several months to visit friends.

She knew that Damon had planned to be in France and Della wanted to be there when he arrived. Later she had learned that Damon had been there and returned to Sardinia without even calling on her. Angry with him, she had remained longer, thinking to punish him for his inattentiveness and expecting him to miss her greatly.

So where did this—this *creature* come from! And dressed in boys' clothing, no less! This child could not be more than seventeen years old, *maybe* eighteen. Damon had been so busy in his training camp that he had not been getting into town, Della thought, and he must have turned to a servant girl. Well, the servant girl would soon learn that Damon belonged to only one woman, and that woman was Della Fruge!

Now Damon turned to Della, his arm protectively about the girl.

"Temple, this is Della Fruge, Pierre's sister and longtime friend of the family." Della bristled at the casualness in Damon's voice. Longtime friend, indeed, she thought angrily.

"Della," Damon went on, "May I present my wife, Temple."

Della was shocked speechless; then her green eyes blazed with open hostility. Temple was appalled by the cold fury in those eyes, noting the hatred in the depths of Della's jade gaze. Temple shivered involuntarily and Damon tightened his embrace.

"Wife!" Della hissed. "Your *wife?*"

"Yes, Della, Temple is my wife," Damon confirmed, annoyed at the woman's rudeness.

"When—how long have you been married?" the redhead demanded.

"It will soon be three months," Temple ventured to answer the question addressed to Damon. "We were wed in France on the second of February." She bestowed on Della a warm smile that did not quite reach her brown eyes. This green-eyed woman will *never* be a friend to me, Temple silently acknowledged, and she must never know that the marriage was not of their choosing and that it had been a marriage by proxy.

"February? You were wed while you were in France?" Della cried, icy green eyes on Damon. "Was that your reason for going to France?"

"That is correct," he stated tersely.

Della's long nails dug into her palms as she clenched her fists. She fought to control her temper. She must not show her hand, she reminded herself, she must not show that she was shaken by the announcement.

"Well, how nice," she said, her voice suddenly

honeyed. "I must congratulate you both. I was—
that is, the news came as such a surprise. You
see," she explained to Temple, "I have only just
returned from France myself and had not heard
the—ah—news. My stepfather and Pierre were
not at home, and the butler told me that my
brother was here with Damon, so I just rode out.
I could hardly wait to see them. After all, four
months is a long time to be away from my loved
ones."

Although Della now was making a show of
appearing to be happy for Damon and his new
bride, Temple was not at all convinced of her
sincerity. She knew that the woman was furious
and that the hatred that flashed in her emerald
eyes was very real. Temple also accepted the fact
that, without a doubt, Della was her enemy and
that she should be on guard at all times. On the
heels of that thought came another—*and so
should Damon!* Why she thought of *Damon's*
safety at that moment, she did not know, but the
thought frightened her.

"Tomorrow night, then," Damon's voice broke
into Temple's worried thoughts. "About seven?"

"Seven will be fine," Della agreed and, with a
slight nod, she walked toward a copper-colored
mare and mounted to seat herself in the sidesad-
dle. "Unless your wife would prefer that we come
another day or another time," Della called out,
fairly spitting the words 'your *wife,*' her cold stare
on Temple.

"No," Temple put in sweetly. "Whatever pleases Damon." And groaned inwardly at her display of wifely submissiveness. How Rosco would gloat if he had heard, Temple thought, and turned to see the amused expression on her husband's face.

"'Whatever pleases Damon'?" he queried in mock perplexity.

"That woman is impossible!" Temple said heatedly, ignoring his comment.

"You have no idea *how* impossible," Damon responded. Taking her hand in his, he led her to the tent from which he and Della had emerged earlier and they entered its cool duskiness.

Seating her in a straight chair, Damon moved to sit behind a crude wooden desk. "I have some paperwork to get done but it will take only a few minutes. I want you where I can keep an eye on you. I cannot have you walking about the camp distracting my men from their training duties."

Temple smiled, stretched her feet out before her and bent down to remove her boots. She wriggled her cramped toes and tucked her feet beneath her.

Damon watched her graceful movements fondly. Lord, but she was full of surprises. A woman of wonder as well as beauty. And she was his!

The hall clock was striking seven when the party of three arrived at the Villa Silone. Emil showed them into the library after taking their wraps.

Louis Torre was a handsome man in his late fifties, with blue eyes like his son's and gray hair that had once been light brown. He spoke with a joviality and merriment that won Temple's liking instantly.

Della floated in, wearing a dinner dress of apple-green velvet fringed with ice-green satin, her feet shod in satin slippers the same shade of ice green. Her russet hair was a mass of uneven curls about her head, a pearl- and emerald-studded comb behind her right ear. She exuded a scent that was chokingly musty.

When Damon inquired about the unusual scent, Della threw him an intimate smile and purred, "Oh, you noticed. It is called 'Sandalwood' and is sinfully expensive." She lifted her wrist to her nose and sniffed. "It comes from Asian trees. Unusual, do you not agree?"

"I would say that 'breathtaking' is more the word for it!" Damon replied, and Temple choked on her wine. Damon turned to her quickly and began patting none too gently on her back, but it did nothing to alleviate the spasm of coughing that claimed her.

Damon excused them and guided her up the stairs to their room. When Temple had regained control, she turned to her husband who sat close by her side on their bed, his face concerned.

"You should not gulp your wine, Temple," he admonished.

"Really, Damon." She gave him an accusing look. "It is your fault that I choked."

"My fault?" Damon echoed in surprise.

"Yes, yours! That comment about Della's perfume—'I would say that 'breathtaking' is more the word for it!'" she mimicked.

"Well, 'unusual' certainly was not adequate to define something that damned near chokes the breath from a body!" he informed her, and they both broke into a gale of laughter.

Dinner was announced as they descended the stairs arm in arm and everyone proceeded into the dining hall.

Pierre and Damon spoke of the training progress and of the approaching war, with Rosco and Louis joining in the conversation. At intervals Della broke into the talk with some remark that she cooed directly to Damon, causing both his and Rosco's faces to darken. Louis pressed his lips together in disapproval and Pierre seethed at his stepsister's brazenness.

But Temple took Della's behavior with good grace. Damon's hand often found hers beneath the table, clasping it tightly. Twice he lifted it to his lips and kissed her fingertips, earning them both stabbing looks from the green-eyed vixen seated opposite. Very sure now that Damon had no personal interest in the red head, Temple determined not to let Della distress her and she refused to flinch under the snapping green eyes.

All in all, dinner went well and they rose to

retire to the library for brandy. The guests entered first, and then Damon took Temple's hand, halting her just outside the library door.

"It has been a pleasant evening, my friends," Damon told them, his manner friendly yet casual. "I have had a long day and I must rise early. My wife and I shall now bid you good night."

He gave no heed to Della's "But, Damon!"

"Good night, sir," he addressed his father. "Pierre, I shall see you on the morrow. And Louis, it was good seeing you, sir. Della, welcome back."

Temple smiled warmly at her husband's friends and bade them all good night. Then the young *Signore* Silone mounted the stairs with his lady, his arm encircling her slender waist. A stony-faced Della stood watching through narrowed lids from the library doorway, her fists clenched in fury.

Only Pierre was aware of the danger in Della. He appointed himself to watch her closely—very closely.

Chapter Thirteen

DAMON HAD BEEN SUMMONED BY MESSENGER TO meet with his superiors regarding the looming war and Temple spent a sleepless night without his warmth beside her. Often at night he would reach out to her in his sleep, pull her close to him, whispering her name. She missed him dreadfully.

Never would she have believed that a relationship such as theirs could develop between two people who had started out at odds with each other. But as time had gone by, a closeness had grown between Temple and Damon and she had let herself come to hope that he cared about her, maybe even loved her in some way.

Temple rose late in the morning to ride out to the hillside as was her habit. She was fascinated with the activities of the camp, observing but never interfering with the training. She loved watching Damon in action and her heart would soar when he would break from his duties and ride across the clearing to join her on the knoll.

She chuckled at the memory of the day she had

dressed in young Mario's old clothes and ridden into camp. The look on Damon's face had been priceless. He had not known whether to be angry, amused or happy—shocked was probably the most accurate word. But he had allowed her to stay and later, at her insistence, he had begun to teach her to handle a pistol. "There may come a time when my ability to use a gun will be a necessity," she had insisted stubbornly. And in a very few days Temple had become quite a marksman. Damon had been both surprised and proud of her accomplishment.

Now, as she watched the mock battle from her hillside vantage point, she found that she had no interest whatsoever in what transpired down there. It just was not the same without Damon in the midst of the action.

Temple mounted Spirit and rode back to the villa. Leaving her horse at the stables, she decided to take a leisurely walk and chose a direction she had never before been. She walked along an overgrown path that led to a small lake. Here she stopped to rest for a while and enjoy the peaceful surroundings, to listen to the gentle sounds of the land.

Her eyes took in the mysteriously beautiful place. The earth bore a soft carpet of grass and the stately trees rose proudly toward the vividly blue sky. A broken marble bench with ivy clinging about it lay just beyond and Temple moved it.

Then she saw the gravestone. With leaden steps Temple approached the marble structure and, leaning forward, reached out to brush aside the green ferns that laced the sides of the stone. She read:

Our Beloved LaDonna
Only Daughter of Rosco and Candida,
Sister of Damon
Taken from us too soon,
gone before we were ready to lose her.
God has called, she has answered
and in His gentle embrace he holds our angel.
She was loved passionately, she is greatly missed.

So it was here that the gentle beauty now slept forever, here beneath the ivory-colored stone. With tears on her cheeks, Temple rose and stood looking down at the mound. She shivered as the wind stirred and crossed her arms about her.

Gazing about her once more, she drank in the peaceful serenity of this idyllic place. This must have been LaDonna's private refuge in life, Temple thought. It must have been here in this garden that she had spent her time. That was why Rosco had chosen to let her rest here.

Temple knelt before the marble crypt.

"I understand your love now, LaDonna," she whispered brokenly. "I understand, for I love your brother with the same fathomless passion."

She began to pull the overgrown foliage away from the marble, reverently dusting the smooth stone with her hand.

Suddenly Temple heard voices and stopped to listen.

"Silone will be in the village for some time," a deep voice said. "I will station a few men about the outskirts of his camp—"

A murmured voice broke in, but Temple could not make out the words and she sat motionless, her breath still in her throat.

"It is the perfect time," the deep voice came again. "We will strike at high noon, after our men have had time to get into the camp. There will be only a handful of them there, and they will not stand a chance!" The man laughed cruelly.

"And Damon?" the other questioned in a muffled voice.

"He is due back within two days' time. Forbes and Combs will be waiting for him just past the stone wall. They have instructions to take care of him—permanently!"

Again came the murmur.

"It will be clean—quick!" answered the first voice.

"Like the fire?" asked the other.

"That was unfortunate. Combs was not fast enough. He thought he heard someone coming and panicked."

"Well, this time he had better—"

"Silone will be disposed of, you can count on it. That is why I am sending Forbes along." The voice was positive and assured.

Then the voices moved away, leaving Temple crouching by the grave afraid to move, even to breathe. Oh, God, she thought in horror, someone was going to attack the camp at noon tomorrow. And Damon! Dear God, *Damon*—they were planning to kill him! She had to do something, get help from somewhere. She must warn the camp—warn Damon!

Temple forced herself to wait for a few minutes for the unseen intruders to get far enough away not to hear her. Then, coming to her feet, she broke into a run toward the house. Suppose it were someone at the house who was involved in this demonic plot, she thought as she ran. Whom could she really trust, other than Erin and Rosco?

But what could Erin do that she, Temple, could not? And Rosco? He probably would not believe her. Emil? No, he was only a servant and would not have the authority to do anything. So who was left?

Pierre! She must get word to Pierre!

Entering the house and racing to the study, Temple pulled open a desk drawer in search of writing paper. Grasping the ink quill, she scrawled a note to Pierre, sealed it in an envelope and ran to the stables.

Mario was the only one about and she instructed him to ride like the wind to the Villa Torre and see that *Signore* Pierre—and *only Signore* Pierre —received the letter. The boy, noting the quiet urgency in the *Signora's* voice, quickly saddled a horse and rode off toward the neighboring villa.

As the long hours of the evening slowly ticked by, Temple paced the floor impatiently. She wrung her hands in frustration and chewed on her lower lip. After what she had overheard today, it was imperative that she meet with Pierre and either get his advice on what to do with the information or allow him to handle the situation.

Damon was not expected to return for at least another day, perhaps two. She had no one to turn to except Pierre and she prayed fervently that he would heed her summons.

Temple opened the door, looking out into the night. Where was Pierre? She had sent the letter hours ago and Mario had returned with the assurance that he had handed the letter straight to *Signore* Pierre. What could be keeping him?

She stepped back into the hall, closing the door behind her, and resumed her restless pacing. The hall clock struck nine and with each stroke Temple's heart sank and tomorrow moved nearer. With a deep, ragged sigh of defeat, Temple sank to the lowest stair to think. She would have to devise another plan, she decided, ready to give up on Pierre.

Suddenly she heard the pounding of a horse's hooves shattering the quiet of the night. She sprang from the step, ran to the door, and rushed out.

Temple's eyes focused on Pierre as he dismounted just within the circle of lamplight that illuminated the veranda and she flew to meet him, throwing herself into his arms as she cried out his name.

"Oh, Pierre, Pierre!" she choked, clinging to him.

He gently pushed her from him to take her face in his hands, brushing back the golden hair. Tears streamed down her cheeks and her cry tore at his heart.

"Temple, what has happened?" he demanded in an uneven voice, shaking her slightly in his anxiety. "Tell me!"

"They are going to kill Damon! Attack the camp!" Her voice came in panting gasps. "Oh, Pierre! We must do something. *We have to do something to stop them!*"

Pierre folded Temple in his arms and held her for a moment, attempting to comprehend what she had told him and how she had come to be in possession of such knowledge. Temple clung to him in gratitude for his very presence. Right now he was her tower of strength, a haven in her torment. Pierre began walking toward the front door of the villa, his arm supporting the distraught girl.

A stately figure sat motionless astride his horse, watching the scene from the surrounding darkness. His heart felt crushed within his breast, his body was rigid, his teeth were clenched and his dark eyes glittered dangerously, a mighty storm brewing in their ebony depths.

Damon had finished his business in record time in order to return home. One night away from Temple had been endless and sleepless. Another night away from her was more than he wanted to endure. He had hoped that she might have missed him as well, and had pushed Shadow to his limit in order to arrive home before midnight.

Only in the last mile had Damon slowed his pace to rest his mount, knowing that he would be home soon. He, too, had heard the pounding of hooves coming from the opposite direction and had waited warily in the shadows to see who was headed toward the villa in such a hurry. Damon's life had been threatened several times by those who would side with their enemies, and he preferred to take no chances.

He recognized the horse and rider as they pulled up in the lamplight and had been about to urge Shadow forward when the front door opened and Temple dashed out to meet Pierre. There was something odd about this late-night visit from his friend and it was certainly strange that Temple should rush out so eagerly to greet him, almost as if she had expected his arrival and impatiently awaited it.

So, Damon thought bitterly, he had hastened home only to witness his wife rushing out to fling herself into the arms of his best friend. He knew that neither of them had expected him home before late on the morrow. He clenched his teeth furiously and gritted out an oath, his hands balling into fists.

Upon entering the study, Pierre seated Temple in a comfortable chair, poured her a brandy and returned to kneel before her.

"Drink this," he urged, handing to her the snifter of amber liquid.

"We must warn Damon," Temple cried, pushing the snifter away. "We cannot just—"

"Drink, Temple, it will calm you."

"I do not wish to be calm, Pierre. We must find a way to warn Damon!" she insisted in desperation.

Pierre set the snifter down and, taking both her hands in his, spoke to her in a reassuring tone. "Temple, I cannot possibly help unless you calm down and tell me what you know."

She heard his gentle tone and his words began to sink in. Taking a deep breath, she repeated what she had overheard, word for word. It seemed that the words had been etched into her memory, she could even hear the conversation again in her mind—the words, the tone of voice and, above all, the cruel laugh of the demon who planned the death of her beloved Damon!

"Oh, Pierre," Temple cried in conclusion, "they are going to kill Damon. 'Quick—clean' is what he said. I cannot bear it. You must help me, Pierre, you *must!*"

And again she was in his arms, her tears soaking his shirt front. Pierre's hand gently smoothed the honey-colored hair.

"May I inquire, Pierre," Damon's steel-edged voice sliced through the silence, "what is going on between you and my wife?"

"Damon!" Temple pushed herself away from Pierre and flew across the room to Damon, but he reached out a hand and stayed her as she would have thrown herself into his arms. He spat an oath and pushed Temple from him with such force that she staggered backward and would have fallen if Pierre, who had followed her, had not steadied her.

"What the hell is wrong with you, Damon?" Pierre asked indignantly, his face an angry red. "You had no right—"

"I have *every* damned right where *my wife* is concerned, Torre! *Every right!*" Damon lashed out, his tone hard, his black eyes cold as they turned on Temple.

"D-Damon . . . you do not understand. You—" she gasped.

"I have eyes in my head, Temple. I have no trouble seeing," he hissed, his fists clenched threateningly. "I saw you run out to meet your lover—my *friend!*"

"No!" Temple cried, tears glistening on her flushed cheeks. "No, Damon, please—" But her

words died in her throat as she met the rage in his eyes.

He would not hear her—he was not listening. His fury was too great. Fear rose in her and with a cry she tried to pass Damon to flee the room. He clutched her arm in a grip of iron that seared pain along her upper arm and shoulder.

Temple cried out and Pierre stepped toward them, only to be stopped by Damon's deadly calm voice.

"Do not meddle in my affairs, Torre!"

Blue eyes locked with black-violet ones and Temple could see the rapid rise and fall of Damon's broad chest, could feel the violence being unleashed.

"You are making a big mistake, Damon," Pierre stated flatly. "You will regret your actions—"

"I am warning you, Torre!" Damon's body shook with suppressed rage as he rasped the words through clenched teeth.

The atmosphere was charged and Temple realized that an explosion was threatening. She knew that she had to do something, say something, to divert and calm Damon. He was beyond reason, blind to the truth in his fury.

She reached up a trembling hand and touched Damon's colorless cheek and he flinched, his eyes darting to hers. Her lips trembled and tears wet her face.

"I love you, Damon Silone," she told him softly, her voice filled with emotion. "I love you with a passion that frightens me, a love so intense that I would die if ever I should lose you."

Damon stared at her, his bewildered eyes never leaving hers. Her low voice seemed overly loud in the dead silence of the room.

"It is because of that love that I sent for Pierre, the only person I could trust, that I *would* trust with your life." She moved closer to him. "Someone is planning to kill you, even now is plotting your death. I could not bear it," she choked. "I did not know how to reach you, to warn you, and I *had* to do something, Damon. If I did not love you, I would not have cared. Maybe I am wrong in that. Perhaps I should *not* love you, should *not* care!"

And with those words Temple ran from the room in tears, her heart breaking. Her sobs floated back from the hallway as she fled.

Damon stood stunned, unable to speak. After an endless moment he sank into the chair, burying his white face in his hands.

"My God!" he whispered. "My God!" Temple had said she loved him. Dear God! The very words he had hoped for, had prayed to hear, had longed to hear falling from her sweet lips.

She had feared for his life. "Someone is planning to kill you, even now is plotting your death," she had told him in agony. "I could not bear it."

That is why Pierre is here, Damon thought, the realization penetrating his rage-inflamed brain. Temple had sent for him, knowing he could be trusted because he was Damon's friend. His dark head lifted slowly and he looked at Pierre, his black eyes filled with pain and remorse. He could not find the words he sought.

Pierre understood. He knew his friend well. Reaching over, he retrieved the snifter of brandy he had poured for Temple and placed it in Damon's shaking hand.

"I think you need this, my friend," Pierre told him.

Damon mumbled a weak 'thank you' and tossed down the brandy, the fiery liquid burning his throat. He sat staring down at the empty snifter, studying the small amber droplets in its bottom.

"Pierre, I am sorry," Damon said quietly after an interminable silence.

"You should be saying that to Temple, my friend," Pierre replied bluntly. He seated himself on the settee and stretched his long legs out in front of him. "I know you, I know your unreasonable temper. I should, since I have been on the receiving end of it many times over the years and will be, I am sure, again. But my God, Damon, you did not even give Temple a chance to explain and you would not listen to me!"

Remembering the gross unfairness of the entire

situation, Pierre suddenly became angry himself and bounded up to stand above the dejected Damon. Pointing an accusing finger at his friend, Pierre vented his frustration. He knew from past experience that Damon's anger was now spent, and that he could now speak his mind and be heard and that there would be no physical violence between the two of them. It had always been thus for the two close friends.

". . . and you walked in at that point," Pierre concluded his tirade, "you walked in and saw something you did not understand, something you refused to understand, and you jumped to the *wrong* conclusions. God Almighty, Damon, any fool can see that your wife loves you!" Pierre ended, running his hands through his blond hair in anger and frustration.

"You say that as if you are not pleased with the fact," Damon remarked, hearing the despair in Pierre's voice. "Would you prefer that she loved someone else—yourself, for instance?"

There was a long, poignant silence. Neither man moved. Finally, Pierre sighed heavily and looked straight at Damon, his blue eyes not wavering from the black ones that studied him shrewdly.

"I am your friend, Damon, and I value our friendship. Because of that I have curbed my feelings for Temple, I have allowed them to be no more than the love and friendship that I have for her husband. I will admit, however, that if it were any other man . . ." Pierre let the words trail into silence.

He needed nothing more than tonight's events to know that Damon was very much in love with Temple. Pierre too had fallen deeply in love with her, yet he had come to terms with himself, had reasoned that he could not, *would* not, harbor a love for the wife of his best friend. Therefore he had firmly relegated his love for Temple to the back recesses of his heart, willing it to remain there, safe and unsuspected. Now Pierre was keenly aware that his love for Temple was as deep and as strong as his love and friendship for Damon. Pierre knew that he would gladly give his life to save either of them.

Damon did not voice the uncomfortable stirring of jealousy that touched his heart at Pierre's disclosure, at his admission that he could love Temple as any man would if he had not valued Damon as a friend. Now anger and jealousy had threatened their relationship, and Damon saw clearly that he could easily lose both his wife and his best friend. The thought tore at him, giving him a sick feeling.

After another lengthy silence, Pierre seated himself once more and looked at Damon with clear blue eyes.

"Now that you have calmed the storm raging in you, would you care to hear exactly what Temple overheard, what so deeply disturbed her?" Pierre asked quietly.

Damon nodded his dark head mutely and settled back to listen carefully.

Temple had fled to her room, great sobs wracking her slender body. Damon had been livid! The fury in his body, in his words, in his snapping ebony eyes! She had honestly feared for her life and for Pierre's as well. How could Damon dare think that she and Pierre—oh, how *could* he!

And in spite of her fright, she had so boldly declared her love for Damon. *"I love you, Damon Silone,"* she had told him in a choked gasp, *"I love you with a passion that frightens me."* Sweet Christ! Had Damon heard her words, had he believed her?

Rolling over on her back, Temple pressed a hot hand to her quivering lips. She closed her eyes only to see Damon's piercing gaze, angry and accusing. Suddenly she felt cold. Drawing the covers about her, she buried her face in the pillow, smothering the sobs that again claimed her.

After a long time, Temple fell into a deep and troubled sleep.

Damon entered the bedroom quietly, his footfall noiseless on the carpeted floor. He stood silently beside the bed looking down at Temple, his heart aching in his breast. She lay on her back, her honey-gold mane fanned over her pillow. Damon leaned over to gently brush a stray curl from her brow and caught his breath at her sheer beauty. Her flushed cheeks still held the dampness of tears. She breathed slowly and deeply and, as he stood watching, a tiny whimper escaped her lips and she shuddered.

"Oh, God, little one!" Damon choked and sank down on the bed. Taking Temple in his arms, he whispered, "Please, my love, forgive me. Please forgive my stupidity, my jealousy!"

Temple stirred, then turned in his arms and her own arms lifted to encircle Damon's neck. She gave a long, shuddering sigh and her body trembled.

"Damon," she breathed drowsily. "Hold me, hold me close."

He held her close, feeling her warmth, and kissed her tenderly. "My love," he murmured softly.

And Damon continued to hold her, finally closing his eyes in sleep some hours later.

With the information Temple gave them, Pierre and Damon were prepared for the attack on the camp. Urging his friend to go to Temple to straighten out the misunderstanding, Pierre had gone straight from the Villa Silone to the camp to warn their troops and make ready for the expected attack. Damon rose to meet him there before dawn the next morning.

Temple and Erin were waiting nervously in the small sitting room when horses rode onto the villa grounds and loud voices entered the open window. The two women hurried into the front hall. As they reached it, the door burst open and Damon and Pierre strode in, followed by some men carrying a wounded man.

Immediately Emil was summoned and sent to fetch Doctor Vecchi. Temple had breathed a sigh of profound relief when Damon walked in and now she stood beside him, her gaze upon his drawn face.

"Are you all right?" she asked softly, her brown eyes concerned. He turned to her and smiled.

"I am well, little one," he replied, taking her small hand in his. "Thanks to you, we were prepared for them. However," he added sadly, "we lost two good men. I pray that this man will be all right."

Erin returned to inform them that she had arranged for food and drink for those who wished it and that a house servant had readied a bath for Damon in his room and one for Pierre in a guest room. The two men thanked Erin and went up the stairs together.

Erin made her way into the dining hall to oversee the preparations and Temple followed, a prayer of thanksgiving in her heart that Damon had returned safely to her.

It could so easily have been different, Temple thought. Damon had returned to the villa from his meeting earlier than had been expected, thereby foiling the plot to ambush him on his way back. If Forbes and Combs had been waiting for him today, they had waited in vain. How exasperated they must have been when Damon failed to show up, and how reluctant to report their failure to the man with the cruel laugh who had planned Damon's execution! And the camp would have been taken by surprise, and many men probably would have been lost had not Temple been fortunate enough to overhear the conspirators.

Apparently LaDonna's resting place was unfrequented, and the plotters had felt it to be a safe place to meet. Temple suddenly remembered that she had been kneeling beside the grave when she heard the voices and realized that, had she been standing, she might have been discovered. A cold shiver rippled down her spine at the thought: She, too, would have been marked for "disposal" had they been aware that she had heard their plans.

The fact that the rendezvous had been near LaDonna's grave again came to Temple's mind. It seemed to have some significance. Slowly it dawned on her that the private garden of the long-gone LaDonna lay very near the boundary line that separated the grounds of the Villa Silone and the Villa Torre. The hidden enemy had to be someone with knowledge of both estates, someone who had access to both, someone who knew about the deserted garden.

A suspicion was slowly forming in Temple's mind as to who that "someone" could be!

Chapter Fourteen

April 1859

DAMON READ THE URGENT MESSAGE THAT HAD JUST been delivered into his hands. He scanned the letter again before tossing the paper to Pierre.

"The time has come," he said tersely, running long, tanned fingers through his black hair.

Pierre picked up the missive and read it carefully.

Austria has issued the following ultimatum: "Piedmont is to disarm and disband the volunteers within three days' time." The ultimatum delivered 23rd of April. The ultimatum refused. War has been declared.

"I will ride to the camp with you," Pierre said. Damon nodded in agreement and the two men moved toward the door.

Temple was about to knock on the closed door of Damon's study when it suddenly opened before her and she stood facing her husband.

"Oh, Damon, I—" She bit off her words when she saw the expression on his face. "What has happened, Damon?" she cried. "What is wrong?"

Placing his hands on her shoulders, Damon replied solemnly, "War has been declared, Temple. We have only just received the word and we must ride to the camp at once."

Temple paled noticeably and bit her lower lip to still the cry of anguish that threatened to escape. She threw her arms about Damon and he bent to kiss her, assuring her that he would take care. He told her that it would most likely be very late when he returned home, then placed the unwelcome letter in her hand.

"Give this to Rosco. I will speak with him when I return."

Then he was gone. Temple followed him to the door to stand staring after him as he and Pierre disappeared into the darkness.

"Well, Cavour, you have your war," she whispered bitterly, a tear slowly coursing down her cheek. "You have succeeded."

"Was that Damon leaving?" Rosco's deep voice came from behind her and Temple turned. She handed him the dreaded letter with a shaking hand. He looked at her stricken face and bent his graying head to read the message.

"My God!" he exclaimed helplessly. "I had hoped—" His words halted and again he read the letter as if to assure himself that he had read it correctly. He said something in his native tongue, shaking his head gravely.

"Damon—he has gone to the camp?" It was both a question and a statement.

"Yes," Temple answered weakly, brushing the tears from her cheeks. "He and Pierre have gone to tell the volunteers. Damon will return later tonight. He asked that I give you the letter and tell you that he will speak with you when he returns," she related tonelessly.

Rosco said nothing. He turned and strode to the study, closing the door firmly behind him.

Temple slowly mounted the long staircase, her feet leaden, her heart heavy.

On April 26 the Austrians advanced on Piedmont. They moved very slowly and by doing so lost their chance for a major victory, for the Piedmontese were prepared for their attack. And on April 29, General Gyulai, commander of the Austrian army on the Italian front, gave the order to cross the Ticino, a river separating Piedmont from Lombardy. Word came that the Piedmontese had obstructed the enemy's operations by flooding the Lomellina plain as well as the lowlands around Novara.

While the Sardinian army remained on the defensive, Garibaldi launched an attack on the Austrians with his legion, the *Cacciatori delle Alpi*. The first engagement took place near Casale.

Word of the war arrived daily and volunteers still poured in. Damon worked long, tiring hours, losing weight as well as sleep, and Temple began to worry about him. He often remarked that he would prefer to be out there in the fighting and, even more often, expressed his desire to be with Garibaldi. He was concerned over the lack of supplies, firearms and clothing sent for the volunteers.

Now Temple sat quietly, watching her husband pace about the room like a caged animal, not touching the tray of food she had placed on his desk. Pierre sat on the edge of the desk, half-heartedly picking at his own food.

"The French did not declare war until the third of May," Damon was saying, running long fingers through his raven hair, his habit when deeply disturbed. "It will be many days before they can get their army across the Alps to join with the Piedmontese."

"Get some sleep, Damon," Pierre advised him. "You are badly in need of rest. And you know that we can only do so much."

Damon whirled to stare blankly at his friend. "Only do so much!" he barked. "What *are* we doing, Pierre? Are we out there, weapons in hand, supporting those men who are? Are we helping those whose blood spills upon the earth, those who cry 'freedom' with their final breath?"

So went the evening. Sometime later Temple quietly left the room, Damon and Pierre still engrossed in their talk of war. She undressed for bed, crawled between the sheets and tried to go to sleep. This war, she thought bitterly, how she wished it had never come about and, now that it had, she prayed that it would soon end. The spilling of blood—where would it lead? What would be the outcome? These and other questions milled around in Temple's mind and sleep eluded her.

She heard the door open and the soft tread of Damon's footsteps. He did not light the lamp and in the shadows she could see him removing his shirt, then heard the soft thud of his boots as they met the floor. His breeches joined the other discarded clothing.

Walking to the window, Damon stared out into the darkness, his hands on the window frame, his brow pressed against the cool pane. Temple remained silent, not wishing to intrude on his private thoughts, although her heart went out to him in his frustration.

After a time, Damon moved to the bed and sat heavily upon it, a weary sigh escaping him. Coming to her knees, Temple reached out and began kneading the taut muscles of his shoulders and back. Then she put her arms about him, pressed her cheek against his warm shoulder and held him.

"I am blessed to have you, Temple," Damon's quiet voice came to her. His hand lifted to stroke her head. "You are the one thing that is real to me, the one part of my life that I cannot do without!" He turned, taking her in his arms, and settled her on his lap.

"You once told me that you loved me," Damon continued, "do you remember?" Temple nodded her head in reply. "We never again spoke about it. I was so angry that night, believing that you cared for Pierre. I was beyond reason. . . . You see, I have a quick temper and I often do not take the time to govern it—but then, you are well aware of that." He paused but Temple made no reply. After a long moment, Damon went on. "How piercing is the sting of pride!" His voice was shaken with emotion.

"You may not always agree with what I say or do, Temple, but you are always there for me. That is very important to me, little one, more important than you know." He brushed her brow with his lips. "I want very much to believe your words of love, Temple, I *need* to believe them." He sighed and traced her lips with his thumb.

"You do not believe that I feel love for you?" she asked bluntly.

"You never spoke them again, after that night," Damon responded, his dark eyes holding hers.

"But that does not mean that I do not love you, Damon," Temple whispered breathlessly. "How could you *not* believe that I love you? There is not a day, not an hour that goes by that I do not tell you so. Oh, not in words, but here." She pointed to her heart. "I show my love when you hold me in your arms at night, when we make love, every time I kiss you. Every time I look at you!"

Placing a hand on each side of his face, Temple pressed her lips tenderly to his. Then her brown gaze lifted to meet his ebony one.

"I have spoken these words to you only once before, but I do not mind saying them as many times as you need to hear them. *I love you,* Damon. With all my heart, with every breath I take, with my very soul—I love you."

With a ragged groan Damon's lips took Temple's. She wrapped her arms about his neck and returned the kiss with abandon. Her body was soft and yielding against his. He breathed her name over and over and her heart tripped against her breast. They sank into the softness of the bed.

Damon's fingers sought the swell of her breasts, gently kneading their fullness and the nipples that already were hardened in arousal. He pressed his fevered flesh along the length of her, setting her afire with desire, and took one rosy nipple in his mouth, tasting its sweetness. The action brought a gasp from Temple.

"Oh, Damon, yes . . . yes . . ." Her voice was passion-filled and came in a panting huskiness that sent Damon's blood racing through his veins. Her nails bit into his skin as she writhed beneath him.

"Easy, little one, easy," he whispered against her heated flesh. "Slowly."

He kissed her deeply, his tongue plundering the moistness of her mouth, and she moaned. His fingers trailed along the silky softness of her thighs, seeking the warmth of her womanhood, and she moved against him, kissing him hungrily.

"Yes, yes," Damon breathed. He enjoyed her response to his gentle lovemaking and she held him tightly, never wanting to let him go.

Then he urged her legs apart and moved against her, taking her completely. She arched against him and Damon moved with deep, slow thrusts, taking her with him to a higher plane of ecstasy. Temple's breath came in short gasps and her hands roamed along Damon's back, feeling the ripple of muscles beneath his skin.

Their bodies moved in unison, a beautiful rhythm vibrating within them. Emotion engulfed them, tossing the lovers into a storm of passion that consumed them, and they reached their pinnacle of fulfillment together, each whispering the name of the other.

Damon's body shuddered involuntarily and he clasped Temple to his breast.

"God," he murmured contentedly, "so good."

They lay as one for some time; then Damon eased his weight from Temple, still holding her closely, and they reveled in the afterglow of their lovemaking. She could feel the steady beat of his heart against her, his breath slowly fanning her brow. His fingers traced a feather-soft pattern on her hip and she smiled as he kissed her shoulder.

Not once had he taken her only to satisfy his need and then roll from her, she thought. Damon never left her after their mating. He would hold her along the length of him, his hands never still upon her body as he stroked with gentle, soothing fingers. Sometimes they talked quietly into the night.

"Asleep, little one?" came his hushed voice.

Temple turned in his arms, her brown eyes gazing up at him. Her love for him overwhelmed her and tears filled her eyes. Her heart lurched suddenly within her.

"Please, Damon," she cried softly, her chin quivering. "Please do not ever leave me!" She buried her face against his chest, clinging to him desperately.

"Oh, Temple," he crooned, hugging her tightly. "I would never—*could* never leave you. You are too much a part of me. Never, my darling, never would I leave you for whom I waited so long!"

"Love me again, Damon," she whispered against his chest. "Love me fiercely."

And Damon quite willingly complied.

Chapter Fifteen

TEMPLE AND ERIN SAT IN THE MORNING ROOM adjoining the library. Erin was mending a pair of Mario's breeches and Temple was reading.

Erin watched her young friend seated across from her, noting that Temple had not turned the page of her book for a long time.

"That boy," Erin began lightly. "He is forever wearing out the knees of his breeches.

Temple made no comment.

"Emil is a good father," Erin went on. "It is a great responsibility to rear a child alone. His beloved wife dying in childbirth was doubtless a great blow to him, yet he—"

Erin stopped, realizing that Temple was not listening. She studied her closely, noting the circles beneath her eyes, her drawn look and pale cheeks.

Life had been hard on Temple, the older woman thought. Losing her dear father so suddenly, being forced into an unwanted marriage with an unknown man and forced to come to an unknown country. Yet Temple had faced her dilemma with great fortitude and strength.

It had not taken long for Erin to see the love that shone in the eyes of both Temple and Damon. It was as if they were destined for each other and there had been no stopping the love that burned like a white-hot flame. Erin felt certain that there would never be anyone else for either of them.

She smiled at the memory, still fresh in her mind, of a day long ago.

It had been a warm day in June and Erin had gone out to call her charge in for lunch. Moving across the lawn, she had seen the girl perched on a tree branch and a young man standing some feet away. Suddenly the girl had come tumbling down from the tree and Erin had clutched her hands to her heart and stood rooted to the spot.

But the young man had moved swiftly, braced his strong legs and raised his arms to catch the child easily in his embrace. He had held Temple close for a moment, then set her on her feet. The two had stood looking at each other for a long moment, then Temple had raised her small hand to touch the young man's brow and had spoken to him.

Erin remembered that as she had begun to run toward them, the girl had reached down and torn a length of cloth from her petticoat and, standing on tiptoe, had placed it against the young man's brow. Then Erin had realized that he had been injured and she had rushed forward, calling Temple's name. But the young man had assured her that he was all right, had bowed to her, turned to leave and, glancing back over his shoulder, had graced her young ward with a heart-stopping smile.

Temple had stood watching the handsome stranger walk away, taking her young heart with him.

Erin had seen the young man again a few times over the years but had never spoken to him or learned his name. Nathan Harris had been a private person, not given to divulging his business. Only once had he opened to her, saying, "I have made mistakes in my life, Erin. Some I have learned from, others I wish I had had the foresight to avoid. The biggest mistake I have made—" He had broken off with a heavy sigh, tapping his fingers on his desk. "Well, let us pray that it will not bring tragedy, but happiness. For Temple deserves happiness."

So Erin had patiently put the pieces of the puzzle together. She had the entire picture now and, although at the beginning it had seemed a jumbled mess, it was a very pretty one, one that pleased her romantic heart.

First, there was Nathan's promise to Rosco those many years before. Second, the nagging certainty that she had seen Damon before. Third, the scar on Damon's brow from the injury sustained on that day, some eight years ago. The tall, handsome stranger had captured Temple's heart then and now.

Nathan, Erin whispered inwardly, I know the answer to your prayer. I wish you could know that Temple loves Damon and Damon loves her and there can only be happiness in a love so profound. Erin smiled as she thought, perhaps you *do* know, Nathan.

Temple sighed and placed the book upon her lap, rubbing her temples with her fingertips.

"Are you not feeling well, my dear?" Erin asked in concern.

"I am so tired, Erin, and I feel a slight headache coming on."

"Then you should go to your room and lie down," the older woman suggested, putting her sewing aside.

"Yes, I think I shall," the girl told her with a weak smile.

"I will bring you up a cup of tea and a cool cloth, if you would like."

"That would be nice, thank you, Erin."

Temple rose somewhat unsteadily, bracing herself with an outstretched hand. She walked slowly toward the door but she suddenly felt dizzy and her stomach lurched. Before she could call out to Erin for help, Temple toppled to the floor.

Erin had noted the unsteadiness and seen Temple pale noticeably, but as Erin rose to rush to her, Temple fainted.

"Temple!" Erin cried out in alarm. "Oh, God!

Emil!" She fell on her knees beside the girl, clasping Temple's limp hand in her own. "Emil!" she cried again. "Someone please help!"

Emil and a servant girl nearly collided in the doorway, both responding to Erin's frantic call. The servant girl looked down to see the young *Signora* lying on the floor, her pretty face pale as death, and she turned and ran down the hall in search of *Signore* Rosco.

Emil lifted Temple in his arms and carried her upstairs to her room with Erin close behind him.

Damon did not wait for Shadow to stop. He hit the ground at a run, flung open the door to the villa and mounted the stairs two at a time. His breath was painfully labored and his heart hammered against his ribs. All he knew was that Mario had come riding into camp like a whirlwind, his words tripping over each other.

"The *Signora!*" Mario had gasped, swallowing hard. "You are to come quickly, *Signore*. Something has happened to the *Signora!*"

The boy could tell him no more and Damon had wasted no time. He had mounted Shadow in a frenzy, his thoughts on his beloved Temple, and ridden as if the devil were at his heels. Dear God, he had prayed fervently, please let her be all right. She is my heart, my life.

Rosco met him in the corridor outside the bedroom. When Damon put his hand on the doorknob, his father stilled it with his own.

"Temple fainted," Rosco said. "Doctor Vecchi is with her. He asked that you wait here."

"Like hell!" Damon stormed, shaking free of Rosco's hold.

"Damon—"

"Temple is my wife, Rosco!" he snapped, his dark eyes filled with emotion. "I must see her. I have to know that she is all right. For God's sake, Rosco, let me pass!"

At that moment the door opened and the doctor stepped into the hall.

"My wife?" Damon implored.

"She is resting," the doctor answered calmly and, with a nod of his gray head, started to walk toward the stairway. But Damon blocked his path, his very silence demanding more information. "Your wife fainted. They sent for me and I have checked her. She is well."

"I want to see her," Damon stated. "I *need* to see her."

"And she *needs* her rest," Doctor Vecchi retorted. Then he smiled. "Go to her, boy, she has been asking for you and she can tell you what you need to know."

Damon turned to the door but looked back at the doctor for reassurance about his beloved Temple.

"She will be all right?" he asked anxiously.

"She will be fine. She needs rest and must take better care of herself from now on. You, Damon, had better see to it that she does!" Winking at Damon, the old doctor added, "A very spirited wife you have there." And with a chuckle he once again headed for the stairs.

Damon entered the room, his eyes seeking Temple. She lay upon the bed and she looked so young and small. She was pale, much too pale for his liking. Had he been so blind that he had not noticed that Temple might be ill?

Erin was sitting in a chair pulled close to the bed. Now she rose and crossed to Damon.

"She is sleeping, but she will want to know that you are here," she told him quietly.

Damon walked to the bed as Erin left the room. He stood looking down at his wife, noticing for the first time the smudgy shadows under her eyes. Why had he not noticed them before? Gold-tipped lashes fanned her high cheekbones and her lush mouth was relaxed in sleep.

He sat on the edge of the bed and smoothed her silken hair away from her brow, then leaned over to kiss her softly. How he loved her, he thought in wonder. Why had he not been able to tell her so? The words had so often formed on his lips, yet he had never spoken them. What was it about a man that he could not, *would* not, allow his emotions to be known—some kind of false pride, a fear of vulnerability?

When a man loved a woman almost to distraction, why, in God's name, could he not simply tell her so? Why had he, Damon, had to come face to face with the fear of losing Temple before he could say "I love you?"

He shook his raven head in bewilderment and exasperation, unable to answer the questions in his troubled mind. "I love you." Three of the simplest words in the vocabulary, yet the most difficult for him to speak.

Temple opened her eyes to see Damon gazing down at her. She smiled at him drowsily and reached out a hand to touch him.

"Hello, little one," Damon said tenderly. "You gave me quite a fright. You have no idea what dire things went through my mind as I rode home. Mario came riding hell-bent into the camp, shouting that something had happened to you. God, Temple, I damned near went out of my mind before I got here!" He shuddered and his hand clasped hers tightly.

"I only fainted, Damon," she told him with a slight smile.

"Only fainted! Sweet Christ, Temple, I did not even know that much until I arrived here. There are people out there plotting to kill me—they have set fire to my property, attacked the training camp. How was I to know that they had not gone so far as to harm that which means most to me!" His voice was shaken by emotion and his eyes shone with the depth of his feelings. "You once told me that should anything happen to me you could not bear it. Do you think that I could bear losing you any easier? You are my life, Temple! My heart!"

"Damon, please," Temple pleaded, seeing his distress, the pain in his eyes. "I am fine. There has been no harm done to me."

"Oh, Temple," he choked, "that is not the point!"

"Then what *is* the point?" she asked him simply.

"The point is that I *could* have lost you, something bad *could* have happened to you, little one. And I—I would never have told you—never said—" He ran his fingers through his thick hair and groaned raggedly. "Temple, you frightened the hell out of me! I would not want to go on living without you."

Taking a long, deep breath as though he were about to plunge into icy waters, Damon declared, "I love you, Temple! My God, how I love you!"

Finally the words were out and they rang across the room. Damon's black-violet gaze locked with his wife's wide, surprised brown one. Temple could scarcely believe she had heard aright and she wanted to ask him to repeat what he had said. But realizing how difficult it had been for him to say it, she merely stared agape, not knowing what to say.

The silence stretched out and Temple felt that she had to break it, so she said the first thing that came to her mind.

"I am sorry that I frightened you, Damon."

That was not what he had expected her to say. He had thought she would be happy, even overjoyed, that she would throw her arms about him in rapturous triumph that at long last he shared the feeling she had expressed to him so beautifully.

So was this it? An unshaken statement of apology—"I am sorry that I frightened you, Damon." Hellfire! Here he had just spilled out his most intimate and innermost feelings, laid his heart bare. Wait, he told himself, perhaps you only imagined that you said those three words because you felt them so strongly. If you had spoken them aloud, surely Temple would have heard them, surely she would have responded in some manner.

He was definitely confused.

"Damon?" Temple's soft whisper broke into the jumble of his thoughts. "Oh, Damon!" she cried. And then she was in his arms. "I—I have *so* longed to hear you say you love me! I have prayed for it! And when you finally said it—oh, Damon, do you mean it? Do you really love me?" The words came in a rush.

Holding her slightly away from him, Damon took her face in his hands and kissed the tip of her small nose.

"I have never loved another woman," he murmured. "I have never before told a woman that I loved her. And I would never have spoken the words if they were not true, if I did not mean them with all my heart." He smiled happily, running his thumb over her parted lips.

"I am glad," she said simply.

"Glad that I love you?"

"No," she replied, then, "I mean, yes. I am more than just glad that you love me! But what I meant was that I am glad that you have never loved another," she explained in a hushed voice.

"I have never thought of loving anyone but you, Temple. You held my heart the first time I looked into those bewitching brown eyes. From that time on, I was lost. No other woman ever had a chance." He looked at his misty-eyed wife, love shining in his eyes, and then he kissed her deeply.

A knock on the door interrupted them and Damon bade the visitor to enter. Erin came in, carrying a tea tray. She looked from one to the other and smiled, pleased with what she saw.

"The doctor said that you should have some tea and toast, Temple. The tea will relax you and the toast will help to combat the nausea."

Damon looked at Temple with new concern. "You said that you had merely fainted, little one." His voice was slightly accusing.

Temple looked at Erin with a sly smile and it was returned, equally mischievously. "That is right, Damon," she returned innocently.

"Then what is this talk about nausea?" he wanted to know.

"Oh, that?" Temple laughed lightly. "Well, I am told that nausea is to be expected when one is with child."

Damon was struck speechless. His mouth dropped open, his eyes widened unbelievingly and he stared first at Temple, then at Erin. Both women burst out laughing.

"W-with child?" he stammered.

Temple nodded, still laughing at his expression, and Damon looked again at Erin, breathing, "A child?"

"So Doctor Vecchi says," Erin replied.

The words snapped Damon back to the reality, and he let out an ear-piercing yell and sprang from the bed.

"My God!" he shouted, a wide grin on his face. "A child! Sweet Mother of God! I am to be a *father!*"

Then once again he had Temple in his arms, raining kisses over her face.

"Oh, little one, there has never been a man whose happiness exceeds mine!" he told her with sheer delight and great pride.

Chapter Sixteen

"Do you have any suspicion as to who the informant might be?" Bates questioned the two men seated before him.

Damon and Pierre answered simultaneously that they did not.

"Well, it is definitely someone who knows the movements of the camp, this much is certain," Bates went on. "Someone is reporting details right down to how many men ride in each day, how many ride out and the number who remain. Dear God!" he shouted, bringing his hand down hard upon the tabletop. "Our men are being attacked before they have traveled more than ten miles from the camp!"

It was tragically true. A group of eight volunteers had been attacked shortly after their departure from the training camp en route to their assigned regiment. Three had been killed and one badly injured. Someone was relaying information of the departures to the enemy, who lay in wait, cutting them down without warning.

Important messages were being intercepted

and false information was reaching both Damon and Bates. The spy was someone who not only knew the area well but could come and go without question, completely unsuspected.

Damon and Pierre trusted no one, spoke to no one else about their movements and their meetings. They had agreed that they would have to be more careful and keep their eyes and ears open for anything the least bit suspicious.

Damon had resigned himself to the fact that, by the process of elimination, the spy was someone at the Villa Silone or the Villa Torre, or one of the four men who were assigned to the camp to assist in the training. He had discussed his theory with Pierre and the two were convinced of its truth.

Bates heaved a sigh of weariness and shook his gray head. "We must find out who is behind this and put a stop to it. I leave it to the two of you. I will be in touch."

And with that Bates left the tent, mounted his horse and rode away, unaware that "someone" would be waiting in the shadows, waiting to cut down another man, removing one more link in the chain leading to Damon Silone.

Temple rode toward the camp. She had packed food for Damon and Pierre and was determined to make them stop their work long enough to eat a decent meal. They could not go on, she thought, if they did not get more rest and take time to eat.

Hearing the faint sound of hooves in the distance, Temple strained her eyes to see who was riding toward her. It was a lone rider and, thinking it might be Damon, she urged Spirit forward. As she topped a knoll she saw the approaching rider on the road below and noted his leisurely gait. There was a glint of sunshine on metal and Temple looked sharply to the side of the road between the lone rider and where she sat.

A gray horse stood hidden behind the trees and astride it was a man who sat motionless, a rifle shouldered and ready. Temple could see that the marksman was drawing a steady bead on the unsuspecting rider and she reined in Spirit, pulling her own rifle from her saddle holster.

Bracing her weapon, Temple sighted, her finger steady as she eased back the trigger. The silence was shattered by a shot and a piercing scream that echoed across the hillside, and the armed man toppled from the gray horse and sprawled upon the ground. Temple's aim had been sure.

Bates had spotted the horse atop the knoll before him, just as the rider aimed his rifle. He had time only to curse himself for a fool not to have been prepared for just such an ambush. Bracing himself for the fiery pain of the bullet that would almost surely take his life, he waited an eternity. Only when the shot rang out and an unexpected scream rent the air did he realize that the marksman before him had aimed at someone else.

Bates rode forward and leaped from his horse

to kneel beside the prone body. He rolled the man over and saw the blood spilling from his side. The wounded man looked up at Bates with pain-glazed eyes but as he opened his mouth to speak, his eyes rolled upward and he gasped his final breath.

The pounding of hooves attracted Bates's attention to the trail behind him and he saw Damon and Pierre riding hard toward him, followed by what looked to be half the camp.

"We heard the shot," Damon called out, reining in Shadow and jumping to the ground. "We thought it was you."

"It was meant to be me," Bates said flatly. "But someone cut him down before he could fire at me."

"Who?" Damon asked in surprise.

"Up there on the knoll," Bates replied, looking in that direction.

All eyes turned toward the hilltop.

"Mother of God!" Damon exclaimed when he saw that it was Temple.

"Damned good shot, little lady. Damned good!"

Bates praised Temple loudly, as he had done for the better part of the past hour.

She sat on the library sofa beside Damon, her husband's arm lovingly draped over her shoulders.

"Thank you, sir," Temple murmured once again in a small voice, and even that was an effort. She had not considered that she might kill the man when she had pulled out her weapon. She had not known which of the two might be her enemy and which her ally, but she had reasoned that no honest man would hide among the trees, his gun aimed at an unsuspecting one. That was taking unfair advantage, and her only thought had been to save the other man's life.

"Temple?" Damon's voice penetrated her thoughts and she looked up at him questioningly. "Bates asked you a question."

"Oh—ah—sorry, sir," she stammered in apology for her inattentiveness.

"Never known her to be without words," Rosco announced from his position by the window. His aloofness and hostility made her stiffen in resentment. Their ongoing battle regarding Damon "reining" her and "bridling her tongue" was a constant irritant to her. She had refrained from going to Damon with the problem, feeling that he had quite enough to worry about. Furthermore, nothing had transpired yet that she had not been able to handle!

"Well, it looks as if my son may have heeded my advice to bridle her tongue. As I said, I have never known her to be without words," Rosco goaded.

Temple sprang to her feet, the light of battle in

her brown eyes. "I have never before killed a man, either, Rosco Silone! Although there is one whom I would dearly love to dispose of!"

Rosco didn't need to be told who she had in mind; he had seen the look of loathing in her eyes often enough to know.

Damon had been ready to leap to Temple's defense against his father's remarks but had not had a chance. Temple had effectively squelched Rosco's barbs. Now glancing at his father, Damon saw that he was ready for a comeback and a battle royal would probably erupt. In an effort to avert it, Damon put out a hand to his wife.

"Now, Temple," he began quietly, only to have her turn on him.

"Do not 'now, Temple' me, Damon Silone!" she bit out. "I am not a child! I am a woman who can think for herself. A woman who can and *will* speak her mind!"

Both Damon and Rosco were taken aback by this sudden display of temper. Damon marked it down to her shaken physical and emotional state. Rosco knew better.

Regaining her composure, Temple turned to Bates and forced a smile. "You must overlook my bad temper, sir. I will not, however, apologize for anything I said, for I meant every word. I am very glad you were not harmed today, sir, and that I was able to prevent it. Now, if you gentlemen— and you, Rosco—will excuse me?"

With her chin tilted, her spine straight and her honey-gold head held high, Temple swept regally from the room, despite the fact that, once again, she was clad in Mario's dusty, worn clothing.

For a long moment the library held a pregnant silence, then Bates threw back his gray head with a shout of laughter, slapping his knee with his hand.

"How smoothly she changed the subject and never slowed down," he laughed. "Heaven forbid that I am ever on the receiving end of that little lady's temper. God Almighty, Damon, but your wife has—"

"Spirit!" Damon beat Bates to the word, a wide smile lighting his handsome face.

The only one not amused was Rosco Silone.

After Bates left, Rosco poured himself a brandy and paced the length of the study.

Damon entered to see his father in a state of agitation.

"Damon, I must speak with you about Temple," Rosco began angrily. "Your wife—"

"That is correct, Rosco, Temple is *my* wife. And I do not choose to discuss her with you." His tone held finality.

"But Damon, you must control her!" his father stormed. "You laugh when your friends call her 'spirited.' My God! The woman needs to learn her place!"

"Temple knows her place," his son countered, black eyes smoldering.

"Apparently not!" Rosco snapped, his face an angry red, his fists clenched. "She goes about dressed in mens' clothing, rides astride her horse, and even bareback at times. She has a tongue as sharp and cutting as a sword. She even swears, Damon, *swears!* And you stand there and tell me she knows her place!" He spat out an oath himself and concluded, "The woman could do with a good lashing. A lashing which I would gladly—"

"You?" Damon shot back. Then he made a slight, mocking bow toward his father. "God's pardon! I had forgotten that the almighty Rosco Silone rules with a rod of iron, that those who do not succumb to his will shall feel his wrath, shall be crunched beneath the heel of his boot! Thy word is law, and all that rot!"

Damon's infamous temper had reared its ugly head and long pent-up emotions, things he had kept inside him for far too long, began boiling to the surface of his mind and spilling from his tongue.

"You held the reins so tightly about my mother's throat that they eventually choked the life from her! In breaking *her* spirit, you led her a life of fear and total unhappiness. Her dying words to *me*, Rosco, to *me*, not to her husband of eighteen years, were these: 'I shall be free, now, Damon. I have spent a lifetime loving your father, loving a man who is incapable of giving or receiving love. Promise me, my son, that he will not break you, will not rule you. Promise me that you will not be like him, that you will love.'"

Damon's voice broke with compassion for the mother whom he *had* loved and still missed. Rosco stared at him, making no move to interrupt the narrative, and Damon swallowed the uncomfortable lump in his throat before he continued.

"She held my hand in a steely grip, weak as she was, and I made her the promises for which she asked. Perhaps this will explain why you have never been able to bully me like you have everyone else. Each time you sought to bend my will to yours, I could see my beloved mother's pleading eyes, could hear her voice saying, 'Promise me that he will not break you, will not rule you.' And you know damned well, Rosco, that I never break a promise."

Damon paused for breath and when Rosco would have spoken, raised a commanding hand.

"I am not finished. My mother loved you, even in death she loved you, Rosco, but my God! she feared you more! Just as LaDonna did! LaDonna loved a father who had her believing that he was God. And feared him, believing him to be the Devil."

"And you, Damon?" Rosco broke in. "What about you?"

Damon looked long at his father, noticing as if

for the first time Rosco's graying hair, the hint of wrinkles about his eyes and never-smiling mouth. He sighed wearily.

"You are my father, Rosco. I am your seed. But you are neither God nor Satan. You are like me—human. You are but a man!"

Damon turned on his heel and left the room, leaving Rosco alone with his thoughts.

Chapter Seventeen

DAMON LAY ON THE TATTERED CANVAS COT IN THE main tent of the training camp. He had been on the road most of the night with Bates and the men who had been assigned to Turin. Only the men who were going had been told their departure time and none were told in what direction they would go. Damon was taking no chances on losing more men.

They had taken six of the volunteers from the camp to a post where a detachment of twenty men waited for them to go on to Turin. Bates and Damon had attended a meeting at the post and had returned safely, escorted by four men assigned to ride with them as guards.

Pierre entered the tent and seated himself behind the crude desk, noting his sleeping friend. Damon needed the sleep, he thought, the man certainly did not get enough rest. But neither did he, for that matter.

He picked up the leather ledger and, taking a key from his pocket, unlocked the clasp that secured it. He thumbed through it and read Damon's last entries:

May 1, 1859
Victor Emmanuel placed himself at the head of his army.

May 12, 1859
Napoleon followed the King's example, riding at the head of his troops.

May 13, 1859
Units moving daily. Franco-Piedmontese to be taken by train to Bella on or about the 16th. Garibaldi has been told to follow his own judgment. He is always ready for a surprise move. Garibaldi is a man who likes to outwit the enemy.

May 20, 1859
Austrians beaten at Montebello; Piedmontese especially responsible for victories.

Dipping the pen in the inkwell, Pierre dated his entry May 27, 1859, and wrote down the events of the previous night, then closed the book and locked it. He leaned back, placed his booted feet atop the desk and took a cheroot from his jacket pocket, lighting it and inhaling deeply.

"I thought you had given those up," Damon said without opening his eyes.

"And I thought you were asleep," Pierre answered with a grin, looking at his friend through the swirling white cloud of smoke.

Damon rolled to his side and raised himself up to rest on his elbow. "Nasty habit," he commented.

"Sleeping?" Pierre queried innocently.

"No. Smoking," Damon corrected, a lazy smile tugging at his lips.

"How is Temple?"

"Very well. She still broods about killing that man, Combs, but she says it is one more of our enemies out of the way. She was not as upset when she learned his identity and realized that he was one of the assassins who was assigned to do away with me."

There was a companionable silence. Shortly Pierre broke it.

"Damon," he began worriedly, "I am quite concerned about you. We know that our enemies have you marked for death and it bothers me that I cannot do a damned thing about it. I wish we knew who to watch out for."

The silence that settled over the tent this time was troubled, each man thinking of the dangers lying in wait. Then Damon stood up to pace back and forth.

"I am not worried for myself so much as I am for Temple," he confided to Pierre. "They just might use her to get to me. They could harm her, perhaps kill her!" He walked to the tent opening and looked out. "Sneed reports that on two occasions in the last two days someone has attempted to follow her."

Della rode back toward the Villa Torre, her face flushed an angry red. How was she to make her move on Temple if someone was following the woman? This was the second day Della had waited for Temple to ride out, and for the second day a rider had ridden out not far behind her.

Perhaps Damon did not trust his little wife, Della mused. And maybe she could place even more doubt in his mind. She knew Damon's temper well and felt that she could feed upon that. If she could trap Temple in a compromising situation and let Damon come upon her— Yes, and Della knew just who to set her up with.

Her scheming mind was working at full speed now, and Della smiled smugly. First she had to meet with Forbes and report what she had learned at the camp. She had Forbes right where she wanted him and as long as she bedded him when necessary and kept him happy, she could use him. Della would need Forbes's help in laying the trap for Temple and then she would be there to watch the jaws of the trap close upon her prey! Della laughed cruelly. If she had to get rid of Temple Silone to obtain Damon for herself, then so be it. Besides, the girl was a bother. She had foiled the attack on Bates. No, Della thought, Temple would not be long for this life, not long at all!

* * *

Most urgent that I see you. Believe I know who is behind the attacks, who is after Damon. Come at once. Meet me at the stone wall at the south border.

The message bore no signature.

The note arrived around noon and after scanning it, Temple dressed quietly in her boys' clothing and, not taking the time to saddle Spirit, rode off bareback toward the stone wall.

When she reached it, no one was there. She dismounted, holding the note clasped in her hand. She waited for some time and had nearly decided she had come here for nothing when a rider emerged from the covering of the trees. It was Pierre Torre, and he wore a puzzled look on his face.

"Temple?" he said questioningly, swinging down from his horse. "Are you the one who sent for me?"

"No," she replied, equally puzzled. "When I saw you I thought that you had sent me the message." She held the note out to him.

Pierre took the folded paper and read it. When he finished, he reached into his pocket to retrieve a paper and, in turn, handed it to Temple.

"Why, it says the exact same thing!" She stared wide-eyed at him. "But who? Why would they send for both of us?"

"Perhaps it was someone who knows that we are the closest to him and who feels that, together, we could help," Pierre suggested, not really able to answer her question.

"Then shall we wait? Or what do we do?" Temple impatiently twisted her hands. Then the thought struck her that the person who had sent the message might have been attacked on his way to their meeting. She turned to Pierre in concern. "Oh, Pierre! Suppose the person who sent the messages was unable to get here, was harmed or even killed to stop him from telling us what he knows?"

Pierre had already thought of the same thing. Besides, he had the uncanny feeling that there was something wrong about the whole situation.

"Well, we have waited long enough. If someone were coming, he would have been here by now. The note said 'come at once' and the person who sent it would certainly have had more time to get here than we, because we had to wait for the messages. I think we should go."

Temple nodded in agreement and rose from the low wall.

Pierre helped her to mount and hoisted himself on his own horse. Even knowing that Damon had a man following Temple at all times, he decided to ride back with her. He remembered Damon's concern that his enemies might try to get to him through Temple and thought that if there should be any trouble, her guard might need his help.

So they rode back together and when Pierre had seen Temple safely close to the house, he returned to the camp. He had decided it was best not to tell Damon of the double messages and had told Temple not to mention them, that there was no need to concern him with anything more than the problems he already had. He assured her that he would tell Damon when the time was right.

Three days later the second message arrived. Again, there was no signature.

Meet me at eleven A.M. Damon is in grave danger. If I am not at the stone wall by noon, leave and wait for a further message. If you don't receive one within two days—I was found out.

As before, Temple and Pierre came upon each other at the stone wall and discovered that their messages were identical.

"Damon is in grave danger." The words went round and round in Temple's mind. She paced before the low wall, thinking that this unknown person knew *something*, yet was unable to tell them. And as the minutes passed, tears began to well in her eyes and her fear for Damon rose in a tide that threatened to engulf her.

Pierre had sat on the wall pondering it all. He had been puzzled from the beginning and was even more concerned when, again, the unknown writer of the messages failed to arrive. He pulled the gold watch from his pocket and read the time. Eleven twenty. Their instructions had been to leave if they had not been contacted by noon.

As the minutes passed slowly, Pierre became more and more bewildered by the strange messages. Twice they had been summoned, twice they had come here and, unless someone showed up soon, both attempts to learn of Damon's pending danger would have been in vain.

Again he checked the time and, though it seemed an eternity of waiting, only a few more minutes had elapsed. He turned his blue eyes on Temple as she paced up and down, twisting her hands in despair, and noted the rain of silent tears that wet her face.

Rising to his feet, Pierre moved to Temple and took both her hands in his, stilling their nervous play. She looked up at him trustingly and his heart went out to her. Taking her in his arms, he held her close, comforting her. His words soft and soothing, he promised that he would never allow anything to happen to Damon, that never would he come to harm if Pierre could prevent it.

Temple accepted Pierre's comfort and leaned on his strength. She trusted his love and friendship for Damon without question, and relief flowed through her at his vehement promise to protect her husband. With a deep sigh, Temple leaned her head against Pierre's chest.

"Damon, surely you are not blind!" Della exclaimed, wide-eyed. "Will you calmly stand by and let your wife fall into the arms of another man?"

"What in God's name are you talking about, Della?" Damon inquired, rising to stand before her.

"Oh, Damon, I am here because I care about you. I do not wish to see you hurt." She took his hand and pressed it to her cheek. "Temple creeps out of the house to meet with him in the groves."

Damon's lips tightened. "Who is it that she supposedly meets, Della?" he asked, trying hard to control the fury beginning to burn in him. He snatched his hand from her grip.

"I cannot bear to tell you," Della replied with feigned reluctance. "I really should not say, but I must. It is—Pierre. But, please, Damon, do not blame him, for she has bewitched him just as surely as she has you."

Damon's eyes became stormy, and his jaw tightened. "You are a fool, Della," he snapped, letting loose his pent-up anger. "Pierre is my friend, a friend I trust. And Temple is my wife, my lover, as well as my friend."

"Damon, these secret liaisons between them

must stop!" she shouted. "You refuse to face the truth. They are together now, at this very moment!"

"I do not believe you, Della!" he grated.

"Then go!" Della taunted him. "They are at the stone wall, as they have been before. Go see for yourself. And why not ask the man you have following your precious wife?"

"Get out, Della!" Damon thundered, his fists clenched in anger. "Get out of here with your lies!"

"You are blind, Damon," she told him sadly. "You do not want to see, because your damned pride—"

"*Get out!*"

Damon took a threatening step toward her and Della fled the tent. In that moment she had sensed a danger in Damon that she had never known existed. He would have struck her, she realized in shock!

"No!" Damon exploded in rage. "No, I do not believe it!" He smote his fist upon the wooden desk, not even feeling the pain in his hand, so great was the pain in his heart.

After a few minutes he left the tent and mounted Shadow, riding toward the stone wall.

Della had not gone far. She had reined in her horse in a wooded glen to wait and see what Damon would do with her information. After a few minutes she was rewarded by seeing Damon dash from the tent and mount his horse, then ride fast toward the stone wall.

A sly smile curved her lips and a glimmer shone in her green eyes. She had planted the seed of doubt. Everything was going beautifully, just as she had planned.

Chapter Eighteen

DAYS PASSED IN AN UNCOMFORTABLE PROCESSION.
Damon rarely spoke and when he did he fairly bit
the servants' heads off. He was abrupt with Erin,
curt to his father and said little to Temple. There
were times that she felt she would rather have him
snap at her than be so aloof.

She did not know what was bothering her
husband, but he was putting a wall between them
that she could not scale. Sometimes Damon barely acknowledged her presence, and often she
looked up to see him watching her coldly. No
longer did his eyes shine with happiness or flame
with desire.

"Oh, Damon," Temple whispered to herself,
"what has happened? What is tearing us apart?
This unnatural silence that hangs between us is
not right. I can feel you slipping away and I do not
know why and I do not know what to do to stop
it." There was a sharp pain in her heart that made
her want to weep.

Damon had spent the past four nights at the

camp, coming home only twice in all that time. But had he been home to sleep in their bed, Temple felt with certainty that he would not have made love to her.

Once when she rode into camp as an excuse to see him, Damon had not had any time for her and she had returned to the villa, her heart breaking. Something was wrong, very wrong!

Damon was at home this night and was drinking more than usual, tossing down brandy after brandy. There was an undercurrent of anger rippling through his body, visible in the tautness of his muscles and the coldness of his eyes. He walked and spoke with rigid control.

A coldness settled over Temple, fear fluttering in her breast. Even Rosco sensed the controlled wrath of his son and for once did not venture to probe.

Temple rose from her seat on the sofa.

"Where are you going, Temple?" Damon snapped, his eyes burning into her.

"I—I am tired, Damon," she said in a small voice. "I am going to retire."

They stood looking at each other. Damon said nothing more and after a moment Temple turned and left the room.

She undressed, slipped into a white satin wrap and stood before the dressing-table mirror, brushing her long hair. Damon entered the room abruptly. Closing the door behind him, he stood leaning against it. In his hand he held a half-filled brandy snifter.

Temple turned toward him and he caught his breath sharply. The soft swell of her high breasts was revealed between the gaping lapels of her wrap. Damon's blood raced in his veins and there was a quickening in his loins. He had been without her for too long. But he had stayed away, far away, for fear that he might harm her, would do something that he would later regret. He knew his own temper.

The memory of Della's visit and its aftermath flashed through his mind. He remembered her words, over and over again: "Go see for yourself." His wife and Pierre lovers! No, he had not believed it, yet something had made Damon ride out to the wall that day to satisfy any doubts.

But as he had reached the rise he had seen them. They stood beyond the wall in a lovers' embrace. He had been livid! Feeling acute hatred rise in his throat and in his heart, he had turned his horse and galloped away, for had he not done so, he would surely have killed them both.

Later he had asked Sneed, whom he had assigned to follow and protect Temple, if his wife and *Signore* Torre had met before. A man of few words, Sneed had only said, "Yes, sir." He had answered the question, and *Signore* Silone had requested no details, asked no other questions.

So, Damon thought, it was true. All that Della

had told him was true. Pierre, his best friend, had sought Damon's wife after all. And Temple, whom he loved and trusted, had welcomed Pierre's advances.

Over the days his hatred and the tremendous anger had festered. He could restrain himself no longer.

"Have you lain with him?" Damon's deadly soft voice cut through the room, his dark eyes boring into Temple.

Temple was taken aback. What in God's name was he talking about?

"Damon, if you would but tell me what it is that has so upset you," Temple began in a frightened whisper, taking a tentative step toward him. "Something is very wrong. If I only knew what it is, what I have done, I could—"

"Have you lain with him?" The words seemed to echo through the room and Temple shivered at the venom in them.

"Damon, I—I do not know what you are talking about." Her voice trembled, and she clutched the satin lapel about her throat.

"Pierre Torre! Your lover!"

"My—" Temple choked on the word. "Pierre is your friend, Damon, he is my friend!"

He spat an ugly oath, his ebony eyes blazing, a muscle working nervously in his jaw.

"I saw you, Temple! I know of your liaison! I know of your rendezvous! I was a fool once, but not again—God, not again!" he stormed, his face a mask of fury. "How long, Temple? How long have you been lovers? Is the child growing in your belly my seed?"

"Damon!" Temple cried out, horrified. Her hand pressed against her lips but did not still the painful cry.

"Tell me, damn you!" Damon thundered. He threw the snifter across the room. The crystal shattered into tiny pieces and the amber liquid trailed down the wall.

"I will tell you nothing!" Temple told him defiantly, her spirit returning. "Nothing! No matter what I say you would not believe me. You have already made your decision, you have judged and found me guilty. Therefore it is a little late for my defense!"

He moved slowly and deliberately toward her, stalking her as a hunter does his prey. Temple was suddenly terrified.

She retreated to the far side of the room in abject fear. Her face was deadly white and her entire body shook. Terror tore through her. He was going to kill her! The man she loved was going to kill her!

Tears streamed down her cheeks and she placed her arms about her stomach in a protective gesture.

"Oh, God! Damon, please!" she cried, terrified. "Please do not kill me!"

Her words struck like a bolt of lightning. He saw the naked terror in her brown eyes, the uncontrollable shudders that wracked her body as she sank to her knees on the floor, sobbing hysterically.

Dear God! What had he done? His heart felt as if someone had torn it from his breast. Temple, his long-loved Temple, was crying, and he had caused her tears.

Damon went on his knees before her and reached out to her. She backed away from him, her brown eyes wide and wild.

"Temple?" Again he reached for her.

"No!" she screamed, beating at his hand with her fists. "No!"

Damon captured her flailing fists and pulled her against him, calling her name over and over. Still she fought against him, not hearing his words.

Suddenly the door was flung open and Erin and Rosco stood in the doorway.

"Leave us!" Damon thundered.

Erin looked at the struggling Temple, hearing her cries, and started to go to her.

"No!" Damon shouted. "I said *leave* us!" There was steel in his voice.

Rosco took Erin's arm and pulled her from the room, closing the door.

Temple's strength was no match for Damon's and in her distraught condition she could not hold up. Damon had both arms about her, holding her in his steely embrace. After a time her strength was spent and her body sagged against him and her cries turned into tiny, broken sobs.

Damon lifted her and carried her to the bed. He sat down, cradling Temple in his lap. He held her thus until the small sobs had subsided and she was silent; then he laid her on the bed, pulled the covers around her and left the room.

His leaden steps carried him down the corridor toward a room he had not entered in many months. Something in his heart called to him and, his steps halting at the door, he opened it and entered. He moved assuredly in the darkness, familiar with the contents of the room.

Damon sat down upon a low chair, sinking into its softness, resting his head against the back. After a moment he reached out and lit the lamp beside him. Its golden glow filled the room, touching the canvas on the wall and LaDonna looked at her brother from the painting.

"LaDonna, if you were but here," Damon whispered, "I could talk to you, you could help me with my dilemma." He ran tanned fingers over the back of his neck, massaging the tightness. "I want to believe, God, how I want to believe! Pierre has been my friend for so many years, since we were but children. Never have I distrusted him, not once have I ever questioned our friendship. But now, in just a few weeks' time, I have come to think him to be false."

Damon stood and paced the room restlessly, his thoughts in a turmoil.

"And Temple—sweet Christ, she is my very life! I love her desperately, yet I am unable to trust her. But I should have to do no more than look into the depths of her warm eyes to see her love, her devotion to me. Yet—"

His words stilled and again he sought the dark eyes of his sister.

"I saw with my own eyes, LaDonna—I saw them at the wall—Temple was in Pierre's embrace."

Suddenly Pierre's words came back to him, the words that had been spoken before when Damon had been assailed by suspicion about his wife and his friend. ". . . you saw something you did not understand, something you refused to understand, and jumped to conclusions . . ."

Dear God! Had he done it again? Had he refused to understand, once again? He could still see the terror in Temple's eyes, the trembling of her body. And—oh, God! Her impassioned plea that he not kill her! She had honestly thought that he was going to kill her!

Damon groaned, a tearing, ragged sound in his throat. His beloved Temple had been terrified of him—afraid for her life—had believed that *he* could take her life from her! A single tear coursed down his cheek and he suddenly felt cold and empty.

"LaDonna, what have I done?" he cried forlornly into the silence.

Finally Damon extinguished the light and made his way to LaDonna's bed and lay heavily across it. And there he spent an interminable, sleepless night, his heart breaking, his thoughts on Temple.

Would she understand? Would she forgive him yet again for his blindness, his stupidity? Would she—*could* she—still love him?

Chapter Nineteen

AS THE FAINTLY TINGED LIGHT OF DAWN STOLE OVER the villa, Damon still lay wide awake upon La-Donna's bed, his head resting on a pink satin pillow. In the soft silence of the night his mind had gone over and over the scene in their bedroom, seeing again Temple's tears, hearing her poignant plea for her life.

Each time he had attempted to close his eyes, the image of Temple had been imprinted on his closed eyelids. He read the awful terror on her face, saw the tears streaming down her cheeks and her eyes—God, the *horror* there was in her eyes!

All through the long hours the voices of the night had seemed to be the whimpers of Temple's heartrending cries, even though he lay in another wing, far removed from where Temple lay in their room.

Restless, Damon rolled over and his outflung hand touched an ivory lace handkerchief. He idly lifted the small square of lace to his nostrils and breathed deeply of its scent. Even now, after all these years, it still held the faint fragrance of roses. It had been LaDonna's favorite scent, he remembered with a pang.

His dark eyes moved over the bed, coming to rest upon the doll with her delicately painted face, the mouth pearly-pink, reminding him of Temple. Damon laid the kerchief aside and picked up the doll.

"Annabella! *An-na-bel-la!*" The distraught cry resounded in his memory. . . . Damon ran into the playroom to see his little sister on her knees, clutching a small bundle of blue silk tightly to her breast. She turned tear-bright eyes to him.

"Oh, Damie," LaDonna's choked voice cried. "Something has happened to Annabella! Oh, Damie, can you fix her?"

Damon reached out to pick up the broken fragments of porcelain that lay scattered upon the floor. He knew that there would be no putting the pieces back together.

"I am sorry, honey, but I do not think Annabella can be fixed," he told her, miserable at the anguish that filled his little sister's eyes.

LaDonna threw herself into Damon's arms and he held her close as great sobs shook her small body.

Then Damon saw Della standing on the other side of the playroom, a sadistic smile on her thin lips. She looked more pleased than concerned. From that moment Damon was convinced that

Della had destroyed the doll, though he knew he could not prove it.

A few weeks later Damon found his sister in her room reading. He handed her a large box wrapped in pink paper.

"Oh, Damie! For me?" she asked delightedly, coming to her knees on the bed, her small hands eagerly outstretched.

When the wrappings were torn aside and the box lid removed, LaDonna stared reverently at what the box held. "Oooooh," she breathed and with gentle fingers lifted the porcelain doll from the box.

"LaDonna," Damon introduced them, "meet AnnaDonna."

Tears of joy welled in her blue-black eyes and spilled over.

"Thank you," LaDonna whispered with heart-felt emotion. "No one will ever hurt AnnaDonna, Damie, *no one.* . . ."

Damon sighed heavily, mentally shaking himself, and brought his thoughts back to the present. He placed AnnaDonna tenderly among the satin pillows, swung his long legs over the side of the bed and sat up. As he did so, he knocked something off the bed onto the floor.

Bending to retrieve the fallen object, he saw that it was LaDonna's diary. In the fall the lock had opened and as he lifted the leather book the pages fluttered open, releasing a pressed rose to drift to the floor.

Damon picked up the rose with a sad smile. It was like his sister to preserve her memories. He slipped the rose back between the pages and, closing the book, placed it back upon the bed and started for the door.

Then his hand stilled on the doorknob and he looked back over his shoulder, his dark eyes resting on the diary. For a long moment he stood motionless, then walked back to sit on the edge of the bed. Without hesitation he reached for LaDonna's diary, opened it at random and began to read.

". . . and she plans to marry Damon. But I know my brother. He will *never* marry Della Fruge, for he sees her for what she is—a rotten, spoiled child. I pray that I am never caught in Della's web of lies!

". . . There is no one I can tell. Damon is gone or I would talk to him. He has always been there when I needed him. Oh, Damie, I wish you were here! Father badgers me each day about marrying Vito Bellini, but how can I even *think* of marrying one man when I love another?"

Damon turned the pages, reading here and there.

". . . so Della told Father that I rode out alone. . . . I do not like Della. . . . and when I walked in, Della was holding my diary. Later I found that the lock had been tampered with. . . . Della Fruge is nothing but trouble. She stalks me, her green eyes watching me, waiting for me to make a mistake.

"I do not trust Della! There is evil in her. . . . and if she cannot have it, then she will see to it that no one else does even if she has to destroy the very thing she wants. Just as she did my darling Annabella years ago."

So, Damon thought, Della *had* broken the porcelain doll. LaDonna had known but had never told.

"I met Nathan in the garden. How I love him! . . . and tonight Nathan asked me to marry him but I cannot. Father would never stand for it. I am afraid Father will harm Nathan if he should learn that we are meeting. . . . so now I am going to have a child—Nathan's child! Such joy and love I feel. . . . Oh, Damie, please hurry home! Tell me what to do, help me!"

The last entry was dated June 6, 1851.

"Della saw Nathan and me in the garden. She smiled spitefully and walked away. I know she told Father for I can see the two of them from my window and Father appears to be very angry. Damie, if you were here you would help me. You would not let Father bring his wrath upon me. I am afraid that I shall never see Nathan again. I love you, Nathan, I love you and I love our child."

That was the last entry in LaDonna's diary. It had been on the evening of that same day that

LaDonna suffered the tragic fall down the stairway. The fall had resulted in her losing the child that nestled in her womb and, in the small hours of the following morning, LaDonna had slipped quietly into eternal sleep.

Damon had not been there, for he had been away in France on business for Rosco. He had never known that LaDonna's thoughts had been on him the last night of her life, wishing that he were with her to comfort her and to protect her from the unreasonable anger of their father.

"Oh, LaDonna, my beloved sister," Damon whispered to her portrait. "I am so sorry that I was not here to help you."

He moved to stand before the painting, the diary in his hand.

"You have helped me, LaDonna, even in death you have helped me by your written hand. Through your long-ago words you have named the person who is behind my distrust of my wife and my best friend.

"'Della is not to be trusted,' that is what you wrote. You knew her, you saw her as I have not. You saw her as a liar, a schemer and a destroyer. And I trust your judgment. Thank you, little sister, for leaving me your words of wisdom and your love!"

Chapter Twenty

DAMON SAT AT HIS DESK IN THE STUDY, LOST IN thought. He had not seen Temple all day. Erin had brought in a supper tray without a word, placing it on the desk and departing as silently as she had come. Damon had nibbled on the veal shank with peas and mushrooms, finally giving up, for his appetite had deserted him. Food had no taste, wine was bitter in his mouth.

The events of last night lay heavy on his mind and even heavier on his heart. He had learned that Doctor Vecchi had been called in earlier that morning to see the *Signora* and had made his way to her door, only to find his way barred by a stony-faced Erin who informed him icily that Temple had no wish to see him.

The entire house was silent, seeming to hold its breath. The servants moved about as quietly as if they were mute. Damon groaned at the thought that they might have learned what had happened last night and hoped that their actions were due to the fact that the young *Signora* was abed and that the doctor had been summoned. He did not want them to know of his display of temper, his cruelty to Temple, whom they adored.

Pierre quietly closed the door to Temple's room, his blood boiling. He had called to see Damon but had been intercepted by Erin with the message that Temple had asked to see him, should he by chance stop by, and that it was imperative that he see her *before* he saw Damon.

Erin had accompanied him up the stairs and to Temple's room. She had remained by Temple's bedside as the girl poured out the story of how, again, Damon had accused her and Pierre of being lovers.

The three of them had discussed this latest catastrophe, going back in their minds to the beginning of Damon's erratic behavior. Pierre reported that for the same number of days that he had been cold and distant with Temple, he had been so with him. At the training camp Damon had seemed to avoid him, had been curt and insulting. Pierre had tried to overlook it, thinking Damon to be preoccupied with the war, the training, Temple's condition.

But now it all fell in place. They all agreed that Damon's behavior had begun on the afternoon Pierre and Temple had made their second attempt to contact the writer of the mysterious notes. Temple still did not know that Damon had provided her with an unseen protector, but Pierre knew, and he thought that Sneed must have reported to Damon about the meetings by the low stone wall.

He rose from his chair, promising Temple that he would set the record straight, once and for all. Pierre stepped out into the hallway, his blood boiling, determined to face Damon Silone. This would be the first time he could remember that *he* would have the first round in an argument with his friend.

The study door burst open without warning and Pierre stormed in. Damon simply stared at his friend, who towered over him in controlled rage. The thought flitted through his mind that the tables had been turned on him. Until now, Damon had always been the aggressor.

Pierre tossed two pieces of paper on the desk. Damon looked at Pierre questioningly.

"Read them!" Pierre ordered.

Damon picked up the first one, then the other, and read them. He laid them down and stated, "They say the same thing."

Pierre did not reply, merely throwing two more papers on the desk. Damon read them and turned his dark gaze on his friend.

"Again, these are the same," he said, not quite comprehending what Pierre was driving at.

"I am glad that you can see *that* much," Pierre said dryly.

"But what is this?" Damon asked, pointing to the papers. "Who sent them?"

"They are 'urgent' messages," Pierre responded acidly. "As to who sent them, I have not a clue. As you have pointed out, there are two copies of each message. Both Temple and I received them. Twice we received these notes, twice we went to meet the writer of said message, twice no one showed."

He paced to the window and stood looking out unseeingly.

"I should have thought that you would learn from your mistakes, Damon," he said bluntly. "But I suppose some people *never* learn. Once before you misjudged an innocent occurrence, judged only by what you saw *at the moment*. You tore into a rage, not giving anyone a chance to explain. It appears that you have done this once again."

Pierre moved from the window to stand in front of Damon, who still sat behind the desk.

"By all that is holy, Damon, does loving a woman also make you blind? Use your intelligence *and* your heart, man!

"Furthermore, what kind of fool do you take *me* for? I am well aware that Sneed follows Temple each time she rides out, that he is always there in the shadows watching over her. Think, Damon! Do you think me an imbecile, that I would keep a romantic tryst with Temple while your man stands watching, reporting to you her every move?

"How could you say the things you said to

Temple? You are insinuating that your own wife has no morals and is no better than a whore!"

"Now, just a damned minute—" Damon sprang from his chair at the words, leaning across the desk menacingly.

"No! No, my friend, you hear me out and, by God, hear me well!" Pierre roared, flattening his palms upon the desk to lean toward Damon, their faces mere inches apart, their eyes locked. *"Your wife loves you!* She has never bedded anyone but you! The child she carries within her womb is yours!

"What you *saw* that day at the stone wall, Damon, was the woman who loves you and the friend who *also* loves you, following the instructions of an urgent message regarding the attempt on your life! Two people who—and God only knows why—care enough about you to try and obtain the information that could save your life!"

"Pierre—"

"I have not had my say, Damon," Pierre barked. "You have jeopardized your marriage and our friendship. You have gravely endangered the life of your unborn child. All because of your false accusations and, above all, your profound stupidity! *You are not Rosco Silone, Damon! Do not emulate him!"*

Pierre's piercing words cut Damon to the quick. He flinched noticeably at the barb, the stinging words leaving him stunned.

Before Damon could recover, Pierre turned

and stalked from the study. With a harsh oath, he slammed the heavy door behind him. The impact seemed to vibrate throughout the entire villa.

Damon sank wearily into his chair and stared vacantly at the closed door, his tired mind in total confusion, his aching heart like a heavy stone within his breast.

Chapter Twenty-one

ROSCO SAT ON THE BROKEN MARBLE BENCH, A bouquet of flowers in his hand. Tears choked his throat as he stared at the mound under which his daughter had been laid to rest.

Over the years, he realized, he had been coming here more and more often. At first he had suffered such guilt that he had stayed away, not liking to be reminded that he was partly at fault for her death. But as the months had gone by, Rosco's loneliness had driven him to the very spot he had once avoided.

Now he rose and moved forward to place the flowers on LaDonna's grave.

"I never meant to hurt you, LaDonna, please believe that," Rosco said aloud, his words tremulous. "If I could call back the years, my love, I would—"

"You would what?"

The harsh words broke the serenity. Rosco turned to see his son standing a few feet away.

"What changes would you make, Rosco?

Would you allow her to love freely, to marry the man she truly loved, the man whose child she carried? No, I think not," Damon sneered.

"Had I known then what I know now—"

"You would do the same thing, Rosco. You have never been known to change—nor will you ever! And as hard as I have tried, as hard as I have fought against it, I have far too much of you in me," his son finished bitterly.

"Not all that you inherited from me is bad, Damon. Your strength, your determination, your pride—"

"It is your unfairness, your hardness and stubbornness that I inherited and bitterly regret. Your fault of not seeing any other view, any opinion save your own. How I have hated you for those traits, and now I must hate myself as well, for I, too, possess them." Damon's words were as bitter as gall as they fell from his lips.

"It is not too late for you to mend the harm that *you* have done, my son." Rosco's words were spoken with deep feeling. "Mine?" He ran a hand over the smooth marble of the gravestone, shaking his graying head sadly. "Mine cannot be rectified."

Rosco turned bleak eyes upon his only son. "You are a much better man than I, Damon, for you have allowed yourself to love, as your mother asked you to. You are stronger than I because you are not afraid to feel, to give. I cannot make a new start with either your mother or LaDonna, but—may I dare hope that, one day, I can make a new start with my son?"

Damon stared into the suffering eyes of his father. Never had he known Rosco to speak thus. Never had he spoken with tenderness in his voice and a plea in his ebony eyes.

It would be difficult to erase the years of animosity and hostility between them, Damon thought. But it was a real challenge and there was a slim chance that it might be possible.

"I do not know, Rosco," he answered truthfully. "I have much to come to terms with, much resentment to overcome. I have many things to forget before I can forgive."

Rosco nodded his dark head in understanding. It was enough, for now, that they were discussing the possibility of a new start.

"There is a deep gulf between Temple and me." Damon changed the subject, running nervous fingers through his hair. "A wide gulf, one of my own doing. I must repair the damage I have done, I must span the gap. She refuses to see me and I cannot make my peace with her."

Damon stooped to pluck a single pink rose from a nearby bush and stepped forward to place it on LaDonna's grave. He was quiet for a moment and Rosco waited patiently, not daring to comment or question; this was the first time that Damon had ever bared his soul to him, allowed him to see his vulnerability.

"I have been called to Cellini's post," Damon

resumed. "It is some hours' ride from here, toward Alghero. Bates and his men are waiting at the camp for me. I shall be away for a week, maybe longer."

Reaching into his pocket, Damon withdrew three sealed envelopes and handed them to his father. Rosco took them without a word, noting his name on one, "Temple" scrawled on another and "Pierre" on the third.

"Put these into the right hands, Rosco; give them to *no one* to deliver. I am entrusting my wife to your care."

Damon picked up a canvas pack from the ground and left the garden without another word. Rosco followed and saw him cross to his horse and tie the pack over the animal's back. Damon cast one last look toward the house, then mounted and rode away.

Rosco looked thoughtfully down at the envelopes in his hand, then walked slowly toward the Villa Silone.

Bates poured the steaming black coffee into two cups. He glanced over at Damon sitting before the fire, idly stirring the coals with a long stick. Bates was worried about his friend. He had never seen the young man in this depressed mood.

"Are you as weary of this war as I, Damon?" he asked conversationally, handing him a cup of the hot coffee.

"Very weary," Damon replied and sipped at his coffee. "But it is for a good cause."

Bates made no reply and the silence grew. The older man studied Damon's features closely, noticing the furrowed brow and drawn face. The boy had more on his mind than the war, he would wager.

"You want to talk about it, boy?" Bates finally asked in a fatherly manner.

Damon's gaze met the older man's kind eyes. He saw no curiosity, merely concern.

"If you want to listen," he replied softly.

So Damon told him the story, starting with the young man watching the small girl in France and returning home to learn that his only sister had died, the years of visiting Nathan Harris and the growing friendship between the two of them, LaDonna's and Nathan's great love and his own profound love for Temple.

His friendship with Nathan had made it easy for him to tell Temple's father how very much he loved her, thereby setting Nathan's mind at rest regarding the rash promise he had made to Rosco. Damon had assured Nathan that he would take good care of Temple for, loving her as he did, he could not do less.

Rosco believed himself avenged for LaDonna's death by the marriage between Damon and Temple, but the union was blessed by Nathan.

"Let Rosco believe he has won," Nathan had told Damon on his deathbed, his weak words spoken for Damon's ears only. "Let him be deluded."

So Damon had stood in the shadows of Nathan's room, stepping forward only to take Temple's hand in marriage. She had not really seen him because of the tears in her eyes and the fact that her full attention was on her dying father. She never knew that it was he who stood beside her in the dimly lit room and did not know, even now, that he had married her because he had long loved her, because *he wanted her,* and that her own dear father had wished it and not because Rosco Silone had decreed it.

Damon remembered Nathan's whispered thank-you as he gave his beloved daughter into the care of his young friend.

Bates listened to the story in astonishment and with great interest. It had begun with love, had somehow become entangled with tragedy and heartache and had finally evolved into love again.

But Damon had not finished. He paused to draw a deep, ragged breath and continued. Bates heard of Temple's arrival at the villa and how the closeness between her and Damon had grown into love on Temple's part and a deeper, abiding love for Damon. Finally Damon related the events of the last few weeks and brought his story to its sad conclusion.

Both men sat in silence, staring into the red-orange flames, both lost in thought. After a long time, Bates stirred and cleared his throat.

"From what you have told me, Damon, this Della woman set out to trap Temple and Pierre in a compromising situation, knowing that you would follow to see with your own eyes the fruit of the lying idea that she had planted in your mind," Bates told him bluntly.

"Why could I not see that, Bates?" Damon asked tiredly.

"Because, my friend, you were too close to the situation. Your heart was involved, your emotions! This Della is clever. She used your temper and your jealousy against you. She knew that if she could make you suspicious enough, your temper would do the rest. All she had to do then was to sit back and watch. She built the fire, then watched it burn. There are those who seem to enjoy stirring up trouble, *big* trouble, for others.

"Della is clever. But she is also dangerous and would bear close watching. If she is as devious as she seems, then you should be on guard at all times against her. I would say that she is not yet finished with you and Temple, my friend."

Damon remained thoughtfully silent. The fire had died down to a bed of glowing embers before Bates roused Damon from his reverie.

"You should be back at the villa, Damon. You should be with your wife."

Temple read the letter over and over, tears blurring her vision.

Pierre has said much, all of which is true. I see Rosco in myself, a side of myself that I do not like. I can only ask that you try to forgive me, my love, that you try to understand me. I make no excuses for my words or actions or for my anger. They are inexcusable. I was wrong.

But you see, my darling, I have never before loved. I could not bear to lose you, yet I have been the one to force the sword of doubt and distrust between us. It is my own doing.

I know that you have not been happy here, that you would prefer to be in France or back in America. You are my wife, which means that you have nothing to fear from Rosco. You repaid your father's 'debt,' you fulfilled his promise, by the union between us. And neither you nor your father owes Rosco anything more.

It is in my power to let you go, Temple, to release you, for I am your husband. I will see that you are well taken care of, whether you choose France or America. You are free to go. All I would ask is that you allow me to see my child when and as often as I can.

You will always be my heart, my love and my life, little one, for I love you passionately —perhaps too much.

Damon

"Oh, Damon," Temple cried aloud. "I do not wish to be anywhere but with you! I need your love every day, *I need you!*" She dissolved into tears, her body wracked with great sobs, Damon's letter crushed in her hand.

"Temple?" Rosco's unusually quiet voice penetrated her grief and she looked up to see him standing in the open doorway. "I knocked but you did not answer and I could hear you crying and—" His words broke off.

Temple dabbed at her flowing eyes. Even through her tears she could see an unaccustomed expression on his face. She fought for composure and waited to see what had brought Rosco to her private quarters for the first time.

"Please, may I come in?" She nodded permission for him to enter. Rosco dropped heavily into a chair by the window and Temple could clearly see that the lines etched in his face were deeper and his bowed head seemed to be grayer than she remembered. She could not understand the feeling of sudden sympathy for the old man that seemed to surge through her.

"We have never been friends, Temple," Rosco began. A gross understatement, Temple thought.

"Oh, I know that you are thinking, 'why should we be friends' or maybe 'how could we be friends.' After all, I hated your father and blamed him for my daughter's death. I forced a marriage between you and my son, a marriage neither of you wanted. And all for the sole purpose of revenge!"

Rosco's voice was low, yet it vibrated across the room. He rose and walked to the bed and stood looking down at Temple. Temple was astonished to realize that, for the first time, she could see no hostility in his black eyes.

"I have made a lot of mistakes, Temple, many mistakes." He shook his head wearily and, to her utter surprise, sat down on the side of her bed. "You have a will of iron, Temple Silone, and, although I admired that will, I also resented it."

Temple could not understand why he was telling her these things. Gone was the acid from his voice, the animosity from his dark eyes. Rosco was attempting to communicate with her but Temple was not sure what she should say to him, so she decided to play it safe and say nothing. She would hear him out.

"My son has brought home a lot of truths to me. He has told me things that I never knew—for instance, my wife's final words. Words she spoke to Damon, not to me. God, I never knew, never believed that Candida loved me. But she did! We were married for eighteen years, Temple, and not once did I say 'I love you' or 'I desire you.'"

Rosco's dark eyes looked into hers and Temple was shocked to see the mist of tears.

"I did, though, I honestly did," he continued. "And I loved my LaDonna. I love my son. Yet I have never shown any emotion other than anger, hatred, arrogance, stubbornness—the list is far too long, Temple. I have never admitted my love for anyone, until now. Ironic, is it not, that *you* should be the first to hear my confessions, the one on whom I am unloading all my guilty feelings!"

Temple remained silent. Somehow she felt that she really was not expected to say anything. Apparently Rosco desperately needed to talk this out, needed someone to listen.

"Damon says that I broke Candida's spirit and that, in so doing, I led her a life of fear and unhappiness. Perhaps that is why she did not live longer. Perhaps I am partially responsible for my wife's early death as well as for my daughter's."

There was a long silence. Rosco seemed to age before her very eyes. A battle was raging within him.

"Do you fear me, Temple?" he asked suddenly.

Taking an uneven breath, she answered as honestly as she could.

"I *have* feared you, Rosco. Some times more than others."

"And do you hate me?"

When Temple did not reply, Rosco laughed shortly, harshly.

"That was not a fair question, Temple, forgive me. How could you do otherwise than hate me? My own son hates me, despises me.

"Damon has not called me 'Father' since his

mother died. I lost him when I lost her. All that was left for me was LaDonna and in the end I destroyed even her."

Rosco stood to walk the length of the room. For several long minutes he paced and the silence was broken only by the steady tread of his footsteps.

"This union, yours and Damon's. Love has come, has it not? You love my son?" Rosco broke from the sad past and returned to the present.

"Yes," Temple answered him, simply and truthfully. "I did not mean to, I vowed that I would not."

Rosco chuckled. "I remember well," he said in amusement and Temple found herself smiling. Suddenly she realized that Rosco was attempting to bridge the gap between them. There was a change in him, a new quietness.

"Damon told me that I am neither God nor Satan, only a man, only human. But do not humans have hearts? Do they not feel, do they not care? Then what am I? I do not have a heart, do not feel nor care! Does that not make me some kind of monster?"

Temple could see the pain in his dark eyes, hear the emotion in his voice, yet she could not answer his question.

Rosco let out a long breath that shook his body.

"I hated your father, Temple. I knew very little of him, but I hated him because he took my LaDonna. I feared that she loved him more than me. But, do you see, I would have hated *any* man for that reason. Nathan Harris just happened to be the one. I hated him before I even knew who he was. All I knew, all that mattered, was that LaDonna's love was being shared. Selfish as I was—as I *am*—I could not accept it."

Rosco's voice trembled. He walked to the window, his back to the room.

"I am not like my son, not as strong as he, nor as wise."

He reached into his breast pocket and retrieved the letter Damon had left for him. Unfolding it, he began to read aloud:

I do not know what I feel for you, Rosco, my own father, but I do not believe it to be hate. It seems to be an emotion that forever floats aimlessly on a tide that never comes in to shore, that never seems to settle.

And my marriage—you believe that I married Temple to help you obtain your revenge on Nathan Harris, that out of a sense of duty I complied with your demands. In truth, Rosco, I married Temple because I wanted to, because I loved her. I have loved her from the first time I saw her more than eight years ago.

Temple's breath stopped in her throat. She could scarcely believe the words that Rosco was reading. Damon had married her because he wanted to, because he loved her—not because of

Rosco's desire for revenge! But she did not understand—she had not known Damon before. Eight years ago—why, she would only have been thirteen years old.

Rosco continued reading and she listened intently.

I knew of LaDonna's love for Nathan. I had gone to visit him, not knowing that he had gone to Sardinia. Upon learning that he was away, I left his home and was walking along the drive when I heard a child's laughter and turned to see the beauty. . . .

As Rosco read on, Temple began to recall that summer day, remembering the handsome stranger who had taken possession of her young heart and walked out of her life. Damon her heart cried, it had been Damon!

From that time on, she had looked for him in the face of every man she met. She had dreamed of him and, as the years passed, his image had grown shadowy, yet his memory had remained.

. . . Nathan knew of my love for his daughter. We became friends through the years that followed. You would have liked him, Rosco, had you taken the time to know him.

Our union had Nathan's blessing. He gave his daughter to me with no reservations for he knew how deeply I loved her. I took her hand gladly that day, not because of any promise or obligation. I stood in the shadows as a stranger because Nathan felt it best. He felt that, given time, Temple would come to love me. She never knew that it was I who stood at her side and spoke the vows.

"Oh, my God!" Temple breathed, reliving that scene in her mind. Damon had been there! It had been his hand that had given her the strength, had comforted her. She remembered thinking that if it were *this* man to whom she was being wed, she would not mind so much. And it had been Damon!

. . . so it is not because I do not love Temple that I am releasing her from this marriage. It is because of that love, for I love her more than life itself.

It is not enough to love someone; you must love them enough to let them go free and to not destroy them with that love. And I have hurt Temple in my love for her. I will hurt her no more.

Rosco finished reading and held the letter out to Temple.

"My son's soul and his heart are in this letter. I have destroyed much. I have hurt many people. I cannot go back and make those things right. I would, if I could, but it is too late. You may not believe that, Temple. Damon did not believe it when I told him as much. But it is true, nonetheless."

Rosco reached down and took Temple's hand in his, a gesture she would never have believed him capable of. She raised her large brown eyes to meet his gaze.

"If you choose to remain with us, Temple, I will try to know you better. I have not given myself a chance to know and like you. I ask you to stay here, because my son loves you, he needs you. Without you, I am very afraid, he will become the man I was." He paused. "Did you hear that, Temple?" Rosco asked with a pleased smile. "I used the past tense without realizing it. Is that not a good omen?"

He was clearly delighted with the thought and Temple found herself responding to his new friendliness. She realized that this was the first time she had ever seen him smile.

Rosco continued, "I am asking you not to leave the Villa Silone for Damon's sake. Within you is his seed—the child who could bring the laughter, the love back into this house. Please consider my son's love for you and yours for him, think of the child. Do not withhold from us the pleasure and enjoyment of again hearing the cries, the laughter of a child."

Temple looked deep into Rosco's ebony eyes and knew that he was sincere in all that he had said. She felt deep sympathy for the old man.

Then he placed something in the palm of her hand and Temple looked down to see a tiny gold locket shining in the lamplight. She recognized it at once. It was the locket LaDonna wore in the portrait.

"Damon asked in his letter that I give this to you. It was LaDonna's. Your father gave it to her."

Temple closed her fingers over the object and clasped her hand to her breast, closing her eyes tightly as tears escaped her golden lashes. When she again opened her eyes, Rosco was gone.

She rose and went to the door, still holding the locket securely. Her feet took her down the long hallway and toward the south wing of the big house, toward LaDonna's room. Without hesitation she opened the door and walked in the duskiness across the bedroom toward the small sitting room where LaDonna's portrait hung. She saw the faint light of a candle within the room and moved with silent steps to the connecting door, which stood partly open.

Rosco stood looking up at his beautiful daughter. The soft glow of the candle's flame illuminated Rosco's face and she saw the glistening of tears on his cheeks.

He sensed her presence and spoke in a hushed voice.

"She was such a gentle, yet spirited child. Her voice was warm and clear and her laughter—" His words broke off momentarily. "Her laughter was like the tinkling of silver bells. LaDonna's eyes were more blue-black than violet like Damon's and mine."

Temple joined him and they stood side by side before the portrait.

"My father never stopped loving her, never stopped grieving," Temple said, and derived some small satisfaction from the shadow of pain that crossed Rosco's face at her words. "Do you truly believe that my father was responsible for her death?" she asked quietly.

"Your father is guilty only of loving her, Temple. I, her own father, am the one who caused her death," Rosco said heavily.

Temple was stunned by his words. What did he mean? Could it be possible that Nathan had suffered the pain of guilt unnecessarily for all those years?

LaDonna's death had been the result of a miscarriage; John Thomas had told Temple about it. And because Nathan had sired the unborn child, Rosco had blamed him for LaDonna's death. So was there more to the story?

"What—what are you saying?" she asked.

"LaDonna died as the result of a miscarriage. From a fall down the stairs." Rosco reached out a shaking hand to touch the canvas lovingly. His voice seemed far away. "I was in a rage! I had suspected that she was seeing someone but was not certain. I rode in from the groves and found Della Fruge waiting for me. She could hardly wait until I had dismounted. '*Signore,*' she said, 'I am so worried about LaDonna, so afraid that she will be hurt. I saw them in the lake garden and they were kissing—'

"I allowed her to say no more. I stormed into the house and straight to LaDonna's room. God, she was so frightened," he remembered, running a hand over his face, his large frame shaking.

"I cursed at her, demanding to know who she was seeing, who her lover was. LaDonna was crying, pleading with me to calm down but I would not listen, I was beyond hearing. Before I knew what she was about, she had run past me and down the hall. I raced after her, even more enraged—she had never before run from me. God, how I wish I had let her go! If I had, she might be here today, here with me."

Rosco turned blindly from the painting as if looking at LaDonna made it more difficult to relate the story. His hands shook badly.

"I caught her at the top of the staircase and turned her to face me, demanding to know the truth. LaDonna screamed that she would never tell me who the man was, not ever, that she would die first. I raised my hand in my anger and she thought I was going to strike her. She cried out, threw up her hands to ward off the blow and stepped backward, away from me. Oh, God! She stepped back and there was nothing to stop her. She had been standing at the edge of the first stair.

"There was nothing I could do. I reached for her but my hands grasped the air. Our screams mingled as she fell. I raced down the stairs and knelt beside her, cradling her in my arms." Rosco looked at Temple with agony in his eyes and his face was a ghostly white. "LaDonna looked up at me with pain-fogged eyes. 'Oh, *Papa*,' she said, 'I hurt myself.' It was what she used to say as a child, when she took a tumble in play. Then she reached out and touched my cheek." Rosco lifted his hand to his cheek in memory.

"She whimpered in pain and closed her eyes and slipped into unconsciousness. Later I learned that she had miscarried. I had not known that she was with child. They had difficulty stopping the bleeding and when, some hours later, they succeeded, it was too late, she was too weak.

"And it was Nathan she called for before she slipped away!"

Temple's heart was breaking, her face was wet with unchecked tears. The pain Rosco suffered had been great; he had carried with him the secret of his own guilt for all these years. She did not judge him and she no longer hated him.

She reached out impulsively and touched his hand. Rosco looked at her, then his gaze fell upon her hand on his. Slowly he clasped it with his own.

It was a start.

Chapter Twenty-two

TEMPLE WALKED ABOUT THE GARDEN, HER thoughts on the last few days, the emotional scene with Rosco, Damon's letter—

It had been a distinct shock to learn that Damon had loved her all these years, that he had married her for love and that her father had welcomed the union. She sat down upon the soft grass, tilting her head back to view the clear blue sky and to watch the drifting white clouds. It had been under a sky such as this, she remembered, on a bed of soft grass that she and Damon had made love for the first time. She wanted to think that it had been then that Damon had planted his seed within her.

There had been misunderstanding, harsh words, pain and tears between them, but above all there had been love. There still was love. Temple wanted nothing more than to take him in her arms and tell him that she never wanted to go away, never wanted to be without him or his love.

Rosco had said that Damon would be gone for a week or more. Temple wanted him *now*. They would talk, they would clear up all the misunderstanding, the bitter words would be forgotten and they would make love. They would lie entwined in each other's arms and talk of their child and of the future.

The Villa Silone would find happiness— laughter would ring through her corridors and soon there would be the happy sound of children's footfalls and youthful chatter.

Temple could visualize a younger version of Damon sliding down the bannister of the long stairway with Erin scolding and Damon laughing. She could even imagine that she could hear Rosco's deep chuckle and mild admonishment to 'Leave the boy be!'

Oh, yes, the future did indeed look bright and wonderful and Temple lay back and closed her eyes, lost in her daydreams.

Pierre watched Della closely, his blue eyes noting her every move. She seemed quite pleased with herself. But then Della always floated about on her cloud of satisfaction when things were going her way.

His green-eyed stepsister must have inherited her wickedness from the man who sired her, whomever that might have been, for Lynette had been the exact opposite of her devious daughter.

Pierre remembered well the lovely Lynette— copper hair and soft green eyes, a gentle voice and a manner almost too shy. Louis Torre had been very lonely following the untimely death of Pierre's mother and had wed Lynette, bringing her and her bastard child, a girl of perhaps ten years, into his home.

Pierre had always liked the gentle Lynette, but Della—well, Della Fruge was an entirely different story. Even as a child she had cleverly wrought destruction and havoc as often as a normal child skinned its knee. He had seen her cunning craftiness during her youth and knew that she had become more vicious through the years.

Pierre had never trusted Della. How he wished that his father had not married Lynette! She had died within a year of their marriage, leaving Louis with the burden and responsibility of the young russet-haired, green-eyed witch.

"You are terribly quiet, Pierre." Della's silky voice broke into his thoughts. She walked up to stand only inches away, her heavy perfume assaulting his nostrils.

"I have much on my mind, Della," he returned coolly and stepped back. Della moved even closer to him, running her fingers over his chest.

"You have been watching me all evening," she cooed. "Since my return from France, my absence for so many months, dare I believe that you finally see me as a woman and not your sister? After all, Pierre, we are not related by blood and there is nothing wrong about such an attraction."

"I could never see you in any other way, Della, than I have all these years," he told her bluntly.

"Come now, Pierre," she teased, "do not tell me that you have not once had the urge to steal into my bedroom at night and share my bed." She ran her hand along his chest and belly, letting it rest daringly low.

He offered no comment, made no move, and his cold blue eyes held hers.

"I have often hoped that you would," she whispered. "I have longed for you to, I would have welcomed you, Pierre. I have lain in my bed just a few steps down the hall from your door, fantasizing about you, running my own hands over my naked flesh pretending they were your hands."

"And in these fantasies of yours, Della," Pierre's voice was low, suggestive, "did I take you with savage thrusts? Did I cause your body to writhe beneath me?"

"Yes, oh yes," she purred, licking her red-painted lips, and Pierre felt her fingers brush against his manhood. "Kiss me, Pierre," Della murmured, her heated body pressing against him.

Pierre bent his head to her, pausing with his lips only a breath away from hers. "When I kiss you, shall you draw me deep into the bottomless pits of passion?"

"Yes!" she breathed, her hands on his body.

"Then shall I strip you naked and take you, here, upon the floor?"

"Yes, yes!" Her red lips parted hungrily.

"Ah, Della, you are a bitch and I want no part

of you!" Pierre told her firmly, pushing her from him in utter disgust.

Della's face suffused with angry color. Her green eyes glittered dangerously, her fingers curled and she struck out at him.

"Damn you!" she snarled. "Damn you to hell!"

Pierre grasped her hands in a steely grip, his eyes burning into her.

"I have had it with you, Della! I have never liked you, much less desired you. Stay out of my way and we will both be better off. You are evil-minded and destructive. No decent man would have you.

"Pull in your claws, you treacherous she-devil! And leave Damon Silone be! He wants you no more than I do. I am onto your fiendish schemes, Della, and Damon soon will be."

Pierre was rewarded for that thrust by a flicker in the green eyes.

"Della, I am warning you—tread softly, lest the stalker become the prey," Pierre finished grimly.

"That sounds very much like a threat to me, Pierre," she said sharply.

"Oh? I did not intend it to *sound* like a threat, Della. *I meant it as one!*"

Pierre released his hold abruptly and she stumbled backward.

"I do not frighten easily, Pierre, you should know that. And you will find that I am a relentless adversary!"

"Crossing swords with you, Della, would give

me much pleasure for I would derive great satisfaction in cutting you down!" With those words Pierre strode from the room.

Della was left standing in the middle of the room rubbing her smarting wrists, her eyes flashing green fire.

"We shall see who will be cut down, Pierre Torre!" she hissed with deadly venom.

The moon drifted in and out of the floating clouds, its silvery glow lighting the sky and stealing across the land. Temple walked down the path toward the lake and stood looking out across the waters, the moonlight shimmering along the blackness of the water.

Picking up a pebble, she skipped the stone over the glimmering surface. She wondered if LaDonna had walked here at night, here in this enchanting place. Had she and Nathan walked hand in hand along the lake, bathed by the glow of the moonlight?

Thoughts of LaDonna caused Temple to turn toward the marble crypt that gleamed blue-white beneath the soft light of the friendly moon.

Suddenly there was a movement. A shadow fell across the stone for a brief moment and was gone. Temple wondered if it had been her imagination, but then she heard the low murmur of voices nearby. She moved slowly, quietly toward the sound.

"I want him dead! Do you hear? *Dead!*" The voice was an angry whisper.

"And the girl?" asked the other.

"Yes, she as well. They stand in the way of what I want. And once Forbes has disposed of them, you will dispose of Forbes."

The voices grew louder as Temple approached. Although they were still only murmurs, one voice touched a chord of recognition in her memory.

"I will have Damon Silone!" the first speaker vowed with determination.

Then Temple remembered the voice and to whom it belonged. Della Fruge! It was Della who wanted Damon dead and the 'girl'—Temple must be the girl Della wanted killed as well. Dear God! She must get back to the villa and tell Rosco or Pierre.

As she whirled to hurry away, the hem of her gown caught on a bush and as she tugged at it, it rustled loudly.

"Shhh—" She heard the whispered warning and her breath caught in her throat. An eerie quiet settled over the garden.

"Forbes, is that you?" Della called out in a hushed voice. There was no answer. "Damn you, Forbes, if that is you, come out!" Moments dragged by.

"It is *not* Forbes," said a deep voice at Temple's ear and she cried out in alarm. She spun about and her wide eyes took in the tall, burly man whose hand grasped her arm. He jerked her hard, tearing her gown loose from the bush and the branches scratched the soft flesh of her leg.

"Well, well, well!" Della walked toward them, her green eyes glittering in the dim light, her arms crossed over her breast. "If it is not *Signora* Silone, mistress of the manor."

"Why, Della?" Temple demanded. "Why do you want Damon dead?"

"Oh, but I do *not* wish Damon dead, my dear. I want him very much alive. Damon was mine, Temple, all these years he was mine. Did you believe that I would step aside and let you have him without a fight? No indeed! Della Fruge will not be defeated by *anyone!*" she declared, a malicious smile on her thin lips. "It was Edson who wanted Damon dead, not I, so I saw to it that it was Edson whose life was taken, rather than Damon's. And you will be taken care of, just as Edson was."

"You plan to kill me?" Temple asked in disbelief.

"Not me, oh dear, no," Della laughed nastily. "Forbes will have the honor. Of course, what he does with you *before* he takes your life will be up to him. After all, he should receive *some* reward for his task!" Again came the diabolical laugh. Then she commanded, "Bring her along, Rogier!"

Temple struggled against the man, but as she opened her lips to scream, his meaty hand clamped over her mouth. He dragged her along, following Della's steps.

Two horses stood waiting in the cover of the trees. Della mounted and watched as the man Rogier slung Temple over his horse, then mounted the steed. And the two captors rode stealthily into the night.

Temple lay upon a dirty canvas cot on the far side of the room in the abandoned cabin to which she had been brought. Her hands and feet were bound and a filthy rag was tied tightly across her mouth.

Della paced the floor, her narrowed eyes darting to Temple every few minutes. Rogier sat at the rickety table playing a one-handed game of cards.

"Once Forbes returns," Della said to the man, "you help him with Pierre's body. Bring it in here so that they will be found together."

"Nice little package you put together, Del," Rogier praised her, spitting a mouthful of tobacco juice. It arced through the air and landed with a loud splat upon the floor. "The two lovers killing themselves to be together in death, seeing as how they could not be together in life." He gave an ugly laugh and added, "You think Silone will believe it?"

"He will believe it once he sees them and reads the note." Della picked up the paper that lay on the table and read aloud:

Damon, love is something one does not plan. The love that Pierre and I share cannot be denied. If we cannot be together in life, then we shall be so in death.

Temple

Della turned to Temple with a sneer.

"Touching, do you not agree? It makes my heart bleed. And when poor Damon finds the bodies of his wife and his best friend lying together upon the floor in their own blood, their hands outstretched to each other—oh, my!" Della sighed mockingly, "He will be so distraught! And I shall be there to comfort him, to say how I had tried to warn him of your unfaithfulness."

Della laughed fiendishly and dropped the note back upon the table.

"Yes, I will comfort Damon and again teach him to love!" she added.

Temple turned her head away. Closing her eyes tightly, she prayed silently and in her heart she called out to Damon and told him how much she loved him.

Chapter Twenty-three

THE MILES PASSED AND DAMON URGED SHADOW on. Bates had told him to go home, where he belonged, and assured him that he could handle the meeting alone. So Damon had saddled his horse and, escorted by two armed men, had turned the black stallion toward the Villa Silone.

As he cleared the groves and took the wide path toward the villa, Damon could see that the grounds about the house and stables were bathed in lamplight. He heard the rising of voices and spurred his horse, not stopping until he had reached the front veranda.

Rosco was coming out of the house with a rifle beneath his arm and a pistol strapped on his hip. Pierre followed, a gun in his hand.

"In God's name!" Damon shouted and leaped from Shadow.

"Damon!" Rosco's relieved voice met him. "That damned fool, Della, has Temple! She is going to kill her!" He gripped his son's shoulder. "It has been Della all along, Damon. She is the informant, the interceptor of our messages. She—"

"Temple?" Damon's eyes were filled with pain and he felt that he could not breathe. All that had registered from Rosco's spate of words was that Della had taken Temple and that she was going to kill her.

A sudden yell rent the night air and a man raced toward them. It was Sneed and he held a scrap of blue silk. Damon snatched it from the man's hand and groaned. It had been torn from Temple's blue gown, he was sure of it, and the silk was stained with blood.

"Oh, dear God!" Damon moaned, his body trembling. He clasped the bit of fabric in his fist.

"*Signore* Silone!" Mario ran from the house. "*Signore* Silone, that man, he died. But he talked and Father heard him—"

At that moment Emil ran out. He, too, carried a rifle and his kindly face was strained.

"*Signore*, the man Forbes, he said they are at the old workers' shack on the Villa Torre!"

Damon and Pierre dashed for their horses and leaped astride them, ready to ride. Rosco hurriedly strapped his rifle into the saddle holster and swung up on Spirit.

"*Signore!*" Emil called out to Rosco. "The *Signora*, she is dear to me. I wish to go with you. Please?"

Rosco saw the entreaty in the eyes of his faithful servant and, without a word, stretched his hand down to help him mount. Emil settled himself behind Rosco and the men rode out. The search party numbered eleven.

Damon's watchful eyes glittered dangerously. His body was taut and alert, like a deadly serpent, readying to strike. He slipped lightly from his saddle, his booted feet soundless upon the ground.

"Pierre," he said in a controlled voice that was a mere whisper, "you cover me—come in behind me. You others spread out. Do not fire on that shack and chance hitting my wife!"

Damon crept noiselessly toward the cabin with Pierre some yards behind him. He glanced about him sharply, noting that the men were carrying out his orders, spreading out to circle the crude house, being careful to keep in the shadows.

"Della!" Damon shouted, his voice ringing loud and authoritative through the night.

Temple watched through half-closed lids as Della sat at the table, her long nails impatiently tapping a monotonous rhythm. Rogier was asleep, his matted head resting on his arms.

Della spat out an obscene oath. She slapped at the cards on the table, sending them flying in all directions. Rogier grunted sleepily and lifted his head, wiping his tobacco-stained mouth with the back of his dirty hand.

"Forbes should have been here by now!" Della snapped. "Damn him—"

Suddenly the air was split by the thunder of Damon's voice, calling Della's name.

"What in hell!" Rogier shouted, jumping up and overturning his chair. He grabbed his gun and stared wide-eyed around the room.

"Shut up, you fool!" Della hissed, her face drained of color.

"Della!" Damon yelled. "Your man, Forbes, is dead. He did not kill Pierre as you had planned."

Temple breathed a prayer of thanks that Damon had come for her and that Pierre was safe. Della's maniacal scheme had not succeeded.

"Just let Temple go, Della. Let her walk out the door to me and I will take her home."

"Never!" Della cried furiously and ran to pull Temple to her feet.

"I have ten men out here, Della. You cannot stay in there with one man and one gun. So just come on out!" Damon reasoned as he approached the shack.

"I do not aim to get myself killed, Del," Rogier barked at the woman, his eyes wide with fear. "Let the girl go, let her go to her husband!"

"No! I will not!" Della gritted out. "If I cannot have him, then Damon sure as hell will not have what *he* wants!"

"Del, this is crazy!" Rogier cried, shaking his head. "My God, woman! There are ten men out there besides Silone. They are just waiting to storm this damned shack. We do not have a chance!"

"Shut up!" Della ordered. "Shut up and let me think!"

After a moment she reached out and yanked the gag from Temple's mouth.

"Call to him!" she commanded. "Call to your beloved. Confess your love so that he may remember your last words!"

Temple glared silently at the other woman, refusing to speak. Della's grip on her arm bit into Temple's soft flesh, her long nails drawing blood. Still Temple made no sound. She would not give Della the satisfaction.

Della turned her narrowed green eyes to Rogier.

"Kill her, Rogier!" she ordered. "Put that gun to her head and pull the trigger!"

Rogier shook his head slowly and, laying the gun on the table, turned toward the door of the cabin.

When Della realized that Rogier was deserting her, she lunged for the gun screaming "No!" Grabbing the gun, she aimed it straight at Rogier's back.

Temple let out a bloodcurdling scream, the bark of gunfire sounded and Rogier fell to the floor.

"Temple!" Damon's anguished call shattered the night. "Temple!" He raced toward the shack, his heart in his throat.

Della turned the gun on Temple, green eyes wild, her teeth bared in a snarl. She stepped closer and Temple could feel the cold steel on her brow.

There was the sound of wood splintering and the door burst open. Damon rushed in, stopping as he saw the gun at Temple's head and her brown eyes filled with terror.

"You will not have her, Damon," Della told him bluntly. Demonic laughter bubbled in her throat. "I told her to call out to you but she refused. I told her to tell you of her love so that you would hear her dying words but she would not. I am glad you came, now you can watch her die—it is ever so much better this way."

In that instant Damon recognized the complete insanity of the green-eyed woman and knew that she was very dangerous, much more dangerous than they had realized.

"Della," he said softly, his hands outstretched. "Please let her go."

Della's cackle of laughter sounded eerie. At that moment a movement caught her attention and her eyes darted to the doorway. Pierre and Rosco stood there.

"Oh, look, Temple!" Della cried. "Your lover is here as well as your dear father-in-law!" Then her mood changed abruptly and she took a deep breath. "Tell them to go away, Damon, darling. This is between just the three of us."

As Damon hesitated, Della cocked the gun.

"For the love of God, Della—"

"Tell them to go away!" she shouted.

"Pierre, Rosco—Della would like you to leave," Damon said softly.

And the two men quietly moved from the doorway, fully realizing that Della was deadly dangerous and that they must comply with Della's wishes and give Damon a chance to outwit the woman.

"Now," Della said, as the two men disappeared into the night. "Temple, tell your husband of your love so that he will remember."

"No!" Damon hissed. "No, Temple."

"If you do not do as I say, Temple, I will turn the gun on Damon first," Della said threateningly.

Temple's wide brown eyes sought Damon. She knew that Della would carry out her threat. She knew that the woman was mad. Temple could not bear to see Damon fall to his death before her eyes while she stood by, unable to help him.

"Tell him!" Della screamed.

"Damon," Temple choked, "Damon, I—"

"No, Temple!" Damon shouted.

"Yes!" Della spat and she whirled to turn the gun on Damon.

Instantly Temple threw herself sideways at Della and the two crashed to the floor. The shot went wild.

Damon shouted Temple's name. Another shot rang out and there was a scream, then silence.

The two women lay still upon the floor and Damon's feet felt like lead.

Then Temple rolled from Della, and Damon saw in horror that her bodice was soaked with blood. Her eyes opened and she gazed at him. There was no terror in her eyes, no pain, only relief, and Damon's taut body relaxed when he realized that she was unharmed.

His eyes moved to Della, who lay quite still, the gun clasped in her hand, the barrel just inches away from her heart. There were black powder burns on the once-white blouse that was fast reddening from the spilling of her blood.

Damon pulled Temple into his arms and held her close for a long moment as she sobbed uncontrollably.

Rosco and Pierre rushed in, followed closely by Emil and the other men. They began laughing and slapping one another's shoulders in their relief that the *Signora* was safe and unharmed.

Pierre bent over Della, then straightened and walked away. His face was expressionless.

Rosco knelt and cut away the rope that bound Temple's ankles. Releasing them, he gently chafed the ugly rope burns and helped to restore the circulation. Then he cut the rope around her wrists and took her freed hands in his, rubbing them gently. Damon noted the gesture, pleased that Rosco was concerned about Temple.

Temple lay exhausted in Damon's arms, her

eyes closed. Rosco searched Damon's face anxiously.

"She is unharmed," Damon told him quietly. He stood with Temple in his arms and walked from the shack.

They had arrived back at the villa to find the entire household waiting for their return, frantic with anxiety about their *Signora*.

Erin had had the foresight to have Mario fetch Doctor Vecchi and he, too, had been waiting. He had examined Temple and pronounced her shaken but unharmed.

Later, bathed and undressed for bed, Temple slid between the sheets with a deep sigh of weariness. Damon slipped into bed beside her and pulled her into his arms. She nestled against him, happy and secure within the circle of his strong arms.

Damon related the events leading up to his appearance at the abandoned shack. He told her how Bates had sent him back home to her, how he had hurried home only to find bedlam at the Villa Silone. He had learned that Temple had been abducted, that Sneed had shot Forbes and that before the man died, Emil had managed to find out where Temple was being held. The rescue party was quickly dispatched. The rest of the story she knew well.

"I love you," Damon said then, with great emotion. "I thought I had lost you. If I—"

Temple placed a finger on his lips.

"I am here, my love. I am where I want to be, safe in your arms, and I will never leave you. Our child is safe and we have each other."

There was a long silence, then Damon spoke in the darkness.

"Father told me of your conversation."

Temple sat bolt upright. Her eyes were wide as she looked down at Damon in the dimness.

"Damon! You called him 'Father'! You have always called him 'Rosco.'" Temple's voice was surprised, yet pleased.

"So I did!" Damon said in wonder. "So I did!" He stroked her cheek gently with the back of his hand. "He has changed, little one, and there may be a chance for all of us."

"There is *always* a chance—*more* than a chance, where there is love."

Damon kissed her tenderly and cradled her close to his heart. He held his beloved one, his heart, his life. Their love was a love so true, so deep, that only death could sever them.

For on that fateful day in Sardinia when one father demanded payment from another, in France a young man had stood watching a child-woman who held his heart capture in destiny's embrace.

Epilogue

The outbreak of war, with Austria on one side and France and Sardinia on the other, lasted from April to July 1859 and constituted the first successful step toward Italian liberation and union.

And on December 3, 1859, Nathan Rosco Silone was born. His lusty cries rang through the corridors of the Villa Silone.

Temple sat in a low rocking chair, nursing her month-old baby. She ran a loving hand through its thatch of black hair. The child stared up at his mother with large, black-violet eyes.

"The Silone hair," Temple whispered, "the Silone eyes!"

She raised her own brown eyes to smile at the tall, handsome man with the same black hair and black-violet eyes. Damon returned the smile as he stood watching the blissful picture of mother and child, both of whom he loved dearly.

Tapestry
HISTORICAL ROMANCES

Breathtaking New Tales

of love and adventure set against
history's most exciting time and
places. Featuring two novels by the
finest authors in the field of romantic fiction—<u>every month.</u>

Next Month From
Tapestry Romances

FIRE AND INNOCENCE
by Sheila O'Hallion
MOTH AND FLAME
by Laura Parker